Anthony Trollope

The Complete Short Stories

VOLUME V
Various Stories

Edited, with introduction, by
Betty Jane Slemp Breyer

Texas Christian University Press
Fort Worth, Texas 76129

Published by Texas Christian University Press

Manufactured in the United States of America

Library of Congress Cataloging in Publication Data
(Revised for volume 5)

Trollope, Anthony, 1815-1882.
  The complete short stories.

    Contents: v. 1. The Christmas stories — v. 2. Editors
and writers — [etc.] — v. 5. Various stories.
    I. Breyer, Betty Jane. II. Title.
PR5682.B73   823'.8   79-15519
ISBN 0-912646-56-X (v. 1)
ISBN 0-912646-79-9 (v. 5)

Contents

Introduction

"OH, FOR SOME MORE BRAVE TROLLOPE," wrote Edward FitzGerald in 1873. There were those among his contemporaries, of course, who thought that there was already a great deal too much of Mr. Anthony Trollope's works before them, but time has been on the side of Mr. FitzGerald. The General Reader over the last hundred years or so has with persistence refused to allow Trollope's works to be neglected. He has read and reread, bought and sold, hoarded and bequeathed Trollope's works, both those well known and those obscure. And in the centenary anniversary of his death, Trollope is as much read and as much discussed as he was when *Framley Parsonage* made the *Fortnightly Review* the best new magazine of the 1860's.

It is beyond the scope of a short introduction to explain the reasons for the lasting success of a writer who, in his own time, though popular, was thought only second best. The reasons for his success may be made as complex or as simple as the critics of the hour choose to make them, but there is that something in Trollope's work which outlasts the varying fashions in criticism. When all tallying up of literary merits and demerits is complete, the final sum is always the same: Trollope is read.

He is read because he knows his reader. He knows that his reader, like his characters, is perfect neither in evil nor in good. He has counted on the fact that there will always be those who will recognize that the stories of men and women whose struggles with the temptation to be worse than they are and their attempts to do better than they have done are drawn from life. Mankind likes nothing so much as to see its own reflection in Art, no matter how distorted that reflection may be. When that reflection is clear and sharp and honest, Mankind pays it the tribute of passing it on from generation to generation. For those in generations to come who know that they should be better than they are and can be better than they have been, Trollope will still hold up a mirror to life. And if there are still those who read in the centuries to come, Trollope will be read.

The world before which he holds his mirror, though the mirror be in a nineteenth-century frame with obvious Victorian gilt, is a world defined by inevitable quotidian choices between the better evil and the lesser good. Again and again, from Thaddy Macdermot and Septimus Harding onward, his characters want to act for the best, if only they knew what that best might be or which course of action open to them might bring about that best. Very few characters use no moral measure but their own self-interest; and they are known to the reader without exception for what they are even if, for a while, society at large may be deceived by such as Lizzie Eustace, Ferdinand Lopez and the Marquis of Brotherton. Evil is always apparent, even if good must always be mixed with uncertainty. His characters struggle on — sometimes choosing the better, sometimes the worse. For Trollope, that struggling on was the real stuff of fiction and of life.

It is easy, he says in *The Eustace Diamonds*, to depict a hero, spotless in virtue and perfect in love, but then that is not the very picture of life. He asks the Reader to consider: ". . . when you have called the dearest of your friends round you to your hospitable table, how many heroes are there sitting at the Board? Your bosom friend, — even if he be a knight without fear, is he a knight without reproach?" A picture of "a King Arthur among men" may do much to show us what man perfected might be, but it does not show us what man is. The man who wishes to portray life must show the man "who is one hour good and the next bad, who aspires greatly, but fails in practice, who sees the higher, but too often follows the lower course." Moreover, Trollope had a talent for creating character of curiously ambiguous moral dimensions. He could draw to life characters who, though they act with malice, pride, envy and meanness, are firmly convinced that they act with moral rectitude for moral aims. No matter how wrong they may be or how much destruction they may spawn, they themselves rarely see their own evil, but rather mistake it for good. It was his particular talent for characterization which allowed him to make the nature of such characters accessible to his readers — to make their evil intelligible and their struggle understandable. To few such characters comes the realization of how the common good and evil may differ from their own views. In one of the most classically dramatic scenes in his work, he portrays such a moment in *The Last Chronicle of Barset* for Mrs. Proudie:

> She had always meant to serve him. She was conscious of that; conscious also in a way that, although she had been industrious, although she had been faithful, although she was clever, yet she had failed. At the bottom of her heart she knew that she had been a bad wife. And yet she had meant to be a pattern wife! She had meant to be a good Christian; but she had so exercised her Christianity that not a soul in the world loved her, or would endure her presence if it could be avoided!

That is the unfortunate end of Mrs. Proudie. Had more life been allotted to her, she could never have been the same Mrs. Proudie. The very mainspring of her character lay in the moral ambiguity with which Trollope invested her. He has succeeded in capturing a very real sense of the complexity of ordinary man's moral struggle. It is both touching and proper that he should lament the passing of such a character even years after the event. He writes in *An Autobiography:* "I have sometimes regretted the deed, so great was my delight in writing about Mrs. Proudie, so thorough was my knowledge of all the little shades of her character . . . Since her time others have grown up equally dear to me, — Lady Glencora and her husband, for instance; but I have never dissevered myself from Mrs. Proudie, and still live much in company with her ghost."

All his characters live and die admidst this struggle between good and evil. It is, in part, this moral landscape that defines the success which he enjoys — that and the sense that there is some direction given to this struggle. Though such a point is not as congenial to the twentieth-century mind as it was to the nineteenth-century one, it is a point still worth making that Trollope believed that the writer of fiction had a special moral obligation to his reader:

To make them and ourselves somewhat better, — not by one spring heavenwards to perfection, because we cannot so use our legs, — but by slow climbing, is, we may presume, the object of all teachers, leaders, legislators, spiritual pastors, and masters. He who writes tales such as this, probably also has, very humbly, some such object distantly before him . . . The true picture of life as it is, if it could be adequately painted, would show men what they are, and how they might rise, not indeed, to perfection, but one step first, and then another on the ladder.

Reading Trollope's stories brings one a sense of the endless variety of humanity and its problems with good and evil. Some writers have only one story to tell and although they may write volumes, always the characters, the situations, the underlying tensions are the same, varied only by time, place and circumstances. Trollope, on the other hand, never left off dissecting the society in which men and women live and struggle. Having said as much, one must hasten to add, lest such evaluation sound deceptively grim, that while the struggle is certainly there, there is also present a sense of the innate comedy of man's situation. There is a sharpness of dry wit — a quality like alum, Carlyle said — about Trollope's writing which constantly calls the reader to laugh as well as sympathize. He has dressed his fare with a piquant sauce composed partly of satire, partly of good-humored irony and a good deal of comic insight into life.

The stories in this volume offer an excellent sample of that variety which is the real foundation for Trollope's success and which is so often forgotten by those who remember only the Trollope of Barsetshire. These stories point to a Trollope far away from the purlieus of Barchester Close, both in spirit and in scene. It is true that he was an accurate recorder of the minutiae of the social framework which shaped and held the curiosities of Victorianism, but it is also true that he could portray with precision ugliness and degradation, decadence and decay, and the workings of a mind tortured to madness. Hawthorne notwithstanding, all Trollope's works are not beef and ale.

In the first story in this volume, he skillfully balances the implacability of Frau Frohmann's Toryism against the inexorable results of inflation — certainly not an untimely theme. It goes without saying that in the end inflation wins, and thence the title, "Why Frau Frohmann Raised Her Prices." But the struggle is a fierce one and the story is among his best. Though it is inevitable that Frau Frohmann should lose, he has chronicled her struggle with all the attention to detail which that battle deserves. He has understood the nature of Man to cling to that which has served in the past and the reluctance to give up the pride of being right, even when one is wrong. The last story of this volume, "The Journey to Panama," is one of the most startling stories he ever wrote. It is a story whose complexity arises from the setting — a world which allows the forms and manners of ordinary behavior to be discarded — and from the use of character development which depends on increasing emotional and sexual tensions. Nowhere else has Trollope studied more closely or with more sensitivity the interaction of men and women released from the restraints of conventional society. Nowhere else has he dealt more frankly with the plight of that peculiar Victorian phenomenon, the middle-class 'lady' without means. In Emily Viner he has created the embodiment of a 'woman problem' far more important to the mid-Victorian woman than the issue of women's rights or women's suffrage — the problem of survival. Because she is a 'lady' the rules of convention and society require that she be imprisoned between her poverty on the one hand and her respectability on the other. With bitterness she explains exactly what her real position is: "The fact is, Mr. Forrest, that there are people who have no business to live at all." It is a terrible and honest comment on her world. Michael Sadleir has called this story the "most courageously 'unfinished' of them all." Courageous it may be; unifnished it is not.

This volume also contains that one *lusus naturae* of Trollope's career, "The Gentle Euphemia; or, Love Shall Still Be Lord of All." Just what sort of story it is is difficult to say. It is not a medieval romance; it is not exactly a parody of a medieval romance; it is not a fairy tale; but it is one piece of fun throughout. It is a compendium of pseudo-archaic language, quotations from famous poets, comically stilted style and droll little barbs of satire shot out in many directions. The point of telling the story lies not in the plot, or the characterization, or the theme; for the story has hardly any of these. The point of telling the story seems to be to include in the shortest possible space the largest number of trappings of as many romances as possible. Taken as a spoof of the stock in trade of the romance writers, it is not only readable, but clever. The story is a credit to Trollope's mastery of the language, his intrepidity in experiment, and his genuine sense of fun. The story is a different Trollope, one seen only here, but one still known, as though accidentally met in disguise but still recognizable. Nothing could bear better witness to Trollope's comic sense than his willingness to give us a story such as "The Gentle Euphemia."

The diversity and variety of Trollope's talents are nowhere more obvious than in his short stories. They allow the modern reader to see him in a new role and give the reader an opportunity to modify the stereotype of Trollope solely as a purveyor of middle-class mid-Victorianism. They give the master craftsman of the three-volume novel a new medium in which to work. They permit him to say and do things which he would not or could not try in his novels. But best of all they provide the reader with "some more brave Trollope."

Why Frau Frohmann Raised Her Prices

Chapter I
The Brunnenthal Peacock

IF EVER THERE WAS A TORY upon the earth, the Frau Frohmann was a Tory; for I hold that landed possessions, gentle blood, a grey-haired butler behind one's chair, and adherence to the Church of England, are not necessarily the distinguishing marks of Toryism. The Frau Frohmann was a woman who loved power, but who loved to use it for the benefit of those around her, —or any any rate to think that she so used it. She believed in the principles of despotism and paternal government, — but always on the understanding that she was to be the despot. In her heart of hearts she disliked education, thinking that it unfitted the minds of her humbler brethren for the duties of their lives. She hated, indeed, all changes, — changes in costume, changes in hours, changes in cookery, and changes in furniture; but of all changes she perhaps hated changes in prices the most. Gradually there had come over her a melancholy conviction that the world cannot go on altogether unaltered. There was, she felt, a fate in things, — a necessity which, in some dark way within her own mind, she connected with the fall of Adam and the general imperfection of humanity, —which demanded changes, but they were always changes for the worst; and therefore, though to those around her she was mostly silent on this matter, she was afflicted by a general idea that the world was going on towards ruin. That

1

all things throve with her herself was not sufficient for her comfort for, being a good woman with a large heart, she was anxious for the welfare not only of herself and of her children, but that of all who might come after her, at any rate in her own locality. Thus, when she found that there was a tendency to dine at one instead of twelve, to wear the same clothes on week days as on Sundays, to desire easy chairs, and linen that should be bleached absolutely white, thoughts as to the failing condition of the world would get the better of her and make her melancholy.

These traits are perhaps the evidences of the weakness of Toryism; — but then Frau Frohmann also had all its strength. She was thoroughly pervaded by a determination that, in as far as in her lay, all that had aught to do with herself should be "well-to-do" in the world. It was a grand ambition in her mind that every creature connected with her establishment, from the oldest and most time-honoured guest down to the last stray cat that had taken refuge under her roof, should always have enough to eat. Hunger, unsatisfied hunger, disagreeable hunger, on the part of any dependent of hers, would have been a reproach to her. Her own eating troubled her little or not at all, but the cooking of the establishment generally was a great care to her mind. In bargaining she was perhaps hard, but hard only in getting what she believed to be her own right. Aristides was not more just. Of bonds, written bonds, her neighbours knew not much; but her word for twenty miles round was as good as any bond. And though she was perhaps a little apt to domineer in her bargains, — to expect that she should fix the prices and to resent opposition, — it was only to the strong that she was tyrannical. The poor sick widow and the little orphan could generally deal with her at their own rates; on which occasions she would endeavour to hide her dealings from her own people, and would give injunctions to the favoured ones that the details of the transaction should not be made public. And then, though the Frau was, I regret to say, no better than a Papist, she was a thoroughly religious woman, believing in real truth what she professed to believe, and complying, as far as she knew how, with the ordinances of her creed.

Therefore I say that if ever there was a Tory, the Frau Frohmann was one.

And now it will be well that the reader should see the residence of the Frau, and learn something of her condition in life.
In one of the districts of the Tyrol, lying some miles south of
Innsbruck, between that town and Brixen, there is a valley called
the Brunnenthal, a most charming spot, in which all the delights
of scenery may be found without the necessity of climbing up
heart-rending mountains, or sitting in oily steamboats, or paying
for greedy guides, or riding upon ill-conditioned ponies. In this
valley Frau Frohmann kept an hotel called the Peacock, which,
however, though it was known as an inn, and was called by that
name, could hardly be regarded as a house of common public
entertainment. Its purpose was to afford recreation and comfort
to a certain class of customers during the summer months, — persons well enough to do in the world to escape from their town
work and their town residences for a short holiday, and desirous
during that time of enjoying picturesque scenery, good living,
moderate comfort, and some amount of society. Such institutions
have now become so common that there is hardly any one who
has not visited or at any rate seen such a place. They are to be
found in every country in Europe, and are very common in
America. Our own Scotland is full of them. But when the Peacock was first opened in the Brunnenthal they were not so
general.

Of the husband of the Frau there are not many records in the
neighbourhood. The widow has been a widow for the last twenty
years at least, and her children, — for she has a son and daughter,
— have no vivid memories of their father. The house and everything in it, and the adjacent farm, and the right of cutting timber
in the forests, and the neighbouring quarry, are all the undoubted
property of the Frau, who has a reputation for great wealth.
Though her son is perhaps nearly thirty, and is very diligent in
the affairs of the establishment, he has no real authority. He is
only, as it were, the out-of-doors right hand of his mother, as his
sister, who is perhaps five years younger, is an indoors right hand.
But they are only hands. The brain, the intelligence, the mind,
the will by which the Brunnenthal Peacock is conducted and
managed, come all from the Frau Frohmann herself. To this day
she can hardly endure a suggestion either from Peter her son or
from her daughter Amalia, who is known among her friends as

3

Malchen, but is called "the Fraulein" by the Brunnenthal world at large. A suggestion as to the purchase of things new in their nature she will not stand at all, though she is liberal enough in maintaining the appurtenances of the house generally.

But the Peacock is more than a house. It is almost a village; and yet every shed, cottage, or barn at or near the place forms a part of the Frau's establishment. The centre or main building is a large ordinary house of three stories, — to the lower of which there is an ascent by some half-dozen stone steps, —covered with red tiles, and with gable ends crowded with innumerable windows. The ground-flour is devoted to kitchens, offices, the Frau's own uses, and the needs of the servants. On the first-story are the two living rooms of the guests, the greater and by far the more important being devoted to eating and drinking. Here, at certain hours, are collected all the forces of the establishment, — and especially at one o'clock, when, with many ringing of bells and great struggles in the culinary department, the dinner is served. For to the adoption of this hour has the Frau at last been driven by the increasing infirmities of the world around her. The scenery of the locality is lovely; the air is considered to be peculiarly health-compelling; the gossipings during the untrammelled idleness of the day are very grateful to those whose lives are generally laborious; the lovemakings are frequent, and no doubt sweet; skittles and bowls and draughts and dominoes have their devotees; and the smoking of many pipes fills up the vacant hours of the men.

But, at the Brunnenthal, dinner is the great glory of the day. It would be vain for any aesthetical guest who might conceive himself to be superior to the allurements of the table to make little of the Frau's dinner. Such a one had better seek other quarters for his summer's holiday. At the Brunnenthal Peacock it is necessary that you should believe in the paramount importance of dinner. Not to come to it at the appointed time would create, first marvel in the Frau's mind, then pity, — as to the state of your health, — and at last hot anger should it be found that such neglect arose from contempt. What muse will assist me to describe these dinners in a few words? They were commenced of course by soup, — real soup, not barley broth with a strong prevalence of the barley.

Then would follow the boiled meats, from which the soup was supposed to have been made, — but such boiled meat, so good, that the supposition must have contained a falsehood. With this there would be always potatoes and pickled cabbages and various relishes. Then there would be two other kinds of meat, generally with accompaniment of stewed fruit; after that fish, — trout from the neighbouring stream, for the preservation of which great tanks had been made. Vegetables with unknown sauces would follow; — and then would come the roast, which consisted always of poultry, and was accompanied of course by salad. But it was after this that were made the efforts on which the Frau's fame most depended. The puddings, I think, were the subject of her greatest struggles and most complete success. Two puddings daily were, by the rules of the house, required to be eaten; — not two puddings brought together so that you might choose with careless haste either one or the other; but two separate courses of puddings, with an interval between for appreciation, for thought, and for digestion. Either one or both can, no doubt, be declined. No absolute punishment, — such as notice to leave the house, — follows such abstention. But the Frau is displeased, and when dressed in her best on Sundays does not smile on those who abstain. After the puddings there is dessert, and there are little cakes to nibble if you will. They are nibbled very freely. But the heat of the battle is over with the second pudding.

They have a great fame, these banquets; so that ladies and gentlemen from Innsbruck have themselves driven out here to enjoy them. The distance each way is from two to three hours, so that a pleasant holiday is made by a visit to the Frau's establishment. There is a ramble up to the waterfall and a smoking of pipes among the rocks, and pleasant opportunities for secret whispers among young people; — but the Frau would not be well pleased if it were presumed that the great inducement for the visit were not to be found in the dinner which she provides. In this way, though the guests at the house may not exceed perhaps thirty in number, it will sometimes be the case that nearly twice as many are seated at the board. That the Frau has an eye to profit cannot be doubted. Fond of money she is certainly; — fond of prosperity generally. But, judging merely from what comes beneath her eye, the observer will be led to suppose that her sole ambition on these occasions is to see the food which she has provided devoured by her guests. A weak stomach, a halting appetite, conscientious scruples as to the over-enjoyment of victuals, restraint in reference to subsequent excesses or subsequent eatings, — all these things are a scandal to her. If you can't or won't or don't eat your dinner when you get it, you ought not to go to the Brunnenthal Peacock.

This banqueting-hall, or Speise-Saal, occupies a great part of the first-floor; but here also is the drawing-room, or reading-room, as it is called, having over the door "Lese-Saal" painted, so that its purpose may not be doubted. But the reading-room is not much, and the guests generally spend their time chiefly out of doors or in their bedrooms when they were not banqueting. There are two other banquets, breakfast and supper, which need not be specially described; — but of the latter it may be said that it is a curtailed dinner, having limited courses of hot meat, and only one pudding.

On this floor there is a bedroom or two, and a nest of others above; but the accommodation is chiefly afforded in other buildings, of which the one opposite is longer, though not so high, as the central house; and there is another, a little down the road, near the mill, and another as far up the stream, where the baths have been built, — an innovation to which Frau Frohmann did not lend herself without much inward suffering. And there are huge barns and many stables; for the Frau keeps a posting establishment, and a diligence passes the door three times each way in the course of the day and night, and the horses are changed at the Peacock; — or it was so, at any rate, in the days of which I am speaking, not very long ago. And there is the blacksmith's forge, and the great carpenter's shed, in which not only are the carts and carriages mended, but very much of the house furniture is made. And there is the mill, as has been said before, in which the corn is ground, and three or four cottages for married men, and a pretty little chapel, built by the Frau herself, in which mass is performed by her favourite priest once a month, — for the parish chapel is nearly three miles distant if you walk by the mountain path, but is fully five if you have yourself carried round by the coach road. It must, I think, be many years since the Frau can have walked there, for she is a dame of portly dimensions.

Whether the buildings are in themselves picturesque I will not pretend to say. I doubt whether there has been an attempt that way in regard to any one except the chapel. But chance has so grouped them, and nature has so surrounded them, that you can hardly find anywhere a prettier spot. Behind the house, so as to leave only space for a little meadow which is always as green as irrigation can make it, a hill rises, not high enough to be called a mountain, which is pine-clad from the foot to the summit. In front and around the ground is broken, but immediately before the door there is a way up to a lateral valley, down which comes a nameless stream which, just below the house, makes its way into the Ivil, the little river which runs from the mountain to the inn, taking its course through that meadow which lies between the hill and the house. It is here, a quarter of a mile perhaps up this little stream, at a spot which is hidden by many turnings from the road, that visitors come upon the waterfall, — the waterfall which at Innsbruck is so often made to be the excuse of these out-ings which are in truth performed in quest of Frau Frohmann's dinners. Below the Peacock, where the mill is placed, the valley is closely confined, as the sombre pine-forests rise abruptly on each side; and here, or very little lower, is that gloomy and ghost-like pass through the rocks, which is called the Höllenthor; a name which I will not translate. But it is a narrow ravine, very dark in dark weather, and at night as black as pitch. Among the superstitious people of the valley the spot is regarded with the awe which belonged to it in past ages. To visitors of the present day it is simply picturesque and sublime. Above the house the valley spreads itself, rising, however, rapidly; and here modern engineering has carried the road in various curves and turns round knolls of hill and spurs of mountains, till the traveller as he ascends hardly knows which way he is going. From one or two points among these curves the view down upon the Peacock with its various appendages, with its dark-red roofs, and many win-dows glittering in the sun, is so charming, that the tourist is almost led to think that they must all have been placed as they are with a view to effect.

The Frau herself is what used to be called a personable woman. To say that she is handsome would hardly convey a proper idea. Let the reader suppose a woman of about fifty, very tall and of large dimensions. It would be unjust to call her fat, because though very large she is still symmetrical. When she is dressed in her full Tyrolese costume, — which is always the case at a certain hour on Sunday, and on other stated and by no means unfrequent days as to which I was never quite able to learn the exact rule, — when she is so dressed her arms are bare down from her shoulders, and such arms I never saw on any human being. Her back is very broad and her bust expansive. But her head stands erect upon it as the head of some old Juno, and in all her motions, — though I doubt whether she could climb by the mountain path to her parish church, — she displays a certain stately alertness which forbids one to call her fat. Her smile, — when she really means to smile and to show thereby her goodwill and to be gracious, — is as sweet as Hebe's. Then it is that you see that in her prime she must in truth have been a lovely woman. There is at these moments a kindness in her eyes and a playfulness about her mouth which is apt to make you think that you can do what you like with the Frau. Who has not at times been charmed by the frolic playfulness of the tiger? Not that Frau Frohmann has aught of the tiger in her nature but its power. But the power is all there, and not unfrequently the signs of power. If she be thwarted, contradicted, counselled by unauthorised counsellors, — above all if she be censured, — then the signs of power are shown. Then the Frau does not smile. At such times she is wont to speak her mind very plainly, and to make those who hear her understand that, within the precincts and purlieus of the Brunnenthal Peacock, she is an irresponsible despot. There have been guests there rash enough to find some trifling fault with the comforts provided for them, — whose beds perhaps have been too hard, or their towels too limited, or perhaps their hours not agreeably arranged for them. Few, however, have ever done so twice, and they who have so sinned, — and have then been told that the next diligence would take them quickly to Innsbruck if they were discontented, — have rarely stuck to their complaints and gone. The comforts of the house, and the prices charged, and the general charms of the place have generally prevailed, — so that the complainants, sometimes with spoken apologies, have in most cases sought permission to remain. In late years the Frau's certainty of victory has created a feeling that nothing is to be said against the arrangements of the Peacock. A displeased guest can exercise his displeasure best by taking himself away in silence.

The Frau of late years has had two counsellors; for though she is but ill inclined to admit advice from those who have received no authority to give it, she is not therefore so self-confident as to feel that she can live and thrive without listening to the wisdom of others. And those two counsellors may be regarded as representing — the first or elder her conscience, and the second and younger her worldly prudence. And in the matter of her conscience very much more is concerned than simple honesty. It is not against cheating or extortion that her counsellor is apt to her; but rather in regard to those innovations which he and she think to be prejudicial to the manner and life of Brunnenthal, of Innsbruck, of the Tyrol, of the Austrian empire generally, and, indeed, of the world at large. To be as her father had been before her, for her father, too, had kept the Peacock; to let life be cheap and simple, but yet very plentiful as it had been in his days, this was the counsel given by Father Conolin the old priest, who always spent two nights in each month at the establishment, and was not unfrequently to be seen there on other occasions. He had been opposed to many things which had been effected, — that alteration of the hour of dinner, the erection of the bath-house, the changing of plates at each course, and especially certain notifications and advertisements by which foreigners may have been induced to come to the Brunnenthal. The kaplan, or chaplain, as he was called, was particularly adverse to strangers, seeming to think that the advantages of the place should be reserved, if not altogether for the Tyrolese, at any rate for the Germans of Southern Germany, and was probably of opinion that no real good could be obtained by harbouring Lutherans. But, of late, English also had come, to whom, though he was personally very courteous, he was much averse in his heart of hearts. Such had ever been the tendency of his advice, and it had always been received with willing, nay, with loving ears. But the fate of the kaplan had been as in the fate of all such counsellors. Let the toryism of the Tory be ever so strong, it is his destiny to carry out the purposes of his opponents. So it had been, and was, with the Frau. Though she was always in spirit antagonistic to the other counsellor, it was the other counsellor who prevailed with her.

At Innsbruck for many years there had lived a lawyer, or rather a family of lawyers, men always of good repute and moderate means, named Schlessen; and in their hands had been reposed by the Frau that confidence as to business matters which almost every one in business must have in some lawyer. The first Schlessen whom the Frau had known in her youth, and who was then a very old man, had been almost as conservative as the priest. Then had come his son, who had been less so, but still lived and died without much either of the light of progress or contamination of revolutionary ideas from the outer world. But about three years before the date of our tale he also had passed away, and now young Fritz Schlessen sat in the chair of his forefathers. It was the opinion of Innsbruck generally that the young lawyer was certainly equal, probably superior, in attainments and intellect to any of his predecessors. He had learned his business both in Munich and Vienna, and though he was only twenty-six when he was left to manage his clients himself, most of them adhered to him. Among others so did our Frau, and this she did knowing the nature of the man and of the counsel she might expect to receive from him. For though she loved the priest, and loved her old ways, and loved to be told that she could live and thrive on the rules by which her father had lived and thriven before her, — still, still there was always present to her mind the fact that she was engaged in trade, and that the first object of a tradesman must be to make money. No shoemaker can set himself to work to make shoes having as his first intention an ambition to make the feet of his customers comfortable. That may come second, and to him, as a conscientious man, may be essentially necessary. But he sets himself to work to make shoes in order that he may earn a living. That law, — almost of nature we may say, — had become so recognised by the Frau that she felt that it must be followed, even in spite of the priest if need were, and that, in order that it might be followed, it would be well that she should listen to the advice of Herr Schlessen. She heard therefore all that her kaplan would say to her with gracious smiles, and something of what her lawyer would say to her, not always very graciously; but in the long-run she would take the lawyer's advice.

It will have to be told in a following chapter how it was that Fritz Schlessen had a preponderating influence in the Brunnenthal, arising from other causes than his professional soundness and in general prudence. It may, however, be as well to explain here that Peter Frohmann the son sided always with the priest, and attached himself altogether to the conservative interest. But he, though he was honest, diligent, and dutiful to his mother, was lumpy, uncouth, and slow both of speech and action. He understood the cutting of timber and the making of hay, — something perhaps of the care of horses and of the nourishment of pigs; but in money matters he was not efficient. Amalia, or Malchen, the daughter, who was four or five years her brother's junior, was much brighter, and she was strong on the reforming side. British money was to her thinking as good as Austrian, or even Tyrolese. To thrive even better than her forefathers had thriven seemed to her to be desirable. She therefore, though by her brightness and feminine ways she was very dear to the priest, was generally opposed to him in the family conclaves. It was chiefly in consequence of her persistency that the table napkins at the Peacock were now changed twice a week.

Chapter II
The Beginning of Troubles

Of late days, and up to the time of which we are speaking, the chief contest between the Frau, with the kaplan and Peter on one side, and Malchen with Fritz Schlessen on the other, was on that most important question whether the whole rate of charges should not be raised at the establishment. The prices had been raised, no doubt, within the lsat twenty years, or the Frau could not have kept her house open; — but this had been done indirectly. That the matter may not be complicated for our readers, we will assume that all charges are made at the Peacock in zwansigers and kreutzers, and that the zwansiger, containing twenty kreutzers, is worth eight-pence of English money. Now it must be understood that the guests at the Peacock were entertained at the rate of six zwansigers, or four shillings, a day, and that this included everything necessary, — a bed, breakfast, dinner, cup of coffee after dinner, supper, as much fresh milk as anybody chose to drink when the cows were milked, and the use of everything in and about the establishment. Guests who required wine or beer, of course, were charged for what they had. Those who were rich enough to be taken about in carriages paid so much per job, — each separate jaunt having been inserted in a tariff. No doubt there were other possible and probable extras; but an ordinary guest might live for his six zwansigers a day; — and the bulk of them did so live, with the addition of whatever allowance of beer each might think appropriate. From time to time a little had been added to the cost of luxuries. Wine had become dearer, and perhaps the carriages. A bath was an addition to the bill, and certain larger and more commodious rooms were supposed to be entitled to an extra zwansiger per week; —but the main charge had always remained fixed. In the time of the Frau's father guests had been entertained at, let us say, four shillings a head, and guests were so entertained now. All the world, — at any rate all the Tyrolese world south of Innsbruck, — knew that six zwansigers was the charge in the Brunnenthal. It would be like adding a new difficulty to the path of life to make a change. The Frau had always held her head high, — had never been ashamed of looking her neighbour in the face, but when she was advised to rush at once up to seven zwansigers and a half (or five shillings a day), she felt that, should she do so, she would be overwhelmed with shame. Would not her customers then have cause of complaint? Would not they have such cause that they would in truth desert her? Did she not know that Herr Weiss, the magistrate from Brixen, with his wife, and his wife's sister, and the children, who came yearly to the Peacock, could not afford to bring his family at this increased rate of expenses? And the Fraulein Tendel with her sister would never come from Innsbruck if such an announcement was made to her. It was the pride of this woman's heart to give all that was necessary for good living to those who would come and submit themselves to her for four shillings a day. Among the "extras" she could endure some alteration. She did not like extras, and if people would have luxuries they must be made to pay for them. But the Peacock had always been kept open for six zwansigers, and though Fritz Schlessen was very eloquent, she would not give way to him.

Fritz Schlessen simply told her that the good things which she provided for her guests cost at present more than six zwansigers, and could not therefore be sold by her at that price without a loss.

She was rich, Fritz remarked shrugging his shoulders, and having amassed property could if she pleased dispose of it gradually by entertaining her guests at a loss to herself; — only let her know what she was doing. That might be charity, might be generosity, might be friendliness; but it was not trade. Everything else in the world had become dearer, and therefore living at the Peacock should be dearer. As to the Weisses and the Tendels, no doubt they might be shocked, and perhaps hindered from coming. But their places would surely be filled by othes. Was not the house always full from the 1st of June till the end of September? Were not strangers refused admittance week after week from want of accommodation? If the new prices were found to be too high for the Tyrolese and Bavarians, they would not offend the Germans from the Rhine, or the Belgians, or the English. Was it not plain to every one that people now came from greater distances then heretofore?

These were the arguments which Herr Schlessen used; and, though they were very disagreeable, they were not easily answered. The Frau repudiated altogether the idea of keeping open her house on other than true trade principles. When the young lawyer talked to her about generosity she waxed angry, and accused him of laughing at her. "Dearest Frau Frohmann," he said, "it is so necessary you should know the truth! Of course you intend to make a profit; — but if you cannot do so at your present prices, and yet will not raise them, at any rate understand what it is that you are doing." Now the last year had been a bad year, and she knew that she had not increased her store. This all took place in the month of April, when a proposition was being made as to the prices for the coming season. The lawyer had suggested that a circular should be issued, giving notice of an altered tariff. Malchen was clearly in favour of the new idea. She could not see that the Weisses and Tendels, and other neighbours, should be entertained at a manifest loss; and, indeed, she had prepossessions in favour of foreigners, especially of the English, which, when expressed, brought down upon her head sundry hard words from her mother, who called her a "pert hussey," and implied that if Fritz Schlessen wanted to pull the house down she, Malchen, would be willing that it should be done. "Better do that, mother, than keep the roof on at a loss," said Malchen; who upon that was

turned at once out of the little inner room in which the conference was being held.

Peter who was present on the occasion, was decidedly opposed
to all innovations, partly because his conservative nature so
prompted him, and partly because he did not regard Herr Schles-
ser with a friendship so warm as that entertained by his sister. He
was, perhaps, a little jealous of the lawyer. And then he had an
idea that as things were prosperous to the eye, they would certainly come right at last. The fortunes of the house had been
made at the rate of six zwansigers a day, and there was, he
thought, no wisdom more clear than that of adhering to a line of
conduct which had proved itself to be advantageous.

The kaplan was clear against any change of prices; but then he
burdened his advice on the question with a suggestion which was
peculiarly disagreeable to the Frau. He acknowledged the truth of
much that the lawyer had said. It appeared to him that the good
things provided could not in truth be sold at the terms as they
were now fixed. He was quite alive to the fact that it behoved the
Frau as a wise woman to make a profit. Charity is one thing, and
business is another. The Frau did her charities like a Christian,
generally using Father Conolin as her almoner in such matters.
But, as a keeper of a house of public entertainment, it was necessary that she should live. The kaplan was as wide awake to this
as was the Frau herself, or the lawyer. But he thought that the
changes should not be in the direction indicated by Schlessen.
The condition of the Weisses and the Tendels should be considered. How would it be if one of the "meats" and one of the puddings were discontinued, and if the cup of coffee after dinner
were made an extra? Would not that so reduce the expenditure as
to leave a profit? And in that case the Weisses and the Tendels
need not necessarily incur any increased charges.

When the kaplan had spoken the lawyer looked closely into
the Frau's face. The proposition might no doubt for the present
meet the difficulty, but he knew that it would be disagreeable.
There came a cloud upon the old woman's brow, and she frowned
even upon the priest.

"They'd want to be helped twice out of the one pudding, and
you'd gain nothing," said Peter.

"According to that," said the lawyer, "if there were only one course the dinner would cost the same. The fewer the dishes, the less the cost, no doubt."

"I don't believe you know anything about it," said the Frau.

"Perhaps not," said the lawyer. "On those little details no doubt you are the best judge. But I think I have shown that something should be done."

"You might try the cofee, Frau Frohmann," said the priest.

"They would not take any. You'd only save the coffee," said the lawyer.

"And the sugar," said the priest.

"But then they'd never ask for brandy," suggested Peter.

The Frau on that occasion said not a word further, but after a little while got up from her chair and stood silent among them; which was known to be a sign that the conference was dismissed.

All this had taken place immediately after dinner, which at this period of the year was eaten at noon. It had simply been a family meal, at which the Frau had sat with her two children and her two friends. The kaplan on such occasions was always free. Nothing that he had in that house ever cost him a kreutzer. But the attorney paid his way like any one else. When called on for absolute work done, — not exactly for advice given in conference, — he made his charges. It might be that a time was coming in which no money would pass on either side, but that time had not arrived as yet. As soon as the Frau was left alone, she reseated herself in her accustomed arm-chair, and set herself to work in sober and almost solemn sadness to think over it all. It was a most perplexing question. There could be no doubt that all the wealth which she at present owned had been made by a business carried on at the present prices and after the existing fashion. Why should there be any change? She was told that she must make her customers pay more because she herself was made to pay more. But why should she pay more? She could understand that in the general prosperity of the Brunnenthal those about her should have somewhat higher wages. As she had prospered, why should not they also prosper? The servants of the poor must, she thought, be poorer than the servants of the rich. But why should poultry be dearer and meat? Some things she knew were cheaper, as tea and sugar and coffee. She had bought three horses during the winter, and they certainly had been costly. Her father had not given such prices, nor, before this, had she. But that probably had been Peter's fault, who had too rashly acceded to the demands made upon him. And now she remembered with regret that on the 1st of January she had acceded to a petition from the carpenter for an addition of six zwansigers to his monthly wages. He had made the request on the plea of a sixth child, adding also, that journeymen carpenters both at Brixen and at Innsbruck were getting what he asked. She had granted to the coming of the additional baby that which she would probably have denied to the other argument; but it had never occurred to her that she was really paying the additional four shillings a month because carpenters were becoming dearer throughout the world. Malchen's clothes were certainly much more costly than her own had been, when she was young; but then Malchen was a foolish girl, fond of fashion from Munich, and just at this moment was in love. It could hardly be right that those poor Tendel females, with their small and fixed means, should be made to pay more for their necessary summer excursion because Malchen would dress herself in so-called French finery, instead of adhering, as she ought, to Tyrolese customs.

The Frau on this occasion spent an hour in solitude, thinking over it all. She had dismissed the conference, but that could not be regarded as an end to the matter. Herr Schlessen had come out from Innsbruck with a written document in his pocket, which he was proposing to have printed and circulated, and which, if printed and circulated, would intimate to the world at large that the Frau Frohmann had raised her prices. Therein the new rates, seven zwansigers and a half a head, were inserted unblushingly at full length, as though such a disruption of old laws was the most natural thing in the world. There was a flippancy about it which disgusted the old woman. Malchen seemed to regard an act which would banish from the Peacock the old friends and well-known customers of the house as though it were an easy trifle; and almost desirable with that very object. The Frau's heart warmed to the well-known faces as she thought of this. Would she not have infinitely greater satisfaction in cooking good dinners for her simple Tyrolese neighbours, than for rich foreigners who, after all, were too often indifferent to what was done for them? By those Tendel ladies her puddings were recognized as real works of art. They thought of them, talked of them, ate them, and no doubt dreamed of them. And Herr Weiss — how he enjoyed her dinners, and how proud he always was as he encouraged his children around him to help themselves to every dish in succession! And the Frau Weiss — with all her cares and her narrow means — was she to be deprived of that cheap month's holiday which was so necessary for her, in order that the Peacock and the charms of the Brunnenthal generally might be devoted to Jews from Frankfort, or rich shopkeepers from Hamburg, or, worse still, to proud and thankless Englishmen? At the end of the hour the Frau had determined that she would not raise her prices.

But yet something must be done. Had she resolved, even silently resolved, that she would carry on her business at a loss, she would have felt that she was worthy of restraint as a lunatic. To keep a house of public entertainment and to lose by it was to her mind, a very sad idea! To work and be out of pocket by working! To her who knew little or nothing of modern speculation, such a catastrophe was most melancholy. But to work with the intention of losing could be the condition only of a lunatic. And Schlessen had made good his point as to the last season. The money spent had been absolutely more than the money received. Something must be done. And yet she would not raise her prices.

Then she considered the priest's proposition. Peter, she knew, had shown himself to be a fool. Though his feelings were good, he always was a fool. The expenses of the house no doubt might be much diminished in the manner suggested by Herr Conolin. Salt butter could be given instead of fresh at breakfast. Cheaper coffee could be procured. The courses at dinner might be reduced. The second pudding might be discontinued with economical results. But had not her success in these things been the pride of her life; and of what good would her life be to her if its pride were crushed? The Weisses no doubt would come all the same, but how would they whisper and talk of her among themselves, when they found these parsimonious changes! The Tendel ladies would not complain. It was not likely that a breath of complaint would ever pass their humble lips; but she herself, she, Frau Frohmann, who was perhaps somewhat unduly proud of her character for wealth, would have to explain to them why it was that the second pudding had been abolished. She would be forced to declare that she could no longer afford to supply it, a declaration which to her would have in it something of meanness, something of degradation. No! she could not abandon the glory of her dinner. It was as though you should ask a Royal Academician to cease to exhibit his pictures, or an actor to consent to have his name withdrawn from the bills. Thus at last she came to that further resolve. The kaplan's advice must be rejected, as must that of the lawyer.

But something must be done. For a moment there came upon her a sad idea that she would leave the whole thing to others, and retire into obscurity at Schwatz, the village from whence the Frohmanns had originally come. There would be ample means for private comfort. But then who would carry on the Peacock, who would look after the farm, and the timber, and the posting, and the mill? Peter was certainly not efficient for all that. And Malchen's ambition lay elsewhere. There was, too, a cowardice in this idea of running away which was very displeasing to her.

Why need there be any raising of prices at all, — either in one direction or in the other? Had she herself never been persuaded into paying more to others, then she would not have been driven to demand more from others. And those higher payments on her part had, she thought, not been obligatory on her. She had been soft and good-natured, and therefore it was that she was now called upon to be exorbitant. There was something abominable to her in this general greed of the world for more money. At the moment she felt almost a hatred for poor Seppel the carpenter, and regarded that new baby of his as an impertinent intrusion. She would fall back upon the old wages, the old prices for everything. There would be a difficulty with that Innsbruck butcher; but unless he would give way she would try the man at Brixen. In that matter of fowls she would not yield a kreutzer to the entreaties of her poor neighbours who brought them to her door for sale.

Then she walked forth from the house to a little arbour or summer-house which was close to the chapel opposite, in which she found Schlessen smoking his pipe with a cup of coffee before him, and Malchen by his side. "I have made up my mind, Herr Schlessen," she said. It was only when she was very angry with him that she called him Herr Schlessen.

"And what shall I do?" asked the lawyer.

"Do nothing at all; but just destroy that bit of paper." So saying the Frau walked back to the house, and Fritz Schlessen, looking round at Malchen, did destroy that bit of paper.

Chapter III
The Question of the Mitgift

About two months after the events described in the last chapter, Malchen and Fritz Schlessen were sitting in the same little harbour, and he was again smoking his pipe and again drinking his coffee. And they were again alone. When these two were seated together in the arbour, at this early period of the season, they were usually left alone, as they were known to be lovers by the guests who would then be assembled at the Peacock. When the summer had grown into autumn, and the strangers from a distance had come, and the place was crowded, then the ordinary coffee-drinkers and smokers would crowd round the arbour regardless of the loves of Amalia and Fritz.

The whole family of the Weisses were now at the Peacock, and the two Tendel ladies and three or four others, men with their wives and daughters, from Botzen, Brunecken, and places around at no great distance. It was now the end of June; but it is not till July that the house becomes full, and it is in August that the real crowd is gathered at Frau Frohmann's board. It is then that folk from a distance cannot find beds, and the whole culinary resources of the establishment are put to their greatest stress. It was now Monday, and the lawyer had been making a holiday, having come to Brunnenthal on the previous Saturday. On the Sunday there had been perhaps a dozen visitors from Innsbruck who had been driven out after early mass for their dinner and Sunday holiday. Everything had been done at the Peacock on the old style. There had been no diminution either in the number or in the excellence of the dishes, nor had there been any increase in the tariff. It had been the first day of the season at which there had been a full table, and the Frau had done her best. Everybody had known that the sojourners in the house were to be entertained at the old rates; but it had been hoped by the lawyer and the priest, and by Malchen, — even by Peter himself, — that a zwansiger would be added to the charge for dinner demanded from the townspeople. But at the last moment word had come forth that there should be no increase. All the morning the old lady had been very gloomy. She had heard mass in her own chapel, and had then made herself very busy in the kitchen. She had spoken no word to any one till, at the moment before dinner, she gave her instructions to Malchen, who always made out the bills and saw that the money was duly received. There was to be no increase. Then, when the last pudding had been sent in, she went, according to her custom, to her room and decorated herself in her grand costume. When the guests had left the dining-room and were clustereing about in the passages and on the seats in front of the house, waiting for their coffee, she had come forth, very fine, with her grand cap on her head, with her gold and silver ornaments, with her arms bare, and radiant with smiles. She shook Madame Weiss very graciously by the hand and stooped down and kissed the youngest child. To one Fräulein Tendel after another she said a civil word. And when, as it happened, Seppel the carpenter went by, dressed in his Sunday best, with a child in each hand, she stopped him and asked kindly after the baby. She had made up her mind that at any rate for a time she would not submit to the humiliation of acknowledging that she was driven to the necessity of asking increased prices.

That had taken place on the Sunday, and it was on the following day that the two lovers were in the arbour together. Now it must be understood that all the world knew that these lovers were lovers, and that all the world presumed that they were to become husband and wife. There was not and never had been the least secrecy about it. Malchen was four or five and twenty, and he was perhaps thirty. They knew their own minds, and were, neither of them, likely to be persuaded by others either to marry or not to marry. The Frau had given her consent, — not with that ecstasy of joy with which sons-in-law are sometimes welcomed, — but still without reserve. The kaplan had given in his adhesion. The young lawyer was not quite the man he liked, — entertained some of the new ideas about religion, and was given to innovations; but he was respectable and well-to-do. He was a lover against whom he, as a friend of the family, could not lift up his voice. Peter did not like the man, and Peter, in his way, was fond of his sister. But he had not objected. Had he done so, it would not have mattered much. Malchen was stronger at the Brunnenthal than Peter. Thus it may be said that things generally smiled upon the lovers. But yet no one had ever heard that a day was fixed for their marrige. Madame Weiss had once asked Malchen, and Malchen had told her — not exactly to mind her own business, but that had been very nearly the meaning of what she had said.

There was, indeed, a difficulty; and this was the difficulty. The Frau had assented — in a gradual fashion, rather by not dissenting as the thing had gone on, so that it had come to be understood that the thing was to be. But she had never said a word as to the young lady's fortune — as to what mitgift, which in such a case would certainly be necessary. Such a woman as the Frau, in giving her daughter would surely have to give something with her. But the Frau was a woman who did not like parting with her money; — and was such a woman that even the lawyer did not like asking the question. The fraulein had once inquired, but the mother had merely raised her eyebrows and remained silent. Then the lawyer had told the priest that in the performance of her moral duties the Frau ought to settle something in her own mind. The priest had assented, but had seemed to imply that in the performance of such a duty an old lady ought not to be hurried. A year or two, he seemed to think, would not be too much for consideration. And so the matter stood at the present moment.

Perhaps it is that the Germans are a slow people. It may be that the Tyrolese are especially so. Be that as it may, Herr Schlessen did not seem to be driven into any agony of despair by these delays. He was fondly attached to his Malchen; but as to offering to take her without any mitgift — quite empty-handed, just as she stood — that was out of the question. No young man who had anything, ever among his acquaintances, did that kind of thing. Scales should be somewhat equally balanced. He had a good income, and was entitled to some substantial mitgift. He was quite ready to marry her to-morrow, if only this important question could get itself settled.

Malchen was quite as well aware as was he that her mother should be brought to do her duty in this matter; but perhaps, of the two, she was a little the more impatient. If there should at last be a slip between the cup and the lip, the effect to her would be so much more disastrous than to him. He could very easily get another wife. Young women were as plenty as blackberries. So the fraulein told herself. But she might find it difficult to suit herself, if at last this affair were to be broken off. She knew herself to be a fair, upstanding, good-looking lass, with personal attractions sufficient to make such a young man as Fritz Schlessen like her society; but she knew also that her good looks, such as they were, would not be improved by weeping. It might be possible that Fritz should change his mind some day, if he were kept waiting till he saw her becoming day by day more commonplace under his eyes. Malchen had good sense enough not to overrate her own charms, and she knew the world well enough to be aware that she would be wise to secure, if possible, a comfortable home while she was at her best. It was not that she suspected Fritz; but she did not think that she would be justified in supposing him to be more angelic than other young men simply because he was her lover. Therefore, Malchen was impatient, and for the last month or two had been making up her mind to be very "round" with her mother on the subject.

At the present moment, however, the lovers, as they were sitting in the arbour, were discussing rather the Frau's affairs in regard to the establishment than their own. Schlessen had, in truth, come to the Brunnenthal on this present occasion to see what would be done, thinking that if the thin edge of the wedge could have been got in, — if those people from the town could have been made to pay an extra zwansiger each for their Sunday dinner, — then, even yet, the old lady might be induced to raise her prices in regard to the autumn and more fashionable visitors. But she had been obstinate, and had gloried in her obstinacy, dressing herself up in her grandest ornaments and smiling her best smiles, as in triumph at her own victory.

"The fact is, you know, it won't do," said the lawyer to his love. "I don't know how I am to say any more, but anybody can see with half an eye that she will simply go on losing money year after year. It is all very fine for the Weisses and Tendels, and very fine for old Trauss," — old Trauss was a retired linen-draper from Vienna, who lived at Innsbruck, and was accustomed to eat many dinners at the Peacock; a man who could afford to pay a proper price, but who was well pleased to get a good dinner at a cheap rate, — "and very well for old Trauss," continued the lawyer, becoming more energetic as he went on, "to regale themselves at your mother's expense; — but that's what it come to. Everybody knows that everybody has raised the price of everything. Look at the Golden Lion." The Golden Lion was the grand hotel in the town. "Do you think they haven't raised their prices during the last twenty years?"

"Why is it, Fritz?"

"Everything goes up together, of course. If you'll look into old accounts you'll see that three hundred years ago you could buy a sheep at Salzburg for two florins and a half. I saw it somewhere in a book. If a lawyer's clerk then had eighty florins a year he was well off. That would not surprise her. She can understand that there should be an enormous change in three hundred years, but she can't make out why there would be a little change in thirty years."

"But many things have got cheaper, Fritz."

"Living altogether hasn't got cheaper. Look at wages."

"I don't know why we should pay more. Everybody says that bread is lower than it used to be."

"What sort of bread do the people eat now? Look at that man." The man was Seppel, who was dragging a cart which he had just mended out of the shed which was close by, — in which cart was seated his three eldest children, so that he might help their mother as assistant nurse even while he was at his work. 'Don't you think he gets more wheaten flour into his house in a week than his grandfather did in a year? His grandfather never saw white bread."

"Why should he have it?"

"Because he likes it, and because he can get it. Do you think he'd have stayed here if his wages had not been raised?"

"I don't think Seppel ever would have moved out of the Brunnenthal, Fritz."

"Then Seppel would have been more stupid than the cow, which knows very well on which side of the field it can find the best grass. Everything gets dearer; — and if one wants to live one has to swim with the stream. You might as well try to fight with bows and arrows, or with the old-fasioned flint rifles, as to live at the same rate as your grandfather." The young lawyer, as he said this, rapped his pipe on the table to knock out the ashes, and threw himself back on his seat with a full conviction that he had spoken words of wisdom.

"What will it all come to, Fritz?" This Malchen asked with real anxiety in her voice. She was not slow to join two things together. It might well be that her mother should be induced by her pride to carry on the business for a while, so as to lose some of her money, but that she should at least be induced to see the error of her ways before serious damage had been done. Her financial position was too good to be brought to ruin by small losses. But during the period of her discomfiture she certainly would not be got to open her hand in that matter of the mitgift. Malchen's own little affair would never get itself settled till this other question should have arranged itself satisfactorily. There could be no mit-gift from a failing business. And if the business were to continue to fail for the next year or two, where would Malchen be then? It was not, therefore, wonderful that she should be in earnest.

"Your mother is a very clever woman," said the lover.

"It seems to me that she is very foolish about this," said Malchen, whose feeling of filial reverence was not at the moment very strong.

"She is a clever woman, and has done uncommonly well in the world. The place is worth double as much as when she married your father. But it is that very success which makes her obstinate. She thinks that she can see her way. She fancies that she can compel people to work for her and deal with her at the old prices. It will take her, perhaps, a couple of years to find out that this is wrong. When she has lost three or four thousand florins she'll come round."

Fritz, as he said this, seemed to be almost contented with this view of the case, — as though it made no difference to him. But with the fraulein the matter was so essentially personal that she could not allow it to rest there. She had made up her mind to be round with her mother; but it seemed to her to be necessary, also, that something should be said to her lover. "Won't all that be very bad for you, Fritz?"

"Her business with me will go on just the same."

This was felt to be unkind and very unloverlike. But she could not afford at the present moment to quarrel with him. "I mean about our settling," she said.

"It ought not to make a difference."

"I don't know about *ought*, but — but won't it? You don't see her as I do, but, of course, it puts her into a bad temper."

"I suppose she means to give you some fixed sum. I don't doubt but she has it all arranged in her own mind."

"Why doesn't she name it, then?"

"Ah, my dear, — mein schatz, — there is nobody who likes too well to part with his money."

"But when is there to be an end of it?"

"You should find that out. You are her child, and she has only two. That she should hang back is a matter of course. When one has the money of his own one can do anything. It is all in her own hand. See what I bear. When I tell her this or that she turns upon me as if I were nobody. Do you think I should suffer it if she were only just a client? You must persuade her, and be gentle with her; but if she would name the sum it would be a comfort, of course."

The fraulein herself did not in the least know what the sum ought to be; but she thought she did know that it was a matter which should be arranged between her lover and her parent. What she would have liked to have told him was this, — that as there were only two children, and as her mother was at any rate an honest woman, he might be sure that a proper dowry would come at last. But she was well aware that he would think that a mitgift should be a mitgift; the bride should come with it in her hand, so that she might be a comfort to her husband's household. Schlessen would not be at all willing to wait patiently for the Frau's death, or even for some final settlement of her affairs when she might make up her mind to leave the Peacock and betake herself to Schwatz. "You would not like to ask her yourself?" she said.

He was silent for a while, and then he answered her by another question. "Are you afraid of her?"

"Not afraid. But she would just tell me I was impertinent. I am not a bit afraid, but it would do no good. It would be so reasonable for you to do it."

"There is just the difference, Malchen. I am afraid of her."

"She could not bite you."

"No; — but she might say something sharp, and then I might answer her sharply; and then there might be a quarrel. If she were to tell me that she did not want to see me any more in the Brunnenthal, where should we be then? Mein schatz, if you will take my advice, you will just say a word yourself, in your softest, sweetest way." Then he got up and made his way across to the stable, where was the horse which was to take him back to Innsbruck. Malchen was not altogether well pleased with her lover, but she perceived that on the present occasion she must, perforce, follow his advice.

Chapter IV
The Frau Returns to the Simplicity
of the Old Days

Two or three weeks went by in the Brunnenthal without any spcial occurrence, and Malchen had not as yet spoken to her mother about her fortune. The Frau had during this time been in more than ordinary good humour with her own household. July had opened with lovely weather, and the house had become full earlier than usual. The Frau liked to have the house full, even though there might be no profit, and therefore she was in a good humour. But she had been exceptionally busy, and was trying experiments in her housekeeping, as to which she was still in hope that they would carry her through all her difficulties. She had been both to Brixen on one side of the mountain and to Innsbruck on the other, and had changed her butcher. Her old friend Hoff, at the latter place, had altogether declined to make any reduction in his prices. Of course they had been raised within the last five or six years. Who did not know that that had been the case with butchers' meat all the world over? As it was, he charged the Frau less than he charged the people at the Golden Lion. So at least he swore; and when she told him that unless an alteration was made she must take her custom elsewhere — he bade her go elsewhere. Therefore she did make a contract with the butcher at Brixen on lower terms, and seemed to think that she had got over her difficulty. But Brixen was further than Innsbruck, and the carriage was more costly. It was whispered also about the house that the meat was not equally good. Nobody, however, had as yet dared to say a word on that subject to the Frau. And she, though in the midst of her new efforts she was good-humoured herself, — as is the case with many people while they have faith in the efforts they are making, — had become the cause of much unhappiness among others. Butter, eggs, poultry, honey, fruit, and vegetables, she was in the habit of buying from her neighbours, and had been so excellent a customer that she was as good as a market to the valley in general. There had usually been some haggling; but that, I think by such vendors is considered a necessary and almost an agreeable part of the operation. The produce had been bought and sold, and the Frau had, upon the whole, been regarded as a kind of providence to the Brunnenthal. But now there were sad tales told at many a cottage and small farm-stead around. The Frau had declared that she would give no more than three zwansigers a pair for chickens, and had insisted on having both butter and eggs at a lower price than she had paid last year. And she had succeeded, after infinite clamours. She had been their one market, their providence, and they had no other immediate customers to whom to betake themselves. The eggs and the butter, the raspberries and the currants, must be sold. She had been imperious and had succeeded, for a while. But there were deep murmurs, and already a feeling was growing up in favour of Innsbruck and a market cart. It was very dreadful. How were they to pay their taxes, how were they to pay anything, if they were to be crimped and curtailed in this way? One poor woman had already walked to Innsbruck with three dozen eggs and had got nearly twice the money which the Frau had offered. The labour of the walk had been very hard upon her, and the economy of the proceeding generally may have been doubtful; but it had proved that the thing could be done.

Early in July there had come a letter, addressed to Peter, from an English gentleman who, with his wife and daughter, had been at the Brunnenthal on the preceding year. Mr. Cartwright had now written to say, that the same party would be glad to come again early in August, and had asked what were the present prices. Now the very question seemed to imply a conviction on the gentleman's mind that the prices would be raised. Even Peter, when he took the letter to his mother, thought that this would be

27

a good opportunity for taking a step in advance. These were English people, and entitled to no loving forbearance. The Cartwrights need know nothing as to the demands made on the Weisses and Tendels. Peter, who had always been on his mother's side, Peter who hated changes, even he suggested that he might write back word that seven zwansigers and a half was now the tariff. "Don't you know I have settled all that?" said the old woman, turning upon him fiercely. Then he wrote to Mr. Cartwright to say that the charge would be six zwansigers a day, as heretofore. It was certainly a throwing away of money. Mr. Cartwright was a Briton, and would, therefore, almost have preferred to pay another zwansiger or two. So at least Peter thought. And he, even an Englishman, with his wife and daughter, was to be taken in and entertained at a loss! At a loss! — unless, indeed, the Frau could be successful in her new mode of keeping her house. Father Conolin in these days kept away. The complaints made by the neighbours around reached his ears, — very sad complaints, — and he hardly knew how to speak of them to the Frau. It was becoming very serious with him. He had counselled her against any rise in her own prices, but had certainly not intended that she should make others lower. That had not been his plan; and now he did not know what advice to give.

But the Frau, resolute in her attempt, and proud of her success as far as it had gone, constantly adducing the conduct of those two rival butchers as evidence of her own wisdom, kept her ground like a Trojan. All the old courses were served, and the puddings and the fruit were at first as copious as ever. If the meat was inferior in quality, — and it could not be so without her knowledge, for she had not reigned so long in the kitchen of the Peacock without having become a judge in such matters, — she was willing to pass the fault over for a time. She tried to think that there was not much difference. She almost tried to believe that second-rate meat would do as well as first-rate. There should at least be no lack of anything in the cookery. And so she toiled and struggled, and was hopeful that she might have her own way and prove to all her advisers that she knew how to manage the house better than any of them.

There was great apparent good humour. Though she had frowned upon Peter when he had shown a disposition to spoil those Egyptians the Cartwrights, she had only done so in defence of her own resolute purpose, and soon returned to her kind looks. She was, too, very civil to Malchen, omitting for the time her usual girds and jeers as to her daughter's taste for French finery and general rejection of Tyrolese customs. And she said nothing of the prolonged absence of her two counsellors, the priest and the lawyer. A great struggle was going on within her own bosom, as to which she in these days said not a word to anybody. One counsellor had told her to raise her prices; another had advised her to lessen the luxuries supplied. As both the one proposition and the other had gone against her spirit, she had looked about her to find some third way out of her embarrassments. She had found it, and the way was one which recommended itself to her own sense of abstract justice. The old prices should prevail in the valley everywhere. She would extort nothing from Mr. Cartwright, but then neither should her neighbours extort anything from her. Seppel's wife was ill, and she had told him that in consequence of that misfortune the increased wages should be continued for three months, but that after that she must return to the old rate. In the softness of her heart she would have preferred to say six months, but that in doing so she would have seemed to herself to have departed from the necessary rigour of her new doctrine. But when Seppel stood before her, scratching his head, a picture of wretchedness and doubt, she was not comfortable in her mind. Seppel had a dim idea of his own rights, and did not like to be told that his extra zwansigers came to him from the Frau's charity. To go away from the Brunnenthal at the end of the summer, to go away at all, would be terrible to him; but to work for less than fair wages, would that not be more terrible? Of all which the Frau, as she looked at him, understood much.

And she understood much also of the discontent and almost despair which were filling the minds of the poor women all around her. All those poor women were dear to her. It was in her nature to love those around her, and especially those who were dependent on her. She knew the story of every household, — what children each mother had reared and what she had lost, when each had been brought to affliction by a husband's illness or a son's misconduct. She had never been deaf to their troubles; and though she might have been heard in violent discussion, now

29

with one and now with another, as to the selling value of this or that article, she had always been held by them to be a just woman and a constant friend. Now they were up in arms against her, to the extreme grief of her heart.

Nevertheless it was necessary that she should support herself by an outward appearance of tranquility, so that the world around her might know that she was not troubled by doubts as to her own conduct. She had heard somewhere that no return can be made from evil to good courses without temporary disruptions, and that all lovers of justice are subject to unreasonable odium. Things had gone astray because there had been unintentional lapses from justice. She herself had been the delinquent when she had allowed herself to be talked into higher payments than those which had been common in the valley in her young days. She had not understood, when she made these lapses gradually, how fatal would be their result. Now she understood, and was determined to plant her foot firmly down on the old figures. All this evil had come from a departure from the old ways. There must be sorrow and trouble, and perhaps some ill blood, in this return. So she smiled, and refused to give more than three zwansigers a pair for her chickens.

One old woman came to her with the express purpose of arguing it all out. Suse Krapp was the wife of an old woodman who lived high up above the Peacock, among the Pines, in a spot which could only be reached by a long and very steep ascent, and who, being old, and having a daughter and grand-daughters whom she could send down with her eggs and wild fruit, did not very often make her appearance in the valley. But she had known the Frau well for many years, having been one of those to welcome her when she had arrived there as a bride, and had always been treated with exceptional courtesy. Suse Krapp was a woman who had brought up a large family, and had known troubles; but she had always been able to speak her own mind; and when she arrived at the house, empty-handed, with nothing to sell, declaring at once her purpose of remonstrating with the Frau, the Frau regarded her as a delegate from the commercial females of the valley generally; and she took the coming in good part, asking Suse into her own inner room.

After sundry inquiries on each side, respecting the children and the guests, and the state of things in the world at large, the real question was asked: "Ah, meine liebe Frau Frohmann,"—my very dear Mrs. Frohmann, as one might say here, — "why are you dealing with us all in the Brunnenthal after this hard fashion?"

"What do you call a hard fashion, Suse?"

"Only giving half price for everything that you buy. Why should anything be cheaper this year than it was last? Ah, alas! does not everybody know that everything is dearer?"

"Why should anything be dearer, Suse? The people who come here are not charged more than they were twenty years ago."

"Who can tell? How can an old woman say? It is all very bad. The world, I suppose, is getting worse. But it is so. Look at the taxes."

The taxes, whether imperial or municipal, was a matter on which the Frau did not want to speak. She felt that they were altogether beyond her reach. No doubt there had been a very great increase in such demands during her time, and it was an increase against which nobody could make any stand at all. But, if that was all, there had been a rise in prices quite sufficient to answer that. She was willing to pay three zwansigers a pair for chickens, and yet she could remember when they were to be bought for a zwansiger each.

"Yes, taxes," she said; "they are an evil which we must all endure. It is no good grumbling at them. But we have had the roads made for us."

This was an unfortunate admission, for it immediately gave Suse Krapp an easy way to her great argument. "Roads, yes! and they are all saying that they must make use of them to send the things into market. Josephine Bull took her eggs into the city and got two kreutzers a-piece for them.

The Frau had already heard of that journey, and had also heard that poor Josephine Bull had been very much fatigued by her labours. It had afflicted her much, both that the poor woman should have been driven to such a task, and that such an inno-vation should have been attempted. She had never loved Innsbruck dearly, and now she was beginning to hate the place. "What good did she get by that, Suse? None, I fear, She had bet-ter have given her eggs away in the valley."

"But they will have a cart."

"Do you think a cart won't cost money? There must be some-body to drive the cart, I suppose." On this point the Frau spoke feelingly, as she was beginning to appreciate the inconvenience of sending twice a week all the way to Brixen for her meat. There was a diligence, but though the horses were kept in her own sta-bles, she had not as yet been able to come to terms with the proprietor.

"There is all that to think of, certainly," said Suse. "But — Wouldn't you come back, meine liebe Frau, to the prices you were paying last year? Do you not know that they would sooner sell to you than to any other human being in all the world? — and they must live by their little earnings."

But the Frau could not be persuaded. Indeed had she allowed herself to be persuaded, all her purpose would have been brought to an end. Of course there must be trouble, and her refusal of such a prayer as this was a part of her trouble. She sent for a glass of kirsch-wasser to mitigate the rigour of her denial, and as Suse drank the cordial she endeavoured to explain her system. There could be no happiness, no real prosperity in the valley, till they had returned to their old ways. "It makes me unhappy," said the Frau, shaking her head, "when I see the girls making for them-selves long petticoats." Suse quite agreed with the Frau as to the long petticoats; but, as she went, she declared that the butter and eggs must be taken into Innsbruck, and another allusion to the cart was the last word upon her tongue.

It was on the evening of that same day that Malchen, unaware that her mother's feelings had just then been peculiarly stirred up by an appeal from the women of the valley, came at last to the determination of asking that something might be settled as to the mitgift. "Mother," she said, "Fritz Schlessen thinks that some-thing should be arranged."

"Arranged? — as how?"

"I suppose he wants — to be married."

"If he don't, I suppose somebody else does," said the mother smiling.

"Well, mother of course it is not pleasant to be as we are now. You must feel that yourself. Fritz is a good young man, and there is nothing about him that I have a right to complain of. But of course, like all the rest of 'em, he expects some money when he takes a wife. Couldn't you tell him what you mean to give?"

"Not at present, Malchen."

"And why not now? It has been going on two years."

"Nina Cobard at Schwatz was ten years before her people would let it come off. Just at present I am trying a great experiment, and I can say nothing about money till the season is over." With this answer Malchen was obliged to be content, and was not slow in perceiving that it almost contained a promise that the affairs should be settled when the season was over.

Chapter V
A Zwansiger is a Zwansiger

In the beginning of August, the Weisses and the Tendels and Herr Trauss had all left the Brunnenthal, and our friend Frau Frohmann was left with a houseful of guests, who were less intimately known to her, but who not the less demanded and received all her care. But, as those departed whom she had taught herself to regard as neighbours and who were therefore entitled to something warmer and more generous than mere tavern hospitality, she began to feel the hardness of her case in having to provide so sumptuously for all these strangers at a loss. There was a party of Americans in the house who had absolutely made no inquiry whatsoever as to prices till they had shown themselves at her door. Peter had been very urgent with her to mulct the Americans, who were likely, he thought, to despise the house merely because it was cheap. But she would not give way. If the American gentleman should find out the fact and turn upon her, and ask her why he was charged more than others, how would she be able to answer him? She had never yet been so placed as not to be able to answer any complaints, boldly and even indignantly. It was hard upon her; but if the prices were to be raised to any, they must be raised to all.

The whole valley now was in a hubbub. In the matter of butter there had been so great a commotion that the Frau had absolutely gone back to the making of her own, a system which had been abandoned at the Peacock a few years since, with the express object of befriending the neighbours. There had been a dairy with all its appurtenances; but it had come to pass that the women around had got cows, and that the Frau had found that without damage to herself she could buy their supplies. And in this way her own dairy had gone out of use. She had kept her cows, because there had grown into use a great drinking of milk at the Peacock, and as the establishment had gradually increased, the demand for cream, custards, and such luxuries had of course increased also. Now when, remembering this, she conceived that she had a peculiar right to receive submission as the price of butter, and yet found more strong rebellion here than on any other point, she at once took the bull by the horns, and threw not only her energies, but herself bodily into the dairy. It was repaired and whitewashed, and scoured, and supplied with all necessary furniture in so marvellously short a time, that the owners of cows around could hardly believe their ears and their eyes. Of course there was a spending of money, but there had never been any slackness as to capital at the Peacock when good results might be expected from its expenditure. So the dairy was set a going.

But there was annoyance, even shame, and to the old woman's feeling almost disgrace, arising from this. As you cannot eat your cake and have it, so neither can you make your butter and have your cream. The supply of new milk to the milk-drinkers was at first curtailed, and then altogether stopped. The guests were not entitled to the luxury by any contract, and were simply told that as the butter was now made at home, the milk was wanted for that purpose. And then there certainly was a deterioration in the puddings. There had hitherto been a rich plenty which was now wanting. No one complained; but the Frau herself felt the falling off. The puddings now were such as might be seen at other places, — at the Golden Lion for instance. Hitherto her puddings had been unrivalled in the Tyrol.

Then there had suddenly appeared a huckster, a pedlar, an itinerant dealer in the valley who absolutely went round to the old women's houses and bought the butter at the prices which she had refused to give. And this was a man who had been in her own employment, had been brought to the valley by herself, and had once driven her own horses! And it was reported to her that this man was simply an agent for a certain tradesman in Innsbruck. There was an ingratitude in all this which nearly broke her heart.

It seemed to her that those to whom in their difficulties she had been most kind were now turning upon her in her difficulty; and she thought that there was no longer left among the people any faith, any feeling of decent economy, any principle. Disregarding right or wrong, they would all go where they could get half a zwansiger more! They knew what it was she was attempting to do; for had she not explained it all to Suse Krapp? And yet they turned against her.

The poor Frau knew nothing of that great principle of selling in the dearest market, however much the other lesson as to buying in the cheapest had been brought home to her. When a fixed price had become fixed, that, she thought, should not be altered. She was demanding no more than she had been used to demand, though to do so would have been so easy. But her neighbours, those to whom she had even been most friendly, refused to assist her in her efforts to re-establish the old and salutary simplicity. Of course when the butter was taken into Innsbruck, the chickens and the eggs went with the butter. When she learned how all this was she sent for Suse Krapp, and Suse Krapp again came down to her.

"They mean then to quarrel with me utterly?" said the Frau with her sternest frown.

"Meine liebe Frau Frohmann!" said the old woman, embracing the arm of her ancient friend.

"But they do mean it?"

"What can we do, poor wretches? We must live."

"You lived well enough before," said the Frau, raising her fist in the unpremeditated eloquence of her indignation. "Will it be better for you now to deal with strangers who will rob you at every turn? Will Karl Muntz, the blackguard that he is, advance money to any of you at your need? Well; let it be so. I too can deal with strangers. But when once I have made arrangements in the town, I will not come back to the people of the valley. If we are to be severed, we will be severed. It goes sadly against the grain with me, as I have a heart in my bosom."

"You have, you have, my dearest Frau Frohmann."

"As for the cranberries, we can do without them." Now it had been the case that Suse Krapp with her grandchildren had supplied the Peacock with wild fruits in plentiful abundance, which wild fruit, stewed as the Frau knew how to stew them, had been in great request among the guests at the Brunnenthal. Great bowls of cranberries and bilberries had always at this period of the year turned the Frau's modest supper into luxurious banquets. But there must be an end to that now; not in any way because the price paid for the fruit was grudged, but because the quarrel, if quarrel there must be, should be internecine at all points. She had loved them all; but, if they turned against her, not the less because of her love would she punish them. Poor old Suse wiped her eyes and took her departure without any kirschwasser on this occasion.

It all went on from bad to worse. Seppel the carpenter gave her notice that he would leave her service at the end of August. "Why at the end of August?" she asked, remembering that she had promised to give him the higher rate of wages up to a later date than that. Then Seppel explained, that as he must do something for himself, — that is, find another place, — the sooner he did that the better. Now Seppel the carpenter was brother to that Anton who had most wickedly undertaken the huckstering business, on the part of Karl Muntz the dealer in Innsbruck, and it turned out that Seppel was to join him. There was an ingratitude in this which almost drove the old woman frantic. If any one in the valley was more bound to her by kindly ties than another, it was Seppel, with his wife and six children. Wages! There had been no question of wages when Babette, Seppel's wife, had been ill; and Babette had always been ill. And when he had chopped his own foot with his own axe, and had gone into the hospital for six weeks, they had wanted nothing! That he should leave her for a matter of six zwansigers a month, and not only leave her, but become her active enemy, was dreadful to her. As a man, and as a carpenter who was bound to keep up his own respect among carpenters, he could not allow himself to work for less than the ordinary wages. The Frau had been very kind to him, and he and his wife and children were all grateful. But she would not therefore wish him, — this was his argument, — she would not on that account require him to work for less than his due. Seppel put his hand on his heart, and declared that his honour was concerned. As for his brother's cart and his huckstery trade and Karl Muntz, he was simply lending a hand to that till he could get a settled place as carpenter. He was doing the Frau no harm. If he did not look after the cart, somebody else would. He was very submissive and most anxious to avert her anger; but yet would not admit that he was doing wrong. But she towered in her wrath, and would listen to no reason. It was to her all wrong. It was innovation, a spirit of change coming from the source of all evil, bringing with it unkindness, absence of charity, ingratitude! It was flat mutiny, and rebellion against their betters. For some weeks it seemed to the Frau that all the world was going to pieces.

Her position was the more painful because at the time she was without counsellors. The kaplan came indeed as usual, and was as attentive and flattering to her as of yore; but he said nothing to her about her own affairs unless he was asked; and she did not ask him, knowing, that he would not give her palatable counsel. The kaplan himself was not well versed in political economy or questions of money generally; but he had a vague idea that the price of a chicken ought to be higher than it was thirty years ago. Then why not also the price of living to the guests at the Peacock? On that matter he argued with himself that the higher prices for the chickens had prevailed for some time, and that it was at any rate impossible to go back. And perhaps the lawyer had been right in recommending the Frau to rush at once to seven zwansigers and a half. His mind was vacillating and his ideas misty; but he did agree with Suse Krapp when she declared that the poor people must live. He could not, therefore, do the Frau any good by his advice.

As for Schlessen, he had not been at the Brunnenthal for a month, and had told Malchen in Innsbruck that unless he were specially wanted he would not go to the Peacock until something had been settled as to the mitgift. "Of course she is going to lose a lot of money," said Schlessen. "Anybody can see that with half an eye. Everybody in the town is talking about it. But when I tell her so, she is only angry with me."

Malchen of course could give no advise. Every step which her mother took seemed to her to be unwise. Of course the old women would do the best they could with their eggs. The idea that any one out of gratitude should sell cheaper to a friend than to an enemy was to her monstrous. But when she found that her mother was determined to swim against the stream, to wound herself by kicking against the pricks, to set at defiance all the common laws of trade, and that in this way money was to be lost, just at that very epoch of her own life in which it was so necessary that money should be forthcoming for her own advantage, — then she became moody, unhappy, and silent. What a pity it was that all this power should be vested in her mother's hands!

As for Peter, he had been altogether converted. When he found that a cart had to be sent twice a week to Brixen, and that the very poultry which had been carried from the valley to the town had to be brought back from the town to the valley, then his spirit of conservatism deserted him. He went so far as to advise his mother to give way. "I don't see that you do any good by ruining yourself," he said.

But she turned at him very fiercely. "I suppose I may do what I like with my own?" she replied.

Yes; she could do what she liked with her own. But now it was declared by all those around her, by her neighbours in the valley, and by those in Innsbruck who knew anything about her, that it was a sad thing and a bad thing that an old woman should be left with the power of ruining all those who belonged to her, and that there should be none to restrain her! And yet for the last twenty-five years previous to this it had been the general opinion in these parts that nobody had ever managed such a house as well as the Frau Frohmann. As for being ruined, — Schlessen, who was really acquainted with her affairs, knew better than that. She might lose a large sum of money, but there was no fear of ruin. Schlessen was inclined to think that all this trouble would end in the Frau retiring to Schwatz, and that the settlement of the mit-gift might thus be accelerated. Perhaps he and the Frau herself were the only two persons who really knew how well she had thri-ven. He was not afraid, and, being naturally patient, was quite willing to let things take their course.

The worst of it to the Frau herself was that she knew so well what people were saying of her. She had enjoyed for many years all that delight which comes from success and domination. It had not been merely, nor even chiefly, the feeling that money was being made. It is not that which mainly produces the comfortable condition of mind which attends success. It is the sense of respect which it engenders. The Frau had held her head high, and felt herself inferior to none, because she had enjoyed to the full this conviction. Things had gone pleasantly with her. Nothing is so enfeebling as failure; but she, hitherto, had never failed. Now a new sensation had fallen upon her, by which at certain periods she was almost prostrated. The woman was so brave that at her worst moments she would betake herself to solitude, and shed her tears where no one could see her. Then she would come out and so carry herself that none should guess how she suffered. To no ears did she utter a word of complaint, unless her indignation to Seppel, to Suse, and the others might be called complaining. She asked for no sympathy. Even to the kaplan she was silent, feeling that the kaplan, too, was against her. It was natural that he should take part with the poor. She was now, for the first time in her life, driven, alas, to feel that the poor were against her.

The house was still full, but there had of late been a great falling off in the mid-day visitors. It had, indeed, almost come to pass that that custom had died away. She told herself, with bitter regret, that this was the natural consequence of her deteriorated dinners. The Brixen meat was not good. Sometimes she was absolutely without poultry. And in those matters of puddings, cream, and custards we know what a falling off there had been. I doubt, however, whether her old friends had been stopped by that cause. It may have been so with Herr Trauss, who in going to the Bennenthal, or elsewhere, cared for little else but what he might get to eat and drink. But with most of those concerned the feeling had been that things were generally going wrong in the valley, and that in existing circumstances the Peacock could not be pleasant. She at any rate felt herself to be deserted, and this feeling greatly aggravated her trouble.

"You are having beautiful weather," Mr. Cartwright said to her one day when, in her full costume, she came out among the coffee-drinkers in the front of the house. Mr. Cartwright spoke German, and was on friendly terms with the old lady. She was perhaps a little in awe of him as being a rich man, an Englishman, and one with a white beard and a general deportment of dignity.

"The weather is well enough, sir," she said.

"I never saw the place all round look more lovely. I was up at Sustermann's saw-mills this morning, and I and my daughter agreed that it is the most lovely spot we know."

"The saw-mill is a pretty spot, sir, no doubt."

"It seems to me that the house becomes fuller and fuller every year, Frau Frohmann."

"The house is full enough, sir; perhaps too full." Then she hesitated, as though she would say something further. But the words were wanting to her in which to explain her difficulties with sufficient clearness for the foreigner, and she retreated, therefore, back into her own domains. He, of course, had heard something of the Frau's troubles, and had been willing enough to say a word to her about things in general if the occasion arose. But he had felt that the subject must be introduced by herself. She was too great a potentate to have advice thrust upon her uninvited.

A few days after this she asked Malchen whether Schlessen was ever coming out to the Brunnenthal again. This was also tantamount to an order for his presence. "He will come directly, mother, if you want to see him," said Malchen. The Frau would do no more than grunt in answer to this. It was too much to expect that she should say positively that he must come. But Malchen understood her, and sent the necessary word into Innsbruck.

On the following day Schlessen was at the Peacock, and took a walk up to the waterfall with Malchen before he saw the Frau. "She won't ruin herself," said Fritz. "It would take a great deal to ruin her. What she is losing in the house she is making up in the forests and in the land."

"Then it won't matter if it does go on like this?"

"It does matter, because it makes her so fierce and unhappy, and because the more she is knocked about the more obstinate she will get. She has only to say the word, and all would be right to-morrow."

"What word?" asked Malchen.

"Just to acknowledge that everything has got to be twenty-five per cent dearer than it was twenty-five years ago."

"But she does not like paying more, Fritz. That's just the thing."

"What does it matter what she pays?"

"I should think it mattered a great deal."

"Not in the least. What does matter is, whether she makes a profit out of the money she spends. Florins and zwansigers are but names. What you can manage to eat, and drink, and wear, and what sort of a house you can live in, and whether you can get other people to do for you what you don't like to do yourself, — that is what you have got to look after."

"But, Fritz; — money is money."

"Just so; but it is no more than money. If she could find out suddenly that what she has been thinking was a zwansiger was in truth only half a zwansiger, then she would not mind paying two where she has hitherto paid one, and would charge two where she now charges one, — as a matter of course. That's about the truth."

"But a zwansiger is a zwansiger."

"No; — not in her sense. A zwansiger now is not much more than half what it used to be. If the change had come all at once she could have understood it better."

"But why is it changed?"

Here Schlessen scratched his head. He was not quite sure that he knew, and felt himself unable to explain clearly what he himself only conjectured dimly. "At any rate it is so. That's what she has got to be made to understand, or else she must give it up and go and live quietly in private. It'll come to that, that she won't have a servant about the place if she goes on like this. Her own grandfather and grandmother were very good sort of people, but it is useless to try and live like them. You might just as well go back further, and give up knives and forks and cups and saucers."

Such was the wisdom of Herr Schlessen; and when he had spoken it he was ready to go back from the waterfall, near which they were seated, to the house. But Malchen thought that there was another subject as to which he ought to have something to say to her. "It is all very bad for us; — isn't it, Fritz?"

"It will come right in time, my darling."

"Your darling! I don't think you care for me a bit." As she spoke she moved herself a little further away from him. "If you did, you would not take it all so easily."

"What can I do, Malchen?" She did not quite know what he could do, but she was sure that when her lover, after a month's absence, got an opportunity of sitting with her by a waterfall, he

41

should not confine his conversation to a discussion on the value of zwansigers.

"You never seem to think about anything except money now."

"That is very unfair, Malchen. It was you asked me, and so I endeavoured to explain it."

"If you have said all that you've got to say, I suppose we may go back again."

"Of course, Malchen, I wish she'd settle what she means to do about you. We have been engaged long enough."

"Perhaps you'd like to break it off."

"You never knew me to break off anything yet." That was true. She did know him to be a man of a constant, if not of an enthusiastic temperament. And now, as he helped her up from off the rock, and contrived to snatch a kiss in the process, she was restored to her good humour.

"What's the good of that?" she said, thumping him, but not with much violence. "I did speak to mother a little while ago,, and asked her what she meant to do."

"Was she angry?"

"No; — not angry; but she said that everything must remain as it is till after the season. Oh, Fritz! I hope it won't go on for another winter. I suppose she has got the money?"

"Oh, yes; she has got it; but, as I've told you before, people who have got money do not like to part with it." Then they returned to the house; and Malchen, thinking of it all, felt reassured as to her lover's constancy, but was more than ever certain that, though it might be for five years, he would never marry her till the mitgift had been arranged.

Shortly afterwards he was summoned into the Frau's private room, and there had an interview with her alone. But it was very short; and, as he afterwards explained to Malchen, she gave him no opportunity of proffering any advice. She had asked him nothing about prices, and had made no allusion whatever to her troubles with her neighbours. She said not a word about the butcher, either at Innsbruck or at Brixen, although they were both at this moment very much on her mind. Nor did she tell him anything of the wickedness of Anton, nor the ingratitude of Seppel. She had simply wanted so many hundred florins, — for a purpose, as she said, — and had asked him how she might get them with the least inconvenience. Hitherto the money coming in, which had always gone into her own hands, had sufficed for her expenditure, unless when some new building was required. But now a considerable sum was necessary. She simply communicated her desire, and said nothing of the purpose for which it was wanted. The lawyer told her that she could have the money very easily, — at a day's notice, and without any peculiar damage to her circumstances. With that the interview was over, and Schlessen was allowed to return to his lady love, — or to the amusements of the Peacock generally.

"What did she want of you?" asked Peter.

"Only a question about business."

"I suppose it was about business. But what is she going to do?"

"You ought to know that, I should think. At any rate, she told me nothing."

"It is getting very bad here," said Peter with a peculiarly gloomy countenance. "I don't know where we are to get anything, soon. We have not milk enough, and half the time the visitors can't have eggs if they want them. And as for fowls, they have to be bought for double what we used to give. I wonder the folk here put up with it without grumbling."

"It'll come right after this season."

"Such a name as the place is getting!" said Peter. "And then I sometimes think it will drive her distracted. I told her yesterday we must buy more cows; — and, oh, she did look at me!"

Chapter VI
Hoff the Butcher

The lawyer returned to town, and on the next day the money was sent out to the Brunnenthal. Frau Frohmann had not winced when she demanded the sum needed, nor had she shown by any contorted line in her countenance that she was suffering when she asked for it; but, in truth, the thing had not been done without great pain. Year by year she had always added something to her store, either by investing money, or by increasing her property in the valley, and it would generally be at this time of the year that some deposit was made; but now the stream, which had always run so easily and so prosperously in one direction, had begun to flow backwards. It was to her as though she were shedding her blood. But, as other heroes have shed their blood in causes that have been dear to them, so would she shed hers in this. If it were necessary that these veins of her heart should be opened, she would give them to the knife. She had scowled when Peter had told her that more cows must be bought; but before the week was over the cows were there. And she had given a large order at Innsbruck for poultry to be sent out to her, almost irrespective of price. All idea of profit was gone. It was pride now for which she was fighting. She would not give way, at any rate till the end of this season. Then — then — then! There had come upon her mind an idea that some deluge was about to flow over her; but also an idea that even among the roar of the waters she would hold her head high, and carry herself with dignity.

But there had come to her now a very trouble of troubles, a crushing blow, a misfortune which could not be got over, which could not even be endured, without the knowledge of all those around her. It was not only that she must suffer, but that her sufferings must be exposed to all the valley, — to all Innsbruck. When Schlessen was closeted with her, at that very moment, she had in her pocket a letter from that traitorous butcher at Brixen, saying that after such and such a date he could not continue to supply her with meat at the prices fixed. And this was the answer which the man had sent to a remonstrance from her as to the quality of the article! After submitting for weeks to inferior meat she had told him that there must be some improvement and he had replied by throwing her over altogether!

What was she to do? Of all the blows which had come to her this was the worst. She must have meat. She could, when driven to it by necessity, make her own butter; but she could not kill her own beef and mutton. She could send into the town for ducks and chickens, and feel that in doing so she was carrying out her own project, — that, at any rate, she was encountering no public disgrace. But now she must own herself beaten, and must go back to Innsbruck.

And there came upon her dimly a conviction that she was bound, both by prudence and justice, to go back to her old friend Hoff. She had clearly been wrong in this matter of meat. Hoff had plainly told her that she was wrong, explaining to her that he had to give much more for his beasts and sheep than he did twenty years ago, to pay more wages to the men who killed them and cut them up, and also to make a greater profit himself, so as to satisfy the increased needs of his wife and daughters. Hoff had been outspoken, and had never wavered for a moment. But he had seemed to the Frau to be almost insolent, — she would have said, too independent. When she had threatened to take away her custom he had shrugged his shoulders, and had simply remarked that he would endeavour to live without it. The words had been spoken with, perhaps, something of a jeer, and the Frau had left the shop in wrath. She had since repented herself of this, because Hoff had been an old friend, and had attended to all her wishes with friendly care. But there had been the quarrel, and her custom had been transferred to that wretch at Brixen. If it had been simply a matter of forgiving and forgetting she could have made it up with Hoff, easily enough, an hour after her anger had shown itself. But now she must own herself to have been beaten. She must confess that she had been wrong. It was in that matter of meat, from that fallacious undertaking made by the traitor at Brixen, that she, in the first instance, had been led to think that she could triumph. Had she not been convinced of the truth of her own theory by that success, she would not have been led on to quarrel with all her neighbours, and to attempt to reduce Seppel's wages. But now, when this, her great foundation, was taken away from her, she had no ground on which to stand. She had the misery of failure all around her, and, added to that, the growing feeling that, in some step of her argument, she must have been wrong. One should be so very sure of all the steps before one allows oneself to be guided in important matters by one's own theories!

But after some ten days' time the supply of meat from Brixen would cease, and something therefore must be done. The Brixen traitor demanded now exactly the price which Hoff had heretofore charged. And then there was the carriage! That was not to be thought of. She would not conceal her failure from the world by submission so disgraceful as that. With the Brixen man she certainly would deal no more. She took twenty-four hours to think of it, and then she made up her mind that she would herself go into the town and acknowledge her mistake to Hoff. As to the actual difference of price, she did not now care very much about it. When a deluge is coming, one does not fret oneself as to small details of cost; but even when a deluge is coming, one's heart and pride, and perhaps one's courage, may remain unchanged.

On a certain morning it was known throughout the Peacock at an early hour that the Frau was going into town that day. But breakfast was over before any one was told when and how she was to go. Such journeyings, which were not made very often, had always about them something of ceremony. On such occasions her dress would be, not magnificent, as when she was arrayed for festive occasions at home, but yet very carefully arranged and equally unlike her ordinary habiliments. When she was first seen on this day, — after her early visit to the kitchen, which was not a full-dress affair, — she was clad in what may be called the beginnings or substratum of her travelling gear. She wore a very full, rich-looking, dark-coloured merino gown, which came much lower to the ground than her usual dress, and which covered her up high round the throat. Whenever this was seen it was known as a certainty that the Frau was going to travel. Then there was the question of the carriage and the horses. It was generally Peter's duty and high privilege to drive her in to town; and as Peter seldom allowed himself a holiday, the occasion was to him always a welcome one. It was her custom to let him know what was to befall him at any rate the night before; but now not a word had been said. After breakfast, however, a message went out that the carriage and horses would be needed, and Peter prepared himself accordingly, "I don't think I need take you," said the Frau.

"Why not me? There is no one else to drive them. The men are all employed." Then she remembered that when last she had dispensed with Peter's services Anton had driven her, — that Anton who was now carrying the butter and eggs into market. She shook her head, and was silent for a while in her misery. Then she asked whether the boy, Jacob, could not take her. "He would not be safe with those horses down the mountain," said Peter. At last it was decided that Peter should go; — but she yielded unwillingly, being very anxious that no one in the valley should be informed that she was about to visit Hoff. Of course it would be known at last. Everybody about the place would learn whence the meat came. But she could not bear to think that those around her should talk of her as having been beaten in the matter.

About ten they started, and on the whole road to Innsbruck hardly a word was spoken between the mother and son. She was quite resolved that she would not tell him whither she was going, and resolved also that she would pay the visit alone. But, of course, his curiosity would be excited. If he chose to follow her about and watch her, there could be no help for that. Only he had better not speak to her on the subject, or she would pour out upon him all the vials of her wrath. In the town there was a little hostel called the Black Eagle, kept by a cousin of her late husband, which on these journeys she always frequented, and there she and Peter ate their dinner. At table they sat, of course, close to each other; but still not a word was spoken as to her business. He made no inquiry, and when she rose from the table simply asked her whether there was anything for him to do. "I am going — alone — to see a friend," she said. No doubt he was curious, probably suspecting that Hoff the butcher might be the friend; but he asked no further question. She declared that she would be ready to start on the return journey at four, and then she went forth alone.

So great was her perturbation of spirit that she did not take the directest way to the butcher's house, which was not, indeed, above two hundred yards from the Black Eagle, but walked round slowly by the river, studying as she went the words with which she would announce her purpose to the man, — studying, also, by what wiles and subtlety she might get the man all to herself, — so that no other ears should hear her disgrace. When she entered the shop Hoff himself was there, conspicuous with the huge sharpening-steel which hung from his capacious girdle, as though it were the sword of his knighthood. But with him there was a crowd either of loungers or customers, in the midst of whom he stood, tall above all the others, laughing and talking. To our poor Frau it was terrible to be seen by so many eyes in that shop; — for had not her quarrel with Hoff and her dealings at Brixen been so public that all would know why she had come? "Ah, my friend, Frau Frohmann!" said the butcher, coming up to her with hand extended, "this is good for sore eyes. I am delighted to see thee in

47

the old town." This was all very well, and she gave him her hand. As long as no public reference was made to that last visit of hers, she would still hold up her head. But she said nothing. She did not know how to speak as long as all those eyes were looking at her.

The butcher understood it all, being a tender-hearted man, and intelligent also. From the first moment of her entrance he knew that there was something to be said intended only for his ears. "Come in, come in, Frau Frohmann," he said; "we will sit down within, out of the noise of the street and the smell of the carcases." With that he led the way into an inner room, and the Frau followed him. There were congregated three or four of his children, but he sent them away, bidding them join their mother in the kitchen. "And now, my friend," he said, again taking her hand, "I am glad to see thee. Thirty years of good fellowship is not to be broken by a word." By this time the Frau was endeavouring to hide with her handkerchief the tears which were running down her face. "I was thinking I would go out to the valley one of these days, because my heart misgave me that there should be anything like a quarrel between me and thee. I should have gone, but that, day after day, there comes always something to be done. And now thou art come thyself. What, shall the price of a side of beef stand betwixt thee and me?"

Then she told her tale, — quite otherwise than as she had intended to tell it. She had meant to be dignified and very short. She had meant to confess that the Brixen arrangement had broken down, and that she would resort to the old plan and the old prices. To the saying of this she had looked forward with any agony of apprehension, fearing that the man would be unable to abstain from some killing expression of triumph, — fearing that, perhaps, he might decline her offer. For the butcher was a wealthy man, who could afford himself the luxury of nursing his enmity. But his manner with her had been so gracious that she was altogether unable to be either dignified or reticent. Before half an hour was over she had poured out to him, with many tears, all her troubles; — how she had refused to raise her rate of charges, first out of consideration for her poor customers, and then because she did not like to demand from one class more than from another. And she explained how she had endeavoured to reduce her expenditure, and how she had failed. She told him of Seppel and Anton, of Suse Krapp and Josephine Bull, — and, above all, of that traitor at Brixen. With respect to the valley folk Hoff expressed himself with magnanimity and kindness; but in regard to the rival tradesman at Brixen his scorn was so great that he could not restrain himself from expressing wonder that a woman of such experience should have trusted to so poor a reed for support. In all other respects he heard her with excellent patience, putting in a little word here and there to encourage her, running his great steel all the while through his fingers, as he sat opposite to her on a side of the table.

"Thou must pay them for their ducks and chickens as before," he said.

"And you?"

"I will make all that straight. Do not trouble thyself about me. Thy guests at the Peacock shall once again have a joint of meat fit for the stomach of a Christian. But, my friend —"

"My friend!" echoed the Frau, waiting to hear what further the butcher would say to her.

"Let a man who has brought up five sons and five daughters, and who has never owed a florin which he could not pay, tell thee something that shall be useful. Swim with the stream." She looked up into his face, feeling rather than understanding the truth of what he was saying. "Swim with the stream. It is the easiest and the most useful."

"You think I should raise my prices."

"Is not everybody doing so? The Tendel ladies are very good, but I cannot sell them meat at a loss. That is not selling; it is giving. Swim with the stream. When other things are dearer, let the Peacock be dearer also."

"But why are other things dearer?"

"Nay; — who shall say that? Young Schlessen is a clear-headed lad, and he was right when he told thee of the price of sheep in the old days. But why? There I can say nothing. Nor is there reason why I should trouble my head about it. There is a man who has brought me sheep from the Achensee these thirty years, — he and his father before him. I have to pay him now, — ay, more than a third above his first prices."

"Do you give always what he asks?"

"Certainly not that, or there would be no end to his asking. But we can generally come to terms without hard words. When I pay him more for sheep, then I charge more for mutton; and if people will not pay it, then they must go without. But I do sell my meat, and I live at any rate as well now as I did when the prices were lower." Then he repeated his great advice, "Swim with the stream, my friend; swim with the stream. If you turn your head the other way, the chances are you will go backwards. At any rate you will make no progress."

Exactly at four o'clock she started on her return with her son, who, with admirable discretion, asked no question as to her employment during the day. The journey back took much longer than that coming, as the road was up hill all the way, so that she had ample time to think over the advice which had been given her as she leaned back in the carriage. She certainly was happier in her mind than she had been in the morning. She had made no step towards success in her system, — and rather been made to feel that no such step was possible. But, nevertheless, she had been comforted. The immediate trouble as to the meat had been got over without offence to her feelings. Of course she must pay the old prices, — but she had come to understand that the world around her was, in that matter, too strong for her. She knew now that she must give up the business, or else raise her own terms at the end of the season. She almost thought that she would retire to Schwatz and devote the remainder of her days to tranquility and religion. But her immediate anxiety had reference to the next six weeks, so that when she should have gone to Schwatz it might be said of her that the house had not lost its reputation for good living up to the very last. At any rate, within a very few days, she would again have the pleasure of seeing good meat roasting in her oven.

Peter, as was his custom, had walked half up the hill, and then, while the horses were slowly advancing, climbed to his seat on the box. 'Peter," she said, calling to him from the open carriage behind. Then Peter looked back. "Peter, the meat is to come from Hoff again after next Thursday."

He turned round quick on hearing the words. "That's a good thing, mother."

"It is a good thing. We were nearly poisoned by that scoundrel at Brixen."

"Hoff is a good butcher," said Peter.

"Hoff is a good man," said the Frau. Then Peter pricked up, because he knew that his mother was happy in her mind, and became eloquent about the woods, and the quarry, and the farm.

Chapter VII
And Gold Becomes Cheap

"But if there is more money, sir, that ought to make us all more comfortable." This was said by the Frau to Mr. Cartwright a few days after her return from Innsbruck, and was a reply to a statement made by him. She had listened to advice from Hoff the butcher, and now she was listening to advice from her guest. He had told her that these troubles of hers had come from the fact that gold had become more plentiful in the world than heretofore, or rather from that other fact that she had refused to accommodate herself to this increased plenty of gold. Then had come her very natural suggestion. "If there is more money that ought to make us all more comfortable."

"Not at all, Frau Frohmann."

"Well, sir!" Then she paused, not wishing to express an unrestrained praise of wealth, and so to appear too worldly-minded, but yet feeling that he certainly was wrong according to the clearly expressed opinion of the world.

"Not at all. Though you had your barn and your stores filled with gold, you could not make your guests comfortable with that. They could not eat it, nor drink it, nor sleep upon it, nor delight themselves with looking at it as we do at the waterfall, or at the mill up yonder."

"But I could buy all those things for them."

"Ah, if you could buy them! That's just the question. But if everybody had gold so common, if all the barns were full of it, then people would not care to take it for their meat and wine."

"It never can be like that, surely?"

"There is no knowing; probably not. But it is a question of degrees. When you have your hay-crop here very plentiful, don't you find that hay becomes cheap?"

"That's of course."

"And gold becomes cheap. You just think it over, and you'll find how it is. When hay is plentiful, you can't get so much for a load, because it becomes cheap. But you can feed more cows, and altogether you know that such plenty is a blessing. So it is with gold. When it is plentiful, you can't get so much meat for it as you used to do; but, as you can get the gold much easier, it will come to the same thing, — if you will swim with the stream, as your friend in Innsbruck counselled you."

Then the Frau again considered, and again found that she could not accept this doctrine as bearing upon her own case. "I don't think it can be like that here, sir," she said.

"Why not here as well as elsewhere?"

"Because we never see a bit of gold from one year's end to the other. Barns full of it! Why, it's so precious that you English people, and the French, and the Americans, always change it for paper before you come here. If you mean that it is because bank-notes are so common —"

Then Mr. Cartwright scratched his head, feeling that there would be a difficulty in making the Frau understand the increased use of an article which, common as it had become in the great marts of the world, had not as yet made its way into her valley. "It is because bank-notes are less common." The Frau gazed at him steadfastly, trying to understand something about it. "You still use bank-notes in Innsbruck?"

"Nothing else," she said. "There is a little silver among the shops, but you never see a bit of gold."

"And at Munich?"

"At Munich they tell me the French pieces have become — well, not common, but not so very scarce."

"And at Dresden?"

"I do not know. Perhaps Dresden is the same."

"And at Paris?"

"Ah, Paris! Do they have gold there?"

"When I was young it was all silver at Paris. Gold is now as plentiful as blackberries. And at Berlin it is nearly the same. Just here, in Austria, you have not quite got through your difficulties."

"I think we are doing very well in Austria; — at any rate, in the Tyrol."

She did not at all like swimming with the stream. There was something conveyed by the idea which was repugnant to her sense of honour. Did it not mean that she was to increase her prices because other people increased theirs, whether it was wrong or right? She hated the doing of anything because other people did it. Was not that base propensity to imitation the cause of the long petticoats which all the girls were wearing? Was it not thus that all those vile changes were effected which she saw around her on every side? Had it not been her glory, her great resolve, to stand as fast as possible on the old ways? And now in her great attempt to do so, was she to be foiled thus easily?

It was clear to her that she must be foiled, if not in one way, then in another. She must either raise her prices, or else retire to Schwatz. She had been thoroughly beaten in her endeavour to make others carry on their trade in accordance with her theories. On every side she had been beaten. There was not a poor woman in the valley, not one of those who had been wont to be so submissive and gracious to her, who had not deserted her. A proposed reduction of two kreutzers on a dozen of eggs had changed the most constant of humble friends into the bitterest foes. Seppel would have gone through fire and water for her. Anything that a man's strength or courage could do, he would have done. But a threat of going back to the old wages had conquered even Seppel's gratitude. Concurrent testimony had convinced her that she must either yield — or go. But, when she came to think of it in her solitude, she did not wish to go. Schwatz! oh yes; it would be very well to have a quiet place ready chosen for retirement when retirement should be necessary. But what did retirement mean? Would it not be to her simply a beginning of dying? A man, or a woman, should retire when no longer able to do the work of the world. But who in all the world could keep the Brunnenthal Peacock as well as she? Was she fatigued with her kitchen, or worn out with the charge of her guests, or worried inwardly by the anxieties of her position? Not in the least, not at all, but for this later misfortune which had come upon her — a misfortune which she knew how to remedy at once if only she could bring herself to apply the remedy. The kaplan had indiscreetly suggested to her that as Malchen was about to marry and be taken away into the town, it would be a good thing that Peter

"Very well, Frau Frohmann; very well indeed. Pray do
pose that I mean anything to the contrary. But though
en't got into the way of using gold money yourself, the
around you has done so; and, of course, if meat is dear at
because gold won't buy so much there as it used to do, n
be dearer also at Innsbruck, even though you continue t
it with bank-notes."

"It is dearer, sir, no doubt," said the Frau, shaking h
She had endeavoured to contest that point gallantly,
been beaten by the conduct of the two butchers. The
prices of Hoff at Innsbruck had become at any rate bet
the lower prices of that deceitful enemy at Brixen.

"It is dearer. For the world generally that may suffic
friend's doctrine is quite enough for the world at large. Sw
the stream. In buying and selling, — what we call trade, —
arrange themselves so subtly, that we are often driven to
them without quite knowing why they are so. Then we c
swim with the stream. But, in this matter, if you want to
the cause, if you cannot satisfy your mind without know
it is that you must pay more for everything, and must, th
charge more to other people, it is because the gold whi
notes represent has become more common in the world
the last thirty years."

She did want to know. She was not satisfied to swim w
stream as Hoff had done, not caring to inquire, but simply
sure that as things were so, so they must be. That such c
should take place had gone much against the grain of h
servative nature. She, in her own mind, had attributed the
tilently increased expenses to elongated petticoats, Frenc
nets, swallow-tailed coats, and a taste for sour wine. S
imagined that Josephine Bull might have been contente
the old price for her eggs if she would also be contented w
old raiment and the old food. Grounding her resolutions c
belief, she had endeavoured not only to resist further ch
but even to go back to the good old times. But she now wa
aware that in doing so she had endeavoured to swim agaiɪ
stream. Whether it ought to be so or not, she was not as ye
sure, but she was becoming sure that such was the fact an
the fact was too strong for her to combat.

should take a wife, so that there might be a future mistress of the establishment in readiness. The idea caused her to arm herself instantly with renewed self-assertion. So they were already preparing for her departure to Schwatz! It was thus she communed with herself. They had already made up their minds that she must succumb to these difficulties and go! The idea had come simply from the kaplan, without consultation with any one, but to the Frau it seemed as though the whole valley were already preparing for her departure. No, she would not go! With her strength and her energy, why should she shut herself up as ready for death? She would not go to Schwatz yet awhile.

But if not, then she must raise her prices. To waste her substance, to expend the success of her life in entertaining folk gratis who, after all, would believe that they were paying for their entertainment, would be worse even than going to Schwatz. "I have been thinking over what you were telling me," she said to Mr. Cartwright about a week after their last interview, on the day before his departure from the valley.

"I hope you do not find I was wrong, Frau Frohmann."

"As for wrong and right, that is very difficult to get at in this wicked world."

"But one can acknowledge a necessity."

"That is where it is, sir. One can see what is necessary; but if one could only see that it were right also, one would be so much more comfortable."

"There are things so hard to be seen, my friend, that let us do what we will we cannot see clearly into the middle of them. Perhaps I could have explained to you better all this about the depreciation of money, and the nominal rise in the value of everything else, if I had understood it better myself."

"I am sure you understand all about it, — which a poor woman can't ever do."

"But this at any rate ought to give you confidence, that that which you purpose to do is being done by everybody around you. You were talking to me about the Weisses. Herr Weiss, I hear, had his salary raised last spring."

"Had he?" asked the Frau with energy and a little start. For this piece of news had not reached her before.

"Somebody was saying so the other day. No doubt it was found that he must be paid more because he had to pay more for everything he wanted. Therefore he ought to expect to have to pay you more."

This piece of information gave the Frau more comfort than anything she had yet heard. That gold should be common, what people call a drug in the market, did not come quite within the scope of her comprehension. Gold to her was gold, and a zwansiger a zwansiger. But if Herr Weiss got more for his services from the community, she ought to get more from him for her services. That did seem plain to her. But then her triumph in that direction was immediately diminished by a tender feeling as to other customers. "But what of those poor Fraulein Tendels?" she said.

"Ah, yes," said Mr. Cartwright. "There you come to fixed incomes."

"To what?"

"To people with fixed incomes. They must suffer, Frau Frohmann. There is an old saying that in making laws you cannot look after all the little things. The people who work and earn their living are the multitude, and to them these matters adjust themselves. The few who live upon what they have saved or others have saved for them must go to the wall." Neither did the Frau understand this; but she at once made up her mind that, however necessary it might be to raise her prices against the Weisses and the rest of the world, she would never raise them against those two poor desolate frauleins.

So Herr Weiss had had his salary raised, and had said nothing to her about it, no doubt prudently wishing to conceal the matter! He had said nothing to her about it, although he had talked to her about her own affairs, and had applauded her courage and her old conservatism in that she would not demand that extra zwansiger and a half! This hardened her heart so much that she felt she would have a pleasure in sending a circular to him as to the new tariff. He might come or let it alone, as he pleased. Certainly, — certainly he ought to have told her that his own salary had been increased!

But there was more to do than sending out the new circular to her customers. How was she to send a circular round the valley to the old women and the others concerned? How was she to make

Seppel, and Anton, and Josephine Bull understand that they should be forgiven, and have their old prices and their increased wages, if they would come back to their allegiance, and never say a word again as to the sad affairs of the past summer? This circular must be of a nature very different from that which would serve for her customers. Thinking over it, she came to the opinion that Suse Krapp would be the best circular. A day or two after the Cartwrights were gone, she sent for Suse.

Suse was by no means a bad diplomate. When gaining her point she had no desire to triumph outwardly. When feeling herself a conqueror, she was quite ready to flatter the conquered one. She had never been more gracious, more submissive, or more ready to declare that in all matters the Frau's will was the law of the valley than now, when she was given to understand that everything should be bought on the same terms as heretofore, that the dairy should be discontinued during the next season, and that the wild fruits of the woods and mountains should be made welcome at the Peacock as had heretofore always been the case.

"To-morrow will be the happiest day that ever was in the valley," said Suse in her enthusiasm. "And as for Seppel, he was telling me only yesterday that he would never be a happy man again till he could find himself once more at work in the old shed behind the chapel."

Then Suse was told that Seppel might come as soon as he pleased.

"He'll be there the morning after next if I'm a living woman," continued Suse energetically; and then she said another word, "Oh, meine liebe Frau Frohmann! it broke my heart when they told me you were going away."

"Going away!" said the Frau, as though she had been stung. "Who said that I was going away?"

"I did hear it."

"Psha! it was that stupid priest." She had never before been heard to say a word against the kaplan; but now she could hardly restrain herself. "Why should I go away?"

"No, indeed!"

"I am not thinking of going away. It would be a bad thing if I were to be driven out of my house by a little trouble as to the price of eggs and butter! No, Suse Krapp, I am not going away."

"It will be the best word we have all of us heard this many a day, Frau Frohmann. When it came to that, we were all as though we would have broken our hearts." Then she was sent away upon her mission, not, upon this occasion, without a full glass of kirsch-wasser.

On the very day following Seppel was back. There was nothing said between him and his mistress, but he waited about the front of the house till he had an opportunity of putting his hand up to his cap and smiling at her as she stood upon the doorstep. And then, before the week was over, all the old women and all the young girls were crowding round the place with little presents which, on this their first return to their allegiance, they brought to the Frau as peace-offerings.

The season was nearly over when she signified to Malchen her desire that Fritz Schlessen should come out to the valley. This she did with much good humour, explaining frankly that Fritz would have to prepare the new circulars, and that she must discuss with him the nature of the altered propositions which were to be made to the public. Fritz of course came, and was closeted with her for a full hour, during which he absolutely prepared the document for the Innsbruck printer. It was a simple announcement that for the future the charge made at the Brunnenthal Peacock would be seven and a half zwansigers per head per day. It then went on to declare that, as heretofore, the Frau Frohmann would endeavour to give satisfaction to all those who would do her the honour of visiting her establishment. And instructions were given to Schlessen as to sending the circulars out to the public. "But whatever you do," said the Frau, "don't send one to those Tendel ladies."

And something else was settled at this conference. As soon as it was over Fritz Schlessen was encountered by Malchen, who on such occasions would never be far away. Though the spot on which they met was one which might not have been altogether secure from intrusive eyes, he took her fondly by the waist and whispered a word in her ear.

"And will that do?" asked Malchen anxiously; to which question his reply was made by a kiss. In that whisper he had conveyed to her the amount now fixed for the mitgift.

Chapter VIII
It Doesn't Make Any Difference to Any of Them

And so Frau Frohmann had raised her prices, and had acknowledged herself to all the world to have been beaten in her enterprise. There are, however, certain misfortunes which are infinitely worse in their anticipation than in their reality; and this, which had been looked forward to as a terrible humiliation, was soon found to be one of them. No note of triumph was sounded; none at least reached her ear. Indeed, it so fell out that those with whom she had quarrelled for a while seemed now to be more friendly with her than ever. Between her and Hoff things were so sweet that no mention was ever made of money. The meat was sent and the bills were paid with a reticence which almost implied that it was not trade, but an amiable giving and taking of the good things of the world. There had never been a word of explanation with Seppel; but he was late and early about the carts and the furniture, and innumerable little acts of kindness made their way up to the mother and her many children. Suse and Josephine had never been so brisk, and the eggs had never been so fresh or the vegetables so good. Except from the working of her own mind, she received no wounds.

But the real commencement of the matter did not take place till the following summer, — the commencement as regarded the public. The circulars were sent out, but to such letters no answers are returned; and up to the following June the Frau was ignorant what effect the charge would have upon the coming of her customers. There were times at which she thought that her house would be left desolate, that the extra charge would turn away from her the hearts of her visitors, and that in this way she would be compelled to retire to Schwatz.

"Suppose they don't come at all," she said to Peter one day.

"That would be very bad," said Peter, who also had his fears in the same direction.

"Fritz Schlessen thinks it won't make any difference," said the Frau.

"A zwansiger and a half a day does make a difference to most men," replied Peter uncomfortably.

This was uncomfortable; but when Schlessen came out he raised her spirits.

"Perhaps old Weiss won't come," he said, "but then there will be plenty in his place. There are houses like the Peacock all over the country now, in the Engadine, and the Bregenz, and the Salz-kammergut; and it seems to me the more they charge the fuller they are."

"But they are for the grand folk."

"For anybody that chooses. It has come to that, that the more money people are charged the better they like it. Money has become so plentiful with the rich, that they don't know what to do with it."

This was a repetition of Mr. Cartwright's barn full of gold. There was something in the assertion that money could be plentiful, in the idea that gold could be a drug, which savoured to her of innovation, and was therefore unpleasant. She still felt that the old times were good, and that no other times could be so good as the old times. But if the people would come and fill her house, and pay her the zwansiger and a half extra without grumbling, there would be some consolation in it.

Early in June Malchen made a call at the house of the Frauleins Tendel. Malchen at this time was known to all Innsbruck as the handsome Frau Schlessen who had been brought home in the winter to her husband's house with so very comfortable a mitgift in her hand. That was now quite an old story, and there were people in the town who said that the young wife already knew quite as much about her husband's business as she had ever done about her mother's. But at this moment she was obeying one of her mother's commands.

"Mother hopes you are both coming out to the Brunnenthal this year," said Malchen. The elder fraulein shook her head sadly. "Because" Then Malchen paused, and the younger of the two ladies shook her head. "Because you always have been there."

"Yes, we have."

"Mother means this. The change in the price won't have any-thing to do with you if you will come."

"We couldn't think of that, Malchen."

"Then mother will be very unhappy; — that's all. The new cir-cular was not sent to you."

"Of course we heard of it."

"If you don't come mother will take it very bad." Then of course the ladies said they would come, and so that little difficulty was overcome.

This took place in June. But at that time the young wife was staying out in the valley with her mother, and had only gone into Innsbruck on a visit. She was with her mother preparing for the guests; but perhaps, as the Frau too often thought, preparing for guests who would never arrive. From day to day, however, there came letters bespeaking rooms as usual, and when the 21st of June came there was Herr Weiss with all his family.

She had taught herself to regard the coming of the Weisses as a kind of touchstone by which she might judge of the success of what she had done. If he remained away it would be because, in spite of the increase in his salary, he could not encounter the higher cost of this recreation for his wife and family. He was himself too fond of the good living of the Peacock not to come if he could afford it. But if he could not pay so much, then neither could others in his rank of life; and it would be sad indeed to the Frau if her house were to be closed to her neighbour Germans, even though she might succeed in filling it with foreigners from a distance. But now the Weisses had come, not having given their usual notice, but having sent a message for rooms only two days before their arrival. And at once there was a little sparring match between Herr Weiss and the Frau.

"I don't suppose that there would be much trouble as to finding rooms," said Herr Weiss.

"Why shouldn't there be as much trouble as usual?" asked the Frau in return. She had felt that there was some slight in this arrival of the whole family without the usual preliminary inquiries, —as though there would never again be competition for rooms at the Peacock.

"Well, my friend, I suppose that that little letter which was sent about the country will make a difference?"

"That's as people like to take it. It hasn't made any difference with you, it seems."

"I had to think a good deal about it, Frau Frohmann; and I suppose we shall have to make our stay shorter. I own I am a little surprised to see the Tendel women here. A zwansiger and a half a

61

day comes to a deal of money at the end of a month, when there are two or three."

"I am happy to think it won't hurt you, Herr Weiss, as you have had your salary raised."

"That is neither here nor there, Frau Frohmann," said the magistrate, almost with a touch of anger. All the world knew, or ought to know, how very insufficient was his stipend when compared with the invaluable public services which he rendered. Such at least was the light in which he looked at the question.

"At any rate," said the Frau as he stalked away, "the house is like to be as full as ever."

"I am glad to hear it. I am glad to hear it." These were his last words on the occasion. But before the day was over he told his wife that he thought the place was not as comfortable as usual, and that the Frau with her high prices was more upsetting than ever.

His wife, who took delight in being called Madame Weiss at Brixen, and who considered herself to be in some degree a lady of fashion, had nevertheless been very much disturbed in her mind by the increased prices, and had suggested the place should be abandoned. A raising of prices was in her eyes extortion; — though a small raising of salary was simply justice, and, as she thought, inadequate justice. But the living at the Peacock was good. Nobody could deny that. And when a middle-aged man is taken away from the comforts of his home, how is he to console himself in the midst of his idleness unless he has a good dinner? Herr Weiss had therefore determined to endure the injury, and as usual to pass his holiday in the Brunnenthal. But when Madame Weiss saw those two frauleins from Innsbruck in the house, whose means she knew down to the last kreutzer, and who certainly could not afford the increased demand, she thought that there must be something not apparent to view. Could it be possible that the Frau should be so unjust, so dishonest, so extortious as to have different prices for different neighbours! That an Englishman, or even a German from Berlin, should be charged something extra, might not perhaps be unjust or extortious. But among friends of the same district, to put a zwansiger and a half on to one and not to another seemed to Madame Weiss to be a sin for which there should be no pardon. "I am so glad to see you here," she said to the younger fraulein.

"That is so kind of you. But we always are here, you know."

"Yes; — yes. But I feared that perhaps —. I know that with us we had to think more than once about it before we could make up our minds to pay the increased charge. The 'magistrat' felt a little hurt about it." To this the fraulein at first answered nothing, thinking that perhaps she ought not to make public the special benevolence shown by the Frau to herself and her sister. "A zwansiger and a half each is a great deal of money to add on," said Madame Weiss.

"It is, indeed."

"We might have got it cheaper elsewhere. And then I thought that perhaps you might have done so too."

"She has made no increase to us," said the poor lady, who at last was forced to tell the truth, as by not doing so she would have been guilty of a direct falsehood in allowing it to be supposed that she and her sister paid the increased price.

"Soh — oh — oh!" exclaimed Madame Weiss, clasping her hands together and bobbing her head up and down. "Soh — oh — !" She had found it all out.

Then, shortly after that — the next day — there was an uncomfortable perturbation of affairs at the Peacock, which was not indeed known to all the guests, but which to those who heard it, or heard of it, seemed for the time to be very terrible. Madame Weiss and the Frau had — what is commonly called — a few words together.

"Frau Frohmann," said Madame Weiss, "I was quite astonished to hear from Agatha Tendel that you were only charging them the old prices."

"Why shouldn't I charge them just what I please, — or nothing at all, if I pleased?" asked the Frau sharply.

"Of course you can. But I do think, among neighbours, there shouldn't be one price to one and one to another."

"Would it do you any good, Frau Weiss, if I were to charge those ladies more than they can pay? Does it do you any harm if they live here at a cheap rate?"

"Surely there should be one price — among neighbours!"

"Herr Weiss got my circular, no doubt. He knew. I don't suppose he wants to live here at a rate less than it costs me to keep him. You and he can do what you like about coming, — and you and he can do what you like about staying away. You knew my prices. I have not made any secret about the change. But as for interference between me and my other customers, it is what I won't put up with. So now you know all about it."

By the end of her speech the Frau had worked herself up into a grand passion, and spoke aloud, so that all near her heard her. Then there was a great commotion in the Peacock, and it was thought that the Weisses would go away. But they remained for their allotted time.

This was the only disturbance which took place, and it passed off altogether to the credit of the Frau. Something in a vague way came to be understood about fixed incomes; — so that Peter and Malchen, with the kaplan, even down to Seppel and Suse Krapp, were aware that the two frauleins ought not to be made to pay as much as the prosperous magistrate who had had his salary raised. And then it was quite understood that the difference made in favour of those two poor ladies was a kindness shown to them, and could not therefore be an injury to any one else.

Later in the year, when the establishment was full and everything was going on briskly, when the two puddings were at the very height of their glory, and the wild fruits were brought up on the supper-table in huge bowls, when the Brunnenthal was at its loveliest, and the Frau was appearing on holidays in her gayest costume, the Cartwrights returned to the valley. Of course they had ordered their rooms much beforehand; and the Frau, trusting altogether to the wisdom of those counsels which she did not even yet quite understand, had kept her very best apartments for them. The greeting between them was most friendly, — the Frau condescending to put on something of her holiday costume to add honour to their arrival; — a thing which she had never been known to do before on behalf of any guests. Of course there was then time for conversation; but a day or two had not passed before she made known to Mr. Cartwright her later experience. "The people have come, sir, just the same," she said.

"So I perceive."

"It don't seem to make any difference to any of them."

"I didn't think it would. And I don't suppose anybody has complained."

"Well; — there was a little said by one lady, Mr. Cartwright. But that was not because I charged her more, but because another old friend was allowed to pay less."

"She didn't do you any harm, I dare say."

"Harm; — oh dear no! She couldn't do me any harm if she tried. But I thought I'd tell you, sir, because you said it would be so. The people don't seem to think any more of seven zwansigers and a half than they do of six! It's very odd, — very odd indeed. I suppose it's all right, sir?" This she asked, still thinking that there must be something wrong in the world when so monstrous a con-dition of things seemed to prevail.

"They'd think a great deal of it if you charged them more than they believed sufficient to give you a fair profit for your outlay and trouble."

"How can they know anything about it, Mr. Cartwright?"

"Ah, — indeed. How do they? But they do. You and I, Frau Frohmann, must study these matters very closely before we can find out how they adjust themselves. But we may be sure of this, that the world will never complain of fair prices, will never long endure unfair prices, and will give no thanks at all to those who sell their goods at a loss."

The Frau curtseyed and retired, — quite satisfied that she had done the right thing in raising her prices; but still feeling that she had many a struggle to make before she could understand the matter.

"Why Frau Frohmann Raised Her Prices" appeared first in the December issue of *Good Words* for 1877.

Lotta Schmidt

AS ALL THE WORLD KNOWS, the old fortifications of Vienna have been pulled down, — the fortifications which used to surround the centre or kernel of the city; and the vast spaces thus thrown open and forming a broad ring in the middle of the town have not as yet been completely filled up with those new buildings and gardens which are to be there, and which, when there, will join the outside city and the inside city together, so as to make them into one homogeneous whole. The work, however, is going on, and if the war which has come does not swallow everything appertaining to Austria into its maw, the ugly remnants of destruction will be soon carted away, and the old glacis will be made bright with broad pavements and gilded railings, and well-built lofty mansions and gardens beautiful with shrubs — and beautiful with turf also, if Austrian patience can make turf to grow beneath Austrian sky. But if the war that has now begun to rage is allowed to have its way, as most men think that it will, it does not require any wonderful prophet to foretell that Vienna will remain ugly, and that the dust of the brickbats will not be made altogether to disappear for another half century.

No sound of coming war had as yet been heard in Vienna in the days, not yet twelve months since, to which this story refers. On an evening of September, when there was still something left of daylight at eight o'clock, two girls were walking together in the Burgplatz, or large open space which lies between the city palace of the Emperor and the gate which passes thence from the old town out to the new town. Here at present stand two bronze equestrian statues, one of the Archduke Charles, and the other of Prince Eugene. And they were standing there also, both of them, when these two girls were walking round them; but that of the Prince had not as yet been uncovered for the public. There was coming a great gala day in the city. Emperors and empresses, archdukes and grand-dukes, with their archduchessees and grand-duchesses, and princes and ministers, were to be there, and the new statue of Prince Eugene was to be submitted to the art critics of the world. There was very much thought at Vienna of the statue in those days. Well; since that the statue has been submitted to the art critics, and henceforward it will be thought of as little as any other huge bronze figure of a prince on horseback. A very ponderous prince is poised in an impossible position, on an enormous dray horse. But yet the thing is grand, and Vienna is so far a finer city in that it possesses the new equestrian statue of Prince Eugene.

"There will be such a crowd, Lotta," said the elder of the two girls, "that I will not attempt it. Besides, we shall have plenty of time for seeing it afterwards."

"Oh, yes," said the younger girl, whose name was Lotta Schmidt; "of course we shall all have enough of the old prince for the rest of our lives; but I should like to see the grand people sitting up there on the benches; and there will be something nice in seeing the canopy drawn up. I think I shall come. Herr Crippel has said that he would bring me, and get me a place."

"I thought, Lotta, you had determined to have nothing more to say to Herr Crippel."

"I don't know what you mean by that. I like Herr Crippel very much, and he plays beautifully. Surely a girl may know a man old enough to be her father without having him thrown in her teeth as her lover."

"Not when the man old enough to be her father has asked her to be his wife twenty times, as Herr Crippel has asked you. Herr Crippel would not give up his holiday afternoon to you if he thought it was to be for nothing."

"There I think you are wrong, Marie. I believe Herr Crippel likes to have me with him simply because every gentleman likes to have a lady on such a day as that. Of course it is better than being alone. I don't suppose he will say a word to me except to tell me who the people are, and to give me a glass of beer when it is over."

It may be as well to explain at once, before we go any further, that Herr Crippel was a player on the violin, and that he led the musicians in the orchestra of the great beer-hall in the Volksgarten. Let it not be thought that because Herr Crippel exercised his art in a beer-hall therefore he was a musician of no account. No one will think so who has once gone to a Vienna beer-hall, and listened to such music as is there provided for the visitors.

The two girls, Marie Weber and Lotta Schmidt, belonged to an establishment in which gloves were sold in the Graben, and now, having completed their work for the day, — and indeed their work for the week, for it was Saturday evening, — had come out for such recreation as the evening might afford them. And on behalf of these two girls, as to one of whom at least I am much interested, I must beg my English readers to remember that manners and customs differ much in Vienna from those which prevail in London. Were I to tell of two London shop girls going out into the streets after their day's work, to see what friends and what amusement the fortune of the evening might send to them, I should be supposed to be speaking of young women as to whom it would be better that I should be silent; but these girls in Vienna were doing simply that which all their friends would expect and wish them to do. That they should have some amusement to soften the rigours of long days of work was recognized to be necessary; and music, beer, dancing, with the conversation of young men, are thought in Vienna to be the natural amusements of young women, and in Vienna are believed to be innocent.

The Viennese girls are almost always attractive in their appearance, without often coming up to our English ideas of prettiness. Sometimes they do fully come up to our English idea of beauty. They are generally dark, tall, light in figure, with bright eyes, which are however very unlike the bright eyes of Italy and which constantly remind the traveller that his feet are carrying him eastward in Europe. But perhaps the peculiar characteristic in their faces which most strikes a stranger is a certain look of almost fierce independence, as though they had recognized the necessity, and also acquired the power of standing alone, and of pro-

tecting themselves. I know no young women by whom the assistance of a man's arm seems to be so seldom required as the young
women of Vienna. They almost invariably dress well, generally
preferring black, or colours that are very dark; and they wear hats
that are I believe of Hungarian origin, very graceful in form, but
which are peculiarly calculated to add something to that assumed
savageness of independence of which I have spoken.

Both the girls who were walking in the Burgplatz were of the
kind that I have attempted to describe. Marie Weber was older,
and not so tall, and less attractive than her friend; but as her lot
in life was fixed, and as she was engaged to marry a cutter of diamonds, I will not endeavour to interest the reader specially in her
personal appearance. Lotta Schmidt was essentially a Viennese
pretty girl of the special Viennese type. She was tall and slender,
but still had none of that appearance of feminine weakness which
is so common among us with girls who are tall and slim. She
walked as though she had plenty both of strength and courage for
all purposes of life without the assistance of any extraneous aid.
Her hair was jet black, and very plentiful, and was worn in long
curls which were brought round from the back of her head over
her shoulders. Her eyes were blue, — dark blue, — and were clear
and deep rather than bright. Her nose was well formed, but somewhat prominent, and made you think at the first glance of the
tribes of Israel. But yet no observer of the physiognomy of races
would believe for half a moment that Lotta Schmidt was a Jewess.
Indeed, the type of form which I am endeavouring to describe is
in truth as far removed from the Jewish type as it is from the Italian; and it has no connection whatever with that which we ordi-
narily conceive to be the German type. But, overriding everything in her personal appearance, in her form, countenance, and
gait, was that singular fierceness of independence, as though she
were constantly asserting that she would never submit herself to
the inconvenience of feminine softness. And yet Lotta Schmidt
was a simple girl, with a girl's heart, looking forward to find all
that she was to have of human happiness in the love of some
man, and expecting and hoping to do her duty in life as a married
woman and the mother of a family. Nor would she have been at
all coy in saying as much had the subject of her life's prospects
become matter of conversation in any company; no more than

one lad would be coy in saying that he hoped to be a doctor, or another in declaring a wish for the army.

When the two girls had walked twice round the hoarding within which stood all those tons of bronze which were intended to represent Prince Eugene, they crossed over the centre of the Burgplatz, passed under the other equestrian statue, and came to the gate leading into the Volksgarten. There, just at the entrance, they were overtaken by a man with a fiddle-case under his arm, who raised his hat to them and then shook hands with both of them.

"Ladies," he said, "are you coming in to hear a little music? We will do our best."

"Herr Crippel always does well," said Marie Weber. "There is never any doubt when one comes to hear him."

"Marie, why do you flatter him?" said Lotta.

"I do not say half to his face that you said just now behind his back," said Marie.

"And what did she say of me behind my back?" said Herr Crippel. He smiled as he asked the question, or attempted to smile, but it was easy to see that he was much in earnest. He blushed up to his eyes, and there was a slight trembling motion in his hands as he stood with one of them pressed upon the other.

As Marie did not answer at the moment, Lotta replied for her.

"I will tell you what I said behind your back. I said that Herr Crippel had the firmest hand upon a bow; and the surest fingers among the strings in all Vienna, — when his mind was not wool-gathering. Marie, is not that true?"

"I do not remember anything about the wool-gathering," said Marie.

"I hope I shall not be wool-gathering to-night; but I shall doubtless; — shall doubtless, — for I shall be thinking of your judgment. Shall I get you seats at once? There; you are just before me. You see I am not coward enough to fly from my critics." And he placed them to sit at a little marble table, not far from the front of the low orchestra in the foremost place in which he would have to take his stand.

"Many thanks, Herr Crippel," said Lotta. "I will make sure of a third chair, as a friend is coming."

"Oh, a friend!" said he; and he looked sad, and all his sprightliness was gone.

"Marie's friend," said Lotta, laughing. "Do you not know Carl Stobel?"

Then the musician became bright and happy again. "I would have got two more chairs if you would have let me; one for the fraulein's sake, and one for his own. And I will come down presently, and you shall present me, if you will be so very kind."

Marie Weber smiled and thanked him, and declared that she should be very proud; —and the leader of the band went up into his place.

"I wish he had not placed us here," said Lotta.

"And why not?"

"Because Fritz is coming."

"No!"

"But he is."

"And why did you not tell me?"

"Because I did not wish to be speaking of him. Of course you understand why I did not tell you. I would rather it should seem that he came of his own account, — with Carl. Ha, ha!" Carl Stobel was the diamond-cutter to whom Marie Weber was betrothed. "I should not have told you now, — only that I am disarranged by what Herr Crippel has done."

"Had we not better go, — or at least move our seats? We can make any excuse afterwards."

"No," said Lotta. "I will not seem to run away from him. I have nothing to be ashamed of. If I choose to keep company with Fritz Planken, that should be nothing to Herr Crippel."

"But you might have told him."

"No; I could not tell him. And I am not sure Fritz is coming either. He said he would come with Carl if he had time. Never mind; let us be happy now. If a bad time comes by-and-by, we must make the best of it."

Then the music began, and, suddenly, as the first note of a fiddle was heard, every voice in the great beer-hall of the Volksgarten became silent. Men sat smoking, with their long beer-glasses before them, and women sat knitting, with their beer-glasses also before them, but not a word was spoken. The waiters went about with silent feet, but even orders for beer were not given, and money was not received. Herr Crippel did his best, working with his wand as carefully, — and I may say as accurately, — as a leader in a fashionable opera-house in London or Paris. But every now and then, in the course of the piece, he would place his fiddle to his shoulder and join in the performance. There was hardly one then in the hall, man or woman, boy or girl, who did not know, from personal knowledge and judgment, that Herr Crippel was doing his work very well.

"Excellent, was it not?" said Marie.

"Yes; he is a musician. Is it not a pity he should be so bald?" said Lotta.

"He is not so very bald," said Marie.

"I should not mind his being bald so much, if he did not try to cover his old head with the side hairs. If he would cut off those loose straggling locks, and declare himself to be bald at once, he would be ever so much better. He would look to be fifty then. He looks sixty now."

"What matters his age? He is forty-five, just; for I know. And he is a good man."

"What has his goodness to do with it?"

"A good deal. His old mother wants for nothing, and he makes two hundred florins a month. He has two shares in the summer theatre. I know it."

"Bah! what is all that when he will plaster his hair over his old bald head?"

"Lotta, I am ashamed of you." But at this moment the further expression of Marie's anger was stopped by the entrance of the diamond-cutter, and as he was alone, both the girls received him very pleasantly. We must give Lotta her due, and declare that, as things had gone, she would much prefer now that Fritz should stay away, though Fritz Planken was as handsome a young fellow as there was in Vienna, and one who dressed with the best taste, and danced so that no one could surpass him, and could speak French, and was confidential clerk at one of the largest hotels in Vienna, and was a young man acknowledged to be of much general importance, — and had, moreover, in plain language declared his love for Lotta Schmidt. But Lotta would not willingly give unnecessary pain to Herr Crippel, and she was generously glad when Carl Stobel, the diamond-cutter, came by himself. Then there was a second and third piece played, and after that Herr Crippel came down, according to promise, and was presented to Marie's lover.

"Ladies," said he, "I hope I have not gathered wool."

"You have surpassed yourself," said Lotta.

"At wool-gathering?" said Herr Crippel.

"At sending us out of this world into another," said Lotta.

"Ah; go into no other world but this," said Herr Crippel, "lest I should not be able to follow you." And then he went away again to his post.

Before another piece had been commenced, Lotta saw Fritz Planken enter the door. He stood for a moment gazing round the hall, with his cane in his hand and his hat on his head, looking for the party which he intended to join. Lotta did not say a word, nor would she turn her eyes towards him. She would not recognize him if it were possible to avoid it. But he soon saw her, and came up to the table at which they were sitting. When Lotta was getting the third chair for Marie's lover, Herr Crippel, in his gallantry, had brought a fourth, and now Fritz occupied the chair which the musician had placed there. Lotta, as she perceived this, was sorry that it should be so. She could not even dare to look up to see what effect this new arrival would have upon the leader of the band.

The new comer was certainly a handsome young man, — such a one as inflicts unutterable agonies on the hearts of the Herr Crippels of the world. His boots shone like mirrors, and fitted his feet like gloves. There was something in the make and sit of his trousers which Herr Crippel, looking at them as he could not help looking at them, was quite unable to understand. Even twenty years ago Herr Crippel's trousers, as Herr Crippel very well knew, had never looked like that. And Fritz Planken wore a blue frock coat with silk lining to the breast, which seemed to have come from some tailor among the gods. And he had on primrose gloves, and round his neck a bright pink satin handkerchief, joined by a ring, which gave a richness of colouring to the whole thing which nearly killed Herr Crippel, because he could not but acknowledge that the colouring was good. And then the hat! And when the hat was taken off for a moment, then the hair — perfectly black, and silky as a raven's wing, just waving with one curl! And when Fritz put up his hand, and ran his fingers through his locks, their richness and plenty and beauty were conspicuous to all beholders. Herr Crippel, as he saw it, involuntarily dashed his hand up to his own pate, and scratched his straggling lanky hairs from off his head.

"You are coming to Sperl's to-morrow, of course," said Fritz to Lotta. Now Sperl's is a great establishment for dancing in the Leopoldstadt which is always open of a Sunday evening, and which Lotta Schmidt was in the habit of attending with much regularity. It was here she had become acquainted with Fritz. And certainly to dance with Fritz was to dance indeed! Lotta too was a beautiful dancer. To a Viennese such as Lotta Schmidt, dancing is a thing of serious importance. It was a misfortune to her to have to dance with a bad dancer, as it is to a great whist-player among us to sit down with a bad partner. Oh, what she had suffered more than once when Herr Crippel had induced her to stand up with him!

"Yes; I shall go. Marie, you will go?"

"I do not know," said Marie.

"You will make her go, Carl, will you not?" said Lotta.

"She promised me yesterday, as I understood," said Carl.

"Of course we will all be there," said Fritz, somewhat grandly; "and I will give a supper for four."

Then the music began again, and the eyes of all of them became fixed upon Herr Crippel. It was unfortunate that they should have been placed so fully before him, as it was impossible that he should avoid seeing them. As he stood up with his violin to his shoulders, his eyes were fixed on Fritz Planken, and Fritz Planken's boots, and coat, and hat, and hair. And as he drew his bow over the strings he was thinking of his own boots and of his own hair. Fritz was sitting, leaning forward in his chair, so that he could look up into Lotta's face, and he was playing with a little amber-headed cane, and every now and then he whispered a word. Herr Crippel could hardly play a note. In very truth he was wool-gathering. His band became unsteady, and every instrument was mor or less astray.

"Your old friend is making a mess of it to-night," said Fritz to Lotta. "I hope he has not taken a glass too much of schnaps."

"He never does anything of the kind," said Lotta, angrily. "He never did such a thing in his life."

"He is playing awfully badly," said Fritz.

"I never heard him play better in my life than he has played to-night," said Lotta.

"His hand is tired. He is getting old," said Fritz. Then Lotta moved her chair and drew herself back, and was determined that Marie and Carl should see that she was angry with her young lover. In the meantime the piece of music had been finished, and the audience had shown their sense of the performers' inferiority by withdrawing those plaudits which they were so ready to give when they were pleased.

After this some other musician led for a while, and then Herr Crippel had to come forward to play a solo. And on this occasion the violin was not to be his instrument. He was a great favourite among the lovers of music in Vienna, not only because he was good at the fiddle and because with his bow in his hand he could keep a band of musicians together, but also as a player on the zither. It was not often now-a-days that he would take his zither to the music-hall in the Volksgarten; for he would say that he had given up that instrument; that he now played it only in private; that it was not fit for a large hall, as a single voice, the scraping of a foot, would destroy its music. And Herr Crippel was a man who had his fancies and his fantasies, and would not always yield to entreaty. But occasionally he would send his zither down to the public hall; and in the Programme for this evening it had been put forth that Herr Crippel's zither would be there and that Herr Crippel would perform. And now the zither was brought forward, and a chair was put for the zitherist, and Herr Crippel stood for a moment behind his chair and bowed. Lotta glanced up at him and could see that he was very pale. She could even see that the perspiration stood upon his brow. She knew that he was trembling and that he would have given almost his zither itself to be quit of his promised performance for that night. But she knew also that he would make the attempt.

"What, the zither?" said Fritz. "He will break down as sure as he is a living man."

"Let us hope not," said Carl Stobel.

"I love to hear him play the zither better than anything," said Lotta.

"It used to be very good," said Fritz; "but everybody says he has lost his touch. When a man has the slightest feeling of nervousness he is done for the zither."

"H — sh; let him have his chance at any rate," said Marie.

Reader, did you ever hear the zither? When played, as it is sometimes played in Vienna, it combines all the softest notes of the human voice. It sings to you of love, and then wails to you of disappointed love, till it fills you with a melancholy from which there is no escaping, from which you never wish to escape. It speaks to you as no other instrument ever speaks, and reveals to you with wonderful eloquence the sadness in which it delights. It produces a luxury of anguish, a fulness of the satisfaction of imaginary woe, a realization of the mysterious delights of romance, which no words can ever thoroughly supply. While the notes are living, while the music is still in the air, the ear comes to covet greedily every atom of tone which the instrument will produce, so that the slightest extraneous sound becomes an offence. The notes sink and sink so low and low, with their soft sad wail of delicious woe, that the listener dreads that something will be lost in the struggle of listening. There seems to come some lethargy on his sense of hearing, which he fears will shut out from his brain the last, lowest, sweetest strain, the very pearl of the music, for which he has been watching with all the intensity of prolonged desire. And then the zither is silent, and there remains a fond memory together with a deep regret.

Herr Crippel seated himself on his stool and looked once or twice round about upon the room almost with dismay. Then he struck his zither, uncertainly, weakly, and commenced the prelude of his piece. But Lotta thought that she had never heard so sweet a sound. When he paused after a few strokes there was a sound of applause in the room, —of applause intended to encourage by commemorating past triumphs. The musician looked again away from his music to his audience, and his eyes caught the eyes of the girl he loved; and his gaze fell also upon the face of the handsome, well-dresed, young Adonis who was by her side. He, Herr Crippel the musician, could never make himself look like that; he could make no slightest approach to that outward triumph. But then, he could play the zither, and Fritz Planken could only play with his cane! He would do what he could! He would play his best! He had once almost resolved to get up and declare that he was too tired that evening to do justice to his instrument. But there was an insolence of success about his rival's hat and trousers which spirited him on to the fight. He struck his zither again, and they who understood him and his zither knew that he was in earnest.

The old men who had listened to him for the last twenty years declared that he had never played as he played on that night. At first he was somewhat bolder, somewhat louder than was his wont; as though he were resolved to go out of his accustomed track; but, after a while, he gave that up; that was simply the effect of nervousness, and was continued only while the timidity remained present with him. But he soon forgot everything but his zither and his desire to do it justice. The attention of all present soon became so close that you might have heard a pin fall. Even Fritz sat perfectly still, with his mouth open, and forgot to play with his cane. Lotta's eyes were quickly full of tears, and before long they were rolling down her cheeks. Herr Crippel, though he did not know that he looked at her, was aware that it was so. Then came upon them all there an ecstacy of delicious sadness. As I have said above, every ear was struggling that no softest sound might escape unheard. And then at last the zither was silent, and no one could have marked the moment when it had ceased to sing.

For a few moments there was perfect silence in the room, and the musician still kept his seat with his face turned upon his instrument. He knew well that he had succeeded, that his triumph had been complete, and every moment that the applause was suspended was an added jewel to his crown. But it soon came, the loud shouts of praise, the ringing bravos, the striking of glasses, his own name repeated from all parts of the hall, the clapping of hands, the sweet sound of women's voices, and the waving of white handkerchiefs. Herr Crippel stood up, bowed thrice, wiped his face with a handkerchief, and then sat down on a stool in the corner of the orchestra.

"I don't know much about his being too old," said Carl Stobel.

"Nor I either," said Lotta.

"That is what I call music," said Marie Weber.

"He can play the zither, certainly," said Fritz; "but as to the violin, it is more doubtful."

"He is excellent with both, — with both," said Lotta, angrily.

Soon after that the party got up to leave the hall, and as they went out they encountered Herr Crippel.

"You have gone beyond yourself to-night," said Marie, "and we wish you joy."

"Oh no. It was pretty good, was it? With the zither it depends mostly on the atmosphere; whether it is hot, or cold, or wet, or dry, or on I know not what. It is an accident if one plays well. Good-night to you. Good-night, Lotta. Good-night, sir." And he took off his hat, and bowed, — bowed, as it were, expressly to Fritz Planken.

"Herr Crippel," said Lotta, "one word with you." And she dropped behind from Fritz, and returned to the musician. "Herr Crippel, will you meet me at Sperl's to-morrow night?"

"At Sperl's? No. I do not go to Sperl's any longer, Lotta. You told me that Marie's friend was coming to-night; but you did not tell me of your own."

"Never mind what I told you, or did not tell you. Herr Crippel, will you come to Sperl's to-morrow?"

"No; you would not dance with me, and I should not care to see you dance with any one else."

"But I will dance with you."

"And Planken will be there?"

"Yes; Fritz will be there. He is always there. I cannot help that."

"No, Lotta; I will not go to Sperl's. I will tell you a little secret. At forty-five one is too old for Sperl's."

"There are men there every Sunday over fifty, — over sixty, I am sure."

"They are men different in their ways of life from me, my dear. When will you come and see my mother?"

Lotta promised that she would go and see the Frau Crippel before long, and then tripped off and joined her party.

Stobel and Marie had walked on, while Fritz remained a little behind for Lotta.

"Did you ask him to come to Sperl's to-morrow?" he said.

"To be sure I did."

"Was that nice of you, Lotta?"

"Why not nice? Nice or not, I did it. Why should not I ask him, if I please?

"Because I thought I was to have the pleasure of entertaining you; — that it was a little party of my own."

"Very well, Herr Planken," said Lotta, drawing herself a little away from him; "if a friend of mine is not welcome at your little party, I certainly shall not join it myself."

"But, Lotta, does not every one know what it is that Crippel wishes of you?"

"There is no harm in his wishing. My friends tell me that I am very foolish not to give him what he wishes. But I still have the chance."

"O yes; no doubt you still have the chance."

"Herr Crippel is a very good man. He is the best son in the world, and he makes two hundred florins a month."

"O, if that is to count!"

"Of course it is to count. Why should it not count? Would the Princess Theresa have married the other day if the young Prince had had no income to support her?"

"You can do as you please, Lotta."

"Yes, I can do as I please, certainly. I suppose Adela Bruhl will be at Sperl's to-morrow?"

"I should say so, certainly. I hardly ever knew her to miss her Sunday evening."

"Nor I. I, too, am fond of dancing, — very. I delight in dancing. But I am not a slave to Sperl's, and then I do not care to dance with every one."

"Adela Bruhl dances very well," said Fritz.

"That is as one may think. She ought to; for she begins at ten, and goes on till two, always. If there is no one nice for dancing she puts up with some one that is not nice. But all that is nothing to me."

"Nothing, I should say, Lotta."

"Nothing in the world. But this is something; last Sunday you danced three times with Adela."

"Did I? I did not count."

"I counted. It is my business to watch those things, if you are to be ever anything to me, Fritz. I will not pretend that I am indifferent. I am not indifferent. I care very much about it. Fritz, if you dance to-morrow with Adela you will not dance with me again, — either then or ever." And having uttered this threat she ran on and found Marie, who had just reached the door of the house in which they both lived.

Fritz, as he walked home by himself, was in doubt as to the course which it would be his duty as a man to pursue in reference to the lady whom he loved. He had distinctly heard that lady ask an old admirer of hers to go to Sperl's and dance with her; and yet, within ten minutes afterwards, she had preemptorily commanded him not to dance with another girl! Now, Fritz Planken had a very good opinion of himself, as he was well entitled to have, and was quite aware that other pretty girls besides Lotta Schmidt were within his reach. He did not receive two hundred florins a month, as did Herr Crippel, but then he was five-and-twenty instead of five-and-forty; and, in the matter of money, too, he was doing pretty well. He did love Lotta Schmidt. It would not be easy for him to part with her. But she, too, loved him, — as he told himself, and she would hardly push matters to extremities. At any rate, he would not submit to a threat. He would dance with Adela Bruhl, at Sperl's. He thought, at least, that when the time should come, he would find it well to dance with her.

Sperl's dancing saloon, in the Tabor Strasse, is a great institution at Vienna. It is open always of a Sunday evening, and dancing then commences at ten, and is continued till two or three o'clock in the morning. There are two large rooms, in one of which the dancers dance, and in the other the dancers and visitors, who do not dance, eat, and drink, and smoke continually. But the most wonderful part of Sperl's establishment is this, that there is nothing there to offend any one. Girls dance and men smoke, and there is eating and drinking, and everybody is as well behaved as though there was a protecting phalanx of dowagers sitting round the wall of the saloon. There are no dowagers, though there may probably be a policeman somewhere about the place. To a stranger it is very remarkable that there is so little of what we call flirting; — almost none of it. It would seem that to the girls dancing is so much a matter of business, that here at Sperl's they can think of nothing else. To mind their steps, — and at the same time their dresses, lest they be trod upon, — to keep full pace with the music, to make all the proper turns at every proper time, and to have the foot fall on the floor at the exact instant; all this is enough, without further excitement. You will see a girl dancing with a man as though the man were a chair, or a stick, or some necessary piece of furniture. She condescends to use his services, but as soon as the dance is over she sends him away. She hardly speaks a word to him, if a word! She has come there to dance, and not to talk; unless, indeed, like Marie Weber and Lotta Schmidt, she has a recognized lover there of her very own.

At about half-past ten Marie and Lotta entered the saloon, and paid their kreutzers, and sat themselves down on seats in the further saloon, from which, through open archways, they could see the dancers. Neither Carl nor Fritz had come as yet, and the girls were quite content to wait. It was to be presumed that they would be there before the men, and they both understood that the real dancing was not commenced early in the evening. It might be all very well for such as Adela Bruhl to dance with any one who came at ten o'clock, but Lotta Schmidt would not care to amuse herself after that fashion. As to Marie, she was to be married after another week, and of course she would dance with no one but Carl Stobel.

"Look at her," said Lotta, pointing with her foot to a fair girl, very pretty, but with hair somewhat untidy, who at this moment was waltzing in the other room. "That lad is a waiter from the Minden hotel. I know him. She would dance with any one."

"I suppose she likes dancing, and there is no harm in the boy," said Marie.

"No, there is no harm, and if she likes it I do not begrudge it her. See what red hands she has."

"She is of that complexion," said Marie.

"Yes, she is of that complexion all over; look at her face. At any rate she might have better shoes on. Did you ever see anybody so untidy?"

"She is very pretty," said Marie.

'Yes, she is pretty. There is no doubt she is pretty. She is not a native here. Her people are from Munich. Do you know, Marie, I think girls are always thought more of in other countries than in their own."

Soon after this Carl and Fritz came together, and Fritz, as he passed across the end of the first saloon, spoke a word or two to Adela. Lotta saw this, but determined that she would take no offence at so small a matter. Fritz need not have stopped to speak, but his doing so might be all very well. At any rate, if she did quarrel with him she would quarrel on a plain intelligible ground. Within two minutes Carl and Marie were dancing, and Fritz had asked Lotta to stand up.

"I will wait a little," said she, "I never like to begin much before eleven."

"As you please," said Fritz; and he sat down in the chair which Marie had occupied. Then he played with his cane, and as he did so his eyes followed the steps of Adela Bruhl.

"She dances very well," said Lotta.

"H — m — m, yes." Fritz did not choose to bestow any strong praise on Adela's dancing.

"Yes, Fritz, she does dance well, — very well indeed. And she is never tired. If you ask me whether I like her style, I cannot quite say that I do. It is not what we do here, — not exactly."

"She has lived in Vienna since she was a child."

"It is in the blood then, I suppose. Look at her fair hair, all blowing about. She is not like one of us."

"Oh no, she is not."

"That she is very pretty, I quite admit," said Lotta. "Those soft grey eyes are delicious. Is it not a pity she has no eyebrows?"

"But she has eyebrows."

"Ah; you have been closer than I, and you have seen them. I have never danced with her, and I cannot see them. Of course they are there, — more or less."

After a while the dancing ceased, and Adela Bruhl came up into the supper-room, passing the seats on which Fritz and Lotta were sitting.

"Are you not going to dance, Fritz," she said, with a smile, as she passed them.

"Go, go,' said Lotta; "why do you not go? She has invited you."

"No; she has not invited me. She spoke to us both."

"She did not speak to me, for my name is not Fritz. I do not see how you can help going, when she asked you so prettily."

"I shall be in plenty of time presently. Will you dance now, Lotta? They are going to begin a waltz, and we will have a quadrille afterwards."

"No, Herr Planken, I will not dance just now."

"Herr Planken, is it? You want to quarrel with me then, Lotta."

"I do not want to be one of two. I will not be one of two. Adela Bruhl is very pretty, and I advise you to go to her. I was told only yesterday her father can give her fifteen hundred florins of fortune! For me, — I have no father."

"But you may have a husband to-morrow."

"Yes, that is true, and a good one. Oh, such a good one!"

"What do you mean by that?"

"You go and dance with Adela Bruhl, and you shall see what I mean."

Fritz had some idea in his own mind, more or less clearly developed, that his fate, as regarded Lotta Schmidt, now lay in his own hands. He undoubtedly desired to have Lotta for his own. He would have married her there and then, — at that moment had it been possible. He had quite made up his mind that he preferred her much to Adela Bruhl, though Adela Bruhl had fifteen hundred florins. But he did not like to endure tyranny, even from Lotta, and he did not know how to escape the tyranny otherwise than by dancing with Adela. He paused a moment, swinging his cane, endeavoring to think how he might best assert his manhood and yet not offend the girl he loved. But he found that to assert his manhood was now his first duty.

"Well, Lotta," he said, "since you are so cross with me, I will ask Adela to dance." And in two minutes he was spinning round the room with Adela Bruhl in his arms.

"Certainly she dances very well," said Lotta, smiling, to Marie, who had now come back to her seat.

"Very well," said Marie, who was out of breath.

"And so does he."

"Beautifully," said Marie.

"Is it not a pity that I should have lost such a partner for ever?"

"Lotta!"

"It is true. Look here, Marie, there is my hand upon it. I will never dance with him again, — never, — never, — never. Why was he so hard upon Herr Crippel last night?"

"Was he hard upon Herr Crippel?"

"He said that Herr Crippel was too old to play the zither; too old! Some people are too young to understand. I shall go home, I shall not stay to sup with you to-night."

"Lotta, you must stay for supper.'

"I will not sup at his table. I have quarrelled with him. It is all over. Fritz Planken is as free as the air for me."

"Lotta, do not say anything in a hurry. At any rate do not do anything in a hurry."

"I do not mean to do anything at all. It is simply this, — I do not care very much for Fritz after all. I don't think I ever did. It is all very well to wear your clothes nicely, but if that is all, what does it come to? If he could play the zither, now!"

"There are other things except playing the zither. They say he is a good book-keeper."

"I don't like book-keeping. He has to be at his hotel from eight in the morning till eleven at night."

"You know best."

"I am not sure of that. I wish I did know best. But I never saw such a girl as you are. How you change! It was only yesterday you scolded me because I did not wish to be the wife of your dear friend Crippel."

"Herr Crippel is a very good man."

"You go away with your good man! you have got a good man of your own. He is standing there waiting for you, like a gander on one leg. He wants you to dance; go away." Then Marie did go away, and Lotta was left alone by herself. She certainly had behaved badly to Fritz, and she was aware of it. She excused herself to herself by remembering that she had never yet given Fritz a promise. She was her own mistress, and had, as yet, a right to do what she pleased with herself. He has asked her for her love, and she had not told him that he should not have it. That was all. Herr Crippel has asked her a dozen times, and she had at last told him definitely, positively, that there was no hope for him. Herr Crippel, of course, would not ask her again; — so she told herself. But if there was no such person as Herr Crippel in all the world, she would have nothing more to do with Fritz Planken, — nothing more to do with him as a lover. He had given her fair ground for a quarrel, and she would take advantage of it. Then as she sat still while they were dancing, she closed her eyes and thought of the zither and of the zitherist. She remained alone for a long time. The musicians in Vienna will play a waltz for twenty minutes, and the same dancers will continue to dance almost without a pause; and then, almost immediately afterwards, there was a quadrille. Fritz, who was resolved to put down tyranny, stood up with Adela for the quadrille also. "I am so glad," said Lotta to herself. "I will wait till this is over, and then I will say goodnight to Marie, and will go home." Three or four men had asked her to dance, but she had refused. She would not dance to-night at all. She was inclined, she thought, to be a little serious, and would go home. At last Fritz returned to her, and bade her come to supper. He was resolved to see how far his mode of casting off tyranny might be successful, so he approached her with a smile, and offered to take her to his table as though nothing had happened.

"My friend," she said, "your table is laid for four, and the places will all be filled."

"The table is laid for five," said Fritz.

"It is one too many. I shall sup with my friend, Herr Crippel."

"Herr Crippel is not here."

"Is he not? Ah me! then I shall be alone, and I must go to bed supperless. Thank you, no, Herr Planken."

"And what will Marie say?"

"I hope she will enjoy the nice dainties you will give her. Marie is all right. Marie's fortune is made. Woe is me! my fortune is to seek. There is one thing certain, it is not to be found here in this room."

Then Fritz turned on his heel and went away; and as he went Lotta saw the figure of a man, as he made his way slowly and hesitatingly into the saloon from the outer passage. He was dressed in a close frock coat, and had on a hat of which she knew the shape as well as she did the make of her own gloves. "If he has not come after all!" she said to herself. Then she turned herself a little round, and drew her chair somewhat into an archway, so that Herr Crippel should not see her readily.

The other four had settled themselves at their table, Marie having said a word of reproach to Lotta as she passed. Now, on a sudden, she got up from her seat and crossed to her friend.

"Herr Crippel is here," she said.

"Of course he is here," said Lotta.

"But you did not expect him?"

"Ask Fritz if I did not say I would sup with Herr Crippel. You ask him. But I shall not all the same. Do not say a word. I shall steal away when nobody is looking."

The musician came wandering up the room, and had looked into every corner before he had even found the supper-table at which the four were sitting. And then he did not see Lotta. He took off his hat as he addressed Marie, and asked some question as to the absent one.

"She is waiting for you somewhere, Herr Crippel," said Fritz, as he filled Adela's glass with wine.

"For me?" said Herr Crippel, as he looked round. "No, she does not expect me." And in the meantime Lotta had left her seat, and was hurrying away to the door.

"There! there!" said Marie; "you will be too late if you do not run." Then Herr Crippel did run, and caught Lotta as she was taking her hat from the old woman who had the girls' hats and shawls in charge near the door.

"What, Herr Crippel, you at Sperl's? When you told me expressly, in so many words, that you would not come! That is not behaving well to me, certainly."

"What, my coming? Is that behaving bad?"

"No; but why did you say you would not come when I asked you? You have come to meet some one. Who is it?"

"You, Lotta; you."

"And yet you refused me when I asked you! Well, and now you are here, what are you going to do? You will not dance."

"I will dance with you, if you will put up with me."

"No, I will not dance. I am too old. I have given it up. I shall come to Sperl's no more after this. Dancing is a folly."

"Lotta, you are laughing at me now."

"Very well; if you like, you may have it so." By this time he had brought her back into the room, and was walking up and down the length of the saloon with her. "But it is no use our walking about here," she said. "I was just going home, and now, if you please, I will go."

"Not yet, Lotta."

"Yes; now, if you please."

"But why are you not supping with them?"

"Because it did not suit me. You see there are four. Five is a foolish number for a supper party."

"Will you sup with me, Lotta?" She did not answer him at once. "Lotta," he said, "if you sup with me now you must sup with me always. How shall it be?"

"Always? no. I am very hungry now, but I do not want supper always. I cannot sup with you always, Herr Crippel."

"But you will to-night?"

"Yes, to-night."

"Then it shall be always." And the musician marched up to a table, and threw his hat down, and ordered such a supper that Lotta Schmidt was frightened. And when presently Carl Stobel and Marie Weber came up to their table, — for Fritz Planken did not come near them again that evening, — Herr Crippel bowed courteously to the diamond-cutter, and asked him when he was to be married.

"Marie says it shall be next Sunday," said Carl.

"And I will be married the Sunday afterwards," said Herr Crippel. "Yes; and there is my wife." And he pointed across the table with both his hands to Lotta Schmidt.

"Herr Crippel, how can you say that?" said Lotta.

"Is it not true, my dear?"

"In fourteen days! no, certainly not. It is out of the question." But nevertheless what Herr Crippel said came true, and on the next Sunday but one he took Lotta Schmidt home to his house as his wife.

"It was all because of the zither," Lotta said to her old mother-in-law. "If he had not played the zither that night I should not have been here now."

"Lotta Schmidt" appeared first in the August issue of *The Argosy* for 1866.

Father Giles of Ballymoy

I

T IS NEARLY THIRTY YEARS since I, Archibald Green, first entered the little town of Ballymoy, in the west of Ireland, and became acquainted with one of the honestest fellows and best Christians whom it has ever been my good fortune to know. For twenty years he and I were fast friends, — though he was much my elder. As he has now been ten years beneath the sod, I may tell the story of our first meeting.

Ballymoy is a so called town, — or was in the days of which I am speaking, — lying close to the shores of Lough Corrib, in the county Galway. It is on the road to no place, and, as the end of a road, has in itself nothing to attract a traveller. The scenery of Lough Corrib is grand, — but the lake is very large, and the fine scenery is on the side opposite to Ballymoy, and hardly to be reached, or even seen, from that place. There is fishing, but it is lake fishing. The salmon fishing of Lough Corrib is far away from Ballymoy, — where the little river runs away from the lake down to the town of Galway. There was then in Ballymoy one single street, of which the characteristic at first sight most striking to a stranger, was its general appearance of being thoroughly wet through. It was not simply that the rain-water was generally running down its unguttered streets in muddy, random rivulets, hurrying towards the lake with true Irish impetuosity, but that each separate house looked as though the walls were reeking with wet; and the alternated roofs of thatch and slate, — the slated houses being just double the height of those that were thatched, —

assisted the eye and mind of the spectator in forming this opinion. The lines were broken everywhere, and at every break it seemed as though there was a free entrance for the waters of heaven. The population of Ballymoy was its second wonder. There had been no famine then; no rot among the potatoes; and land round the town was let to cottiers for nine, ten, and even eleven pounds an acre. At all hours of the day, and at nearly all hours of the night, able-bodied men were to be seen standing in the streets, with knee-breeches unbuttoned, with stockings rolled down over their brogues, and with swallow-tailed frieze coats. Nor, though thus idle, did they seem to suffer any of the distress of poverty. There were plenty of beggars, no doubt, in Ballymoy, but it never struck me that there was much distress in those days. The earth gave forth its potatoes freely, and neither man nor pig wanted more.

It was to be my destiny to stay a week at Ballymoy, on business, as to the nature of which I need not trouble the present reader. I was not, at that time, so well acquainted with the manners of the people of Connaught as I became afterwards, and I had certain misgivings as I was driven into the village on a jaunting car from Tuam. I had just come down from Dublin and had been informed there that there were two "hotels" in Ballymoy, but that one of the "hotels" might, perhaps, be found deficient in some of those comforts which I, as an Englishman, might require. I was therefore to ask for the "hotel" kept by Pat Kirwan. The other hotel was kept by Larry Kirwan; so that it behoved me to be particular. I had made the journey down from Dublin in a night and a day, travelling, as we then did travel in Ireland, by canal boats and by Bianconi's long cars; and I had dined at Tuam, and been driven over, after dinner on an April evening; and when I reached Ballymoy I was tired to death and very cold.

"Pat Kirwan's hotel," I said to the driver, almost angrily. "Mind you don't go to the other."

"Shure, yer honour, and why not to Larry's? You'd be getting better enthertainment at Larry's, because of Father Giles."

I understood nothing about Father Giles, and wished to understand nothing. But I did understand that I was to go to Pat Kirwan's "hotel," and thither I insisted on being taken.

It was quite dusk at this time, and the wind was blowing down the street of Ballymoy, carrying before it wild gusts of rain. In the west of Ireland March weather comes in April, and it comes with a violence of its own, though not with the cruelty of the English east wind. At this moment my neck was ricked by my futile endeavours to keep my head straight on the side car, and the water had got under me upon the seat, and the horse had come to a standstill half a dozen times in the last two minutes, and my apron had been trailed in the mud, and I was very unhappy. For the last ten minutes I had been thinking evil of everything Irish, and especially Connaught. I was driven up to a queerly-shaped three-cornered house that stood at the bottom of the street, and which seemed to possess none of the outside appurtenances of an inn. "This can't be Pat Kirwan's hotel," said I. "Faix and it is then, yer honour," said the driver. "And barring only that Father Giles —." But I had rung the bell, and as the door was now opened by a barefooted girl, I entered the little passage without hearing anything further about Father Giles.

Could I have a bedroom immediately, — with a fire in it? Not answering me directly, the girl led me into a sitting-room, in which my nose was at once treated by that peculiar perfume which is given out by the relics of hot whisky punch mixed with a great deal of sugar, — and there she left me.

"Where is Pat Kirwan himself?" said I, coming to the door, and blustering somewhat. For, let it be remembered, I was very tired; and it may be a fair question whether in the far west of Ireland a little bluster may not sometimes be of service. "If you have not a room ready, I will go to Larry Kirwan's," said I, showing that I understood the bearings of the place.

"It's right away at the furder end then, yer honour," said the driver, putting in his word, "and we comed by it ever so long since. But shure yer honour wouldn't think of leaving this house for that?" This he said because Pat Kirwan's wife was close behind him.

Then Mrs. Kirwan assured me that I could and should be accommodated. The house, to be sure, was crowded, but she had already made arrangements, and had a bed ready. As for a fire in my bedroom, she could not recommend that, "becase the wind blew so mortial sthrong down the chimney since the pot had blown off—bad cess to it; and that loon, Mick Hackett, wouldn't lend a hand to put it up again, becase there were jobs going on at the big house; — bad luck to every joint of his body, thin," said Mrs. Kirwan, with great energy. Nevertheless she and Mick Hackett the mason were excellent friends.

I professed myself ready to go at once to the bedroom without the fire, and was led away upstairs. I asked where I was to eat my breakfast and dine on the next day, and was assured that I should have the room so strongly perfumed with whiskey all to myself. I had been rather cross before, but on hearing this, I became decidedly sulky. It was not that I could not eat my breakfast in the chamber in question, but that I saw before me seven days of absolute misery, if I could have no other place of refuge for myself than a room in which, as was too plain, all Ballymoy came to drink and smoke. But there was no alternative, at any rate for that night and the following morning, and I therefore gulped down my anger without further spoken complaint, and followed the barefooted maiden upstairs, seeing my portmanteau carried up before me.

Ireland is not very well known now to all Englishmen, but it is much better known than it was in those days. On this my first visit into Connaught, I own that I was somewhat scared lest I should be made a victim to the wild lawlessness and general savagery of the people; and I fancied, as in the wet windy gloom of the night, I could see the crowd of natives standing round the doors of the Inn, and just discern their naked legs and old battered hats, that Ballymoy was probably one of those places so far removed from civilization and law, as to be an unsafe residence for an English Protestant. I had undertaken this service, with my eyes more or less open, and was determined to go through with it; — but I confess that I was by this time alive to its dangers. It was an early resolution with me that I would not allow my portmanteau be out of my sight. To that I would cling; with that ever close to me would I live; on that, if needful, would I die. I therefore required that it should be carried up the narrow stairs before me, and I saw it deposited safely in the bedroom.

The stairs were very narrow and very steep. Ascending them was like climbing into a loft. The whole house was built in a barbarous, uncivilized manner, and as fit to be an hotel as it was to be a church. It was triangular and all corners, — the most uncomfortably arranged building I had ever seen. From the top of the stairs I was called upon to turn abruptly into the room destined for me; but there was a side step which I had not noticed under the glimmer of the small tallow candle, and I stumbled headlong into the chamber, uttering imprecations against Pat Kirwan, Ballymoy, and all Connaught. I hope the reader will remember that I had travelled for thirty consecutive hours, had passed sixteen in a small comfortless canal boat without the power of stretching my legs, and that the wind had been at work upon me sideways for the last three hours. I was terribly tired, and I spoke very uncivilly to the young woman.

"Shure, yer honour, it's as clane as clane, and as dhry as dhry, and has been slept in every night since the big storm," said the girl, good-humouredly. Then she went on to tell me something more about Father Giles, of which, however, I could catch nothing, as she was bending over the bed, folding down the bedclothes. "Feel of 'em," said she, "they's dhry as dhry." I did feel them, and the sheets were dry and clean, and the bed, though very small, looked as if it would be comfortable. So I somewhat softened my tone to her, and bade her call me the next morning at eight. "Shure, yer honour, and Father Giles will call yer hisself," said the girl. I begged that Father Giles might be instructed to do no such thing. The girl, however, insisted that he would, and then left me. Could it be that in this savage place, it was considered to be the duty of the parish priest to go round, with matins perhaps, or some other abominable papist ceremony, to the beds of all the strangers? My mother, who was a strict woman, had warned me vehemently against the machinations of the Irish priests, and I, in truth, had been disposed to ridicule her. Could it be that there were such machinations? Was it possible that my trousers might be refused me till I had taken mass? Or that force would be put upon me in some other shape, perhaps equally disagreeable?

Regardless of that and other horrors, or rather, I should perhaps say, determined to face manfully whatever horrors the night or morning might bring upon me, I began to prepare for bed. There was something pleasant in the romance of sleeping at Pat Kirwan's house in Ballymoy, instead of in my own room in

Keppel-street, Russell-square. So I chuckled inwardly at Pat Kirwan's idea of an hotel, and unpacked my things. There was a little table covered with a clean cloth, on which I espied a small
comb. I moved the comb carefully without touching it, and
brought the table up to my bedside. I put out my brushes and
clean linen for the morning, said my prayers, defying Father Giles
and his machinations, and jumped into bed. The bed certainly
was good, and the sheets were very pleasant. In five minutes I was
fast asleep. How long I had slept when I was awakened, I never
knew. But it was at some hour in the dead of night, when I was
disturbed by footsteps in my room, and on jumping up, I saw a
tall, stout, elderly man standing with his back towards me, in the
middle of the room, brushing his clothes with the utmost care.
His coat was still on his back, and his pantaloons on his legs; but
he was most assiduous in his attention to every part of his body
which he could reach. I sat upright, gazing at him, as I thought
then, for ten minutes, — we will say that I did so perhaps for forty
seconds, — and of one thing I became perfectly certain, —
namely, that the clothes-brush was my own! Whether, according
to Irish hotel law, a gentleman would be justified in entering a
stranger's room at midnight for the sake of brushing his clothes, I
could not say; but I felt quite sure that in such case, he would be
bound at least to use the hotel brush or his own. There was a
manifest trespass in regard to my property.

"Sir," said I, speaking very sharply, with the idea of startling him,
"what are you doing here, in this chamber?"

"'Deed, then, and I'm sorry I've waked ye, my boy," said the
stout gentleman.

"Will you have the goodness, sir, to tell me what you are doing
here?"

"Bedad, then, just at this moment it's brushing my clothes, I
am. It was badly they wanted it."

"I daresay they did. And you were doing it with my clothes-
brush."

"And that's thrue too. And if a man hasn't a clothes-brush of
his own, what else can he do but use somebody else's?"

"I think it's a great liberty, sir," said I.

"I think it's a little one. It's only in the size of it we differ. But
I beg your pardon. There is your brush. I hope it will be none the

worse." Then he put down the brush, seated himself on one of the two chairs which the room contained, and slowly proceeded to pull off his shoes, looking me in the face all the while.

"What are you going to do, sir?" said I, getting a little further out from under the clothes, and leaning over the table.

"I am going to bed," said the gentleman.

"Going to bed! where?"

"Here," said the gentleman; and he still went on untying the knot of his shoestring.

It had always been a theory with me, in regard not only to my own country, but to all others, that civilization displays itself never more clearly than when it ordains that every man shall have a bed for himself. In older days, Englishmen of good positions, — men supposed to be gentlemen, — would sleep together and think nothing of it, as ladies, I am told, will still do. And in outlandish regions, up to this time, the same practice prevails. In parts of Spain you will be told that one bed offers sufficient accommodation for two men, and in Spanish America the traveller is considered to be fastidious who thinks that one on each side of him is oppressive. Among the poorer classes with ourselves this grand touchstone of civilization has not yet made itself felt. For aught I know there might be no such touchstone in Connaught at all. There clearly seemed to be none such at Ballymoy.

"You can't go to bed here," said I, sitting bolt upright on the couch.

"You'll find you are wrong there, my friend,"said the elderly gentleman. "But make yourself aisy, I don't do you the least harm in life, and I sleep as quiet as a mouse."

It was quite clear to me that time had come for action. I certainly would not let this gentleman get into my bed. I had been the first comer, and was for the night, at least, the proprietor of this room. Whatever might be the custom of this country in these wild regions, there could be no special law in the land justifying the landlord in such treatment of me as this.

"You won't sleep here, sir," said I, jumping out of the bed, over the table, on to the floor, and confronting the stranger just as he had succeeded in divesting himself of his second shoe. "You won't sleep here to-night, and so you may as well go away." With that I picked up his two shoes, took them to the door, and chucked them out. I heard them go rattling down the stairs, and I was glad that they made so much noise. He would see that I was quite in earnest. "You must follow your shoes" said I, "and the sooner the better."

I had not even yet seen the man very plainly, and even now, at this time, I hardly did so, though I went close up to him and put my hand upon his shoulder. The light was very imperfect, coming from one small farthing candle, which was nearly burnt out in the socket. And I, myself, was confused, ill at ease, and for the moment unobservant. I knew that the man was older than myself, but I had not recognised him as being old enough to demand or enjoy personal protection by reason of his age. He was tall and big, and burly — as he appeared to me then. Hitherto, till his shoes had been chucked away, he had maintained imperturbable good humour. When he heard the shoes clattering downstairs, it seemed that he did not like it, and he began to talk fast and in an angry voice. I would not argue with him, and I did not understand him, but still keeping my hand on the collar of his coat, I insisted that he should not sleep there. Go away out of that chamber he should.

"But it's my own," he said, shouting the words a dozen times. "It's my own room. It's my own room." So this was Pat Kirwan himself, — drunk probably, or mad.

"It may be your own," said I; "but you've let it to me for tonight, and you sha'n't sleep here." So saying I backed him towards the door, and in so doing I trod upon his unguarded toe.

"Bother you, thin, for a pigheaded Englishman," said he. "You've kilt me entirely now. So take your hands off my neck, will ye, before you have me throttled outright."

I was sorry to have trod on his toe, but I stuck to him all the same. I had him near the door now, and I was determined to put him out into the passage. His face was very round and very red, and I thought that he must be drunk; and since I had found out that it was Pat Kirwan, the landlord, I was more angry with the man than ever. "You sha'n't sleep here, so you might as well go," I said, as I backed him away towards the door. This had not been closed since the shoes had been thrown out, and with something of a struggle between the doorposts, I got him out. I remembered nothing whatever as to the suddenness of the stairs; I had been fast asleep since I came up them, and hardly even as yet knew exactly where I was. So, when I got him through the aperture of the door, I gave him a push, as was most natural, I think, for me to do. Down he went backwards, — down the stairs, all in a heap, and I could hear that in his fall he had tumbled against Mrs. Kir-wan, who was coming up, doubtless to ascertain the cause of all the trouble above her head. A hope crossed my mind that the wife might be of assistance to her husband in this time of trouble. The man had fallen very heavily, I knew, and had fallen back-wards. And I remembered then how steep the stairs were. Heaven and earth! Suppose that he were killed — or even seri-ously injured in his own house. What, in such case as that, would my life be worth in that wild country? Then I began to regret that I had been so hot. It might be that I had murdered a man on my first entrance into Connaught!

For a moment or two I could not make up my mind what I would first do. I was aware that both the landlady and the servant were occupied with the body of the ejected occupier of my cham-ber, and I was aware also that I had nothing on but my night shirt. I returned, therefore, within the door, but could not bring myself to shut myself in and return to bed without making some inquiry as to the man's fate. I put my head out, therefore, and did make inquiry. "I hope he is not much hurt by his fall," I said.

"Ochone, ochone! murdher, murdher! Spake, Father Giles, dear, for the love of God!" Such and many such exclamations I heard from the women at the bottom of the stairs.

"I hope he is not much hurt," I said again, putting my head out from the doorway; "but he shouldn't have forced himself into my room."

"His room, the omadhaun, the born idiot!" said the landlady.

"Faix, ma'am, and Father Giles is a dead man," said the girl, who was kneeling over the prostrate body in the passage below. I heard her say Father Giles as plain as possible, and then I became aware that the man whom I had thrust out was not the landlord, — but the priest of the parish! My heart became sick within me as I thought of the troubles around me. And I was sick also with fear lest the man who had fallen should be seriously hurt. But why — why — why had he forced his way into my room? How was it to

97

be expected that I should have remembered that the stairs of the accursed house came flush up to the door of the chamber?

"He shall be hanged if there's law in Ireland," said a voice down below; and as far as I could see, it might be that I should be hung. When I heard that last voice I began to think that I had in truth killed a man, and a cold sweat broke out all over me, and I stood for a while shivering where I was. Then I remembered that it behoved me as a man to go down among my enemies below, and to see what had really happened, to learn whom I had hurt, — let the consequences to myself be what they might. So I quickly put on some of my clothes, — a pair of trousers, a loose coat, and a pair of slippers, and I descended the stairs. By this time they had taken the priest into the whiskey-perfumed chamber below, and although the hour was late, there were already six or seven persons with him. Among them was the real Pat Kirwan himself, who had not been so particular about his costume as I had.

Father Giles, — for indeed it was Father Giles, the priest of the parish, — had been placed in an old arm-chair, and his head was resting against Mrs. Kirwan's body. I could tell from the moans which he emitted that there was still, at any rate, hope of life. Pat Kirwan, who did not quite understand what had happened, and who was still half asleep, and, as I afterwards learned, half tipsy, was standing over him wagging his head. The girl was also standing by, with an old woman and two men who had made their way in through the kitchen.

"Have you sent for a doctor?" said I.

"Oh, you born blagghuard!" said the woman. "You thief of the world! That the like of you should ever have darkened my door!"

"You can't repent it more than I do, Mrs. Kirwan; but hadn't you better send for the doctor."

"Faix, and for the police too, you may be shure of that, young man. To go and chuck him out of the room like that, his own room too, and he a priest and an ould man; he that had given up the half of it, though I axed him not to do so for a sthranger as nobody knowed nothing about."

The truth was coming out by degrees. Not only was the man I had put out Father Giles, but he was also the proper occupier of the room. At any rate somebody ought to have told me all this before they put me to sleep in the same bed with the priest. I made my way round to the injured man, and put my hand upon his shoulder, thinking that perhaps I might be able to asceratin the extent of the injury. But the angry woman, together with the girl, drove me away, heaping on me terms of reproach, and threatening me with the gallows at Galway. I was very anxious that a doctor should be brought as soon as possible; and as it seemed that nothing was being done, I offered to go and search for one. But I was given to understand that I should not be allowed to leave the house until the police had come. I had there-fore to remain there for half an hour, or nearly so, till a sergeant, with two other policemen, really did come. During this time I was in a most wretched frame of mind. I knew no one at Ballymoy or in the neighbourhood. From the manner in which I was addressed, and also threatened by Mrs. Kirwan, and by those who came in and out of the room, I was aware that I should encounter the most intense hostility. I had heard of Irish murders, and heard also of the love of the people for their priests, and I really began to doubt whether my life might not be in danger.

During this time, while I was thus waiting, Father Giles him-self recovered his consciousness. He had been stunned by the fall, but his mind came back to him, though by no means all at once; and while I was left in the room with him, he hardly seemed to remember all the events of the past hour. I was able to discover from what was said that he had been for some days past, or,as it afterwards turned out, for the last month, the tenant of the room, and that when I arrived he had been drinking tea with Mrs. Kir-wan. The only other public bedroom in the hotel was occupied, and he had, with great kindness, given the landlady permission to put the Saxon stranger into his chamber. All this came out by degrees, and I could see how the idea of my base and cruel ingra-titude rankled in the heart of Mrs Kirwan. It was in vain that I expostulated and explained, and submitted myself humbly to everything that was said around me.

"But, ma'am," I said, "if I had only been told that it was the reverend gentleman's bed!"

"Bed, indeed! To hear the blagghuard talk, you'd think it was axing Father Giles to sleep along with the likes of him we were. And there's two beds in the room as dacent as any Christian iver stretched in."

It was a new light to me. And yet I had known over night, before I undressed, that there were two bedsteads in the room! I had seen them, and had quite forgotten the fact in my confusion when I was woken. I had been very stupid, certainly. I felt that now. But I had truly believed that that big man was going to get into my little bed. It was terrible as I thought of it now. The good-natured priest, for the sake of accommodating a stranger, had consented to give up half of his room, and had been repaid for his kindness by being — perhaps murdered! And yet, though just then I hated myself cordially, I could not quite bring myself to look at the matter as they looked at it. There were excuses to be made, if only I could get any one to listen to them.

"He was using my brush, my clothes-brush, indeed he was," I said. "Not but what he'd be welcome; but it made me think he was an intruder."

"And wasn't it too much honour for the likes of ye?" said one of the women, with infinite scorn in the tone of her voice.

"I did use the gentleman's clothes-brush, certainly," said the priest. They were the first collected words he had spoken, and I felt very grateful to him for them. It seemed to me that a man who could condescend to remember that he had used a clothes-brush, could not really be hurt to death, even though he had been pushed down such very steep stairs as those belonging to Pat Kirwan's hotel.

"And I'm sure you were very welcome, sir," said I. "It wasn't that I minded the clothes-brush. It wasn't, indeed; only I thought, — indeed, I did think that there was only one bed. And they had put me into the room, and had not said anything about anybody else. And what was I to think when I woke up in the middle of the night?"

"Faix, and you'll have enough to think of in Galway gaol, — for that's where you're going to," said one of the bystanders.

I can hardly explain the bitterness that was displayed against me. No violence was absolutely shown to me, but I could not move without eliciting a manifest determination that I was not to be allowed to stir out of the room. Red angry eyes were glowering at me, and every word I spoke called down some expression of scorn and ill-will. I was beginning to feel glad that the police were coming, thinking that I needed protection. I was thoroughly ashamed of what I had done, and yet I could not discover that I had been very wrong at any particular moment. Let any man ask himself the question, what he would do, if he supposed that a stout old gentleman had entered his room at an inn and insisted on getting into his bed? It was not my fault that there had been no proper landing-place at the top of the stairs.

Two sub-constables had been in the room for some time before the sergeant came, and with the sergeant arrived also the doctor, and another priest, — Father Columb he was called, — who, as I afterwards learned, was curate, or coadjutor, to Father Giles. By this time there was quite a crowd in the house, although it was past one o'clock, and it seemed that all Ballymoy knew that its priest had been foully misused. It was manifest to me that there was something in the Roman Catholic religion which made the priests very dear to the people; for I doubt whether in any village in England, had such an accident happened to the rector, all the people would have roused themselves at midnight to wreak their vengeance on the assailant. For vengeance they were now beginning to clamour, and even before the sergeant of police had come, the two sub-constables were standing over me; and I felt that they were protecting me from the people in order that they might give me up — to the gallows!

I did not like the Ballymoy doctor at all, — then or even at a later period of my visit to that town. On his arrival he made his way up to the priest through the crowd, and would not satisfy their affection or my anxiety by declaring at once that there was no danger. Instead of doing so he insisted on the terrible nature of the outrage and the brutality shown by the assailant. And at every hard word he said, Mrs. Kirwan would urge him on. "That's thrue for you, doctor!" "'Deed, and you may say that, doctor; — two as good beds as ever Christian stretched in!" "'Deed, and it was just Father Giles's own room, as you may say, since the big storm fetched the roof off his riverence's house below there." Thus gradually I was learning the whole history. The roof had been blown off Father Giles's own house, and therefore he had gone to lodge at the inn! He had been willing to share his lodging with a stranger; and this had been his reward!

"I hope, doctor, that the gentleman is not much hurt," said I, very meekly.

"Do you suppose a gentleman like that, sir, can be thrown down a long flight of stairs without being hurt?" said the doctor in an angry voice. "It is no thanks to you, sir, that his neck has not been sacrificed."

Then there arose a hum of indignation, and the two policemen standing over me bustled about a little, coming very close to me, as though they thought they should have something to do to protect me from being torn to pieces.

I bethought me that it was my special duty in such a crisis to show a spirit, if it were only for the honour of my Saxon blood among the Celts. So I spoke up again, as loud as I could well speak.

"No one in this room is more distressed at what has occurred than I am. I am most anxious to know, for the gentleman's sake, whether he has been seriously hurt?"

"Very seriously hurt indeed," said the doctor; "very seriously hurt. The vertebrae may have been injured for aught I know at present."

"Arrah, blazes, man," said a voice which I learned afterwards had belonged to an officer of the revenue corps of men which was then stationed at Ballymoy, a gentleman with whom I became afterwards familiarly acquainted; Tom Macdermot was his name, Captain Tom Macdermot, and he came from the county of Leitrim, — "Arrah, blazes, man; do ye think a gentleman's to fall sthrait headlong backwards down such a ladder as that, and not find it inconvanient? Only that he's the priest, and has had his own luck, sorrow a neck belonging to him there would be this minute."

"Be aisy, Tom," said Father Giles himself, — and I was delighted to hear him speak. Then there was a pause for a moment. "Tell the gentleman I ain't so bad at all," said the priest; and from that moment I felt an affection to him which never afterwards waned.

They got him upstairs back into the room from which he had been evicted, and I was carried off to the police station, where I positively spent the night. What a night it was! I had come direct from London, sleeping on my road but once, in Dublin, and now I found myself accommodated with a stretcher in the police barracks at Ballymoy! And the worst of it was that I had business to do at Ballymoy which required that I should hold up my head and make much of myself. The few words which had been spoken by the priest had comforted me, and had enabled me to think again of my own position. Why was I locked up? No magistrate had committed me. It was really a question whether I had done anythig illegal. As that man whom Father Giles called Tom had very properly explained, if people will have ladders instead of staircases in their houses, how is anybody to put an intruder out of the room without risk of breaking the intruder's neck? And as to the fact, — now an undoubted fact, that Father Giles was no intruder, the fault in that lay with the Kirwans, who had told me nothing of the truth. The boards of the stretcher in the police station were very hard, in spite of the blankets with which I had been furnished; and, as I lay there, I began to remind myself that there certainly must be law in county Galway. So I called to the attendant policeman and asked him by whose authority I was locked up.

"Ah, thin, don't bother," said the policeman; "shure, and you've given through enough this night!" The dawn was at that moment breaking, so I turned myself on the stretcher, and resolved that I would put a bold face on it all when the day should come.

The first person I saw in the morning was Captain Tom, who came into the room where I was lying, followed by a little boy with my portmanteau. The sub-inspector of police who ruled over the men at Ballymoy lived, as I afterwards learned, at Oranmore, so that I had not, at this conjuncture, the honour of seeing him. Captain Tom assured me that he was an excellent fellow, and rode to hounds like a bird. As in those days I rode to hounds myself, — as nearly like a bird as I was able, — I was glad to have such an account of my head gaoler. The sub-constables seemed to do just what Captain Tom told them, and there was, no doubt, a very good understanding between the police force and the revenue officer.

"Well, now, I'll tell you what you must do, Mr. Green," said the Captain.

"In the first place," said I, "I must protest that I'm now locked up here illegally."

"Oh, bother; now don't make yourself unaisy."

"That's all very well, Captain —. I beg your pardon, sir, but I didn't catch any name plainly except the Christian name."

"My name is Macdermot, — Tom Macdermot, They call me Captain, — but that's neither here nor there."

"I suppose, Captain Macdermot, the police here cannot lock up anybody they please, without a warrant."

"And where would you have been if they hadn't locked you up? I'm blessed if they wouldn't have had you into the Lough before this time."

There might be something in that, and I therefore resolved to forgive the personal indignity which I had suffered, if I could secure something like just treatment for the future. Captain Tom had already told me that Father Giles was doing pretty well.

"He's as sthrong as a horse, you see, or, sorrow a doubt, he'd be a dead man this minute. The back of his neck is as black as your hat with the bruises, and it's the same way with him all down his loins. A man like that, you know, not just as young as he was once, falls mortial heavy. But he's as jolly as a four-year-old," said Captain Tom, "and you're to go and ate your breakfast with him, in his bedroom, so that you may see with your own eyes that there are two beds there."

"I remembered it afterwards quite well," said I.

"'Deed and Father Giles got such a kick of laughter this morning, when he came to understand that you thought he was going to get into bed alongside of you, that he strained himself all over again, and I thought he'd have frightened the house, yelling with the pain. But anyway you've to go over and see him. So now you'd better get yourself dressed."

This announcement was certainly very pleasant. Against Father Giles, of course, I had no feeling of bitterness. He had behaved well throughout, and I was quite alive to the fact that the light of his countenance would afford me a better aegis against the ill-will of the people of Ballymoy, than anything the law would do for me. So I dressed myself in the barrack-room, while Captain Tom waited without; and then I sallied out under his guidance to make a second visit to Pat Kirwan's hotel. I was amused to see that the police, though by no means subject to Captain Tom's orders, let me go without the least difficulty, and that the boy was allowed to carry my portmanteau back again.

"Oh, it's all right," said Captain Tom, when I alluded to this. "You're not down in the sheet. You were only there for protection, you know." Nevertheless, I had been taken there by force, and had been locked up by force. If, however, they were disposed to forget all that, so was I. I did not return to the barracks again; and when, after that, the policemen whom I had known met me in the street, they always accosted me as though I were an old friend; hoping my honour had found a better bed than when they last saw me. They had not looked at me with any friendship in their eyes when they had stood over me in Pat Kirwan's parlour.

This was my first view of Ballymoy, and of the "hotel," by daylight. I now saw that Mrs. Pat Kirwan kept a grocery establishment, and that the three-cornered house which had so astonished me, was very small. Had I seen it before I entered it I should hardly have dared to look there for a night's lodging. As it was, I stayed there for a fortnight, and was by no means uncomfortable. Knots of men and women were now standing in groups round the door, and, indeed, the lower end of the street was almost crowded.

"They're all here," whispered Captain Tom, "because they've heard how Father Giles has been murdhered during the night by a terrible Saxon; and there isn't a man or woman among them who doesn't know that you are the man who did it."

"But they know also, I suppose," said I, "that Father Giles is alive."

"Bedad, yes, they know that, or I wouldn't be in your skin, my boy. But come along. We mustn't keep the priest waiting for his breakfast." I could see that they all looked at me, and there were some of them, especially among the women, whose looks I did not even yet like. They spoke among each other in Gaelic, and I could perceive that they were talking of me. "Can't you understand, then," said Captain Tom, speaking to them aloud, just as he entered the house, "that Father Giles, the Lord be praised, is as well as ever he was in his life? Shure it was only an accident."

"An accident done on purpose, Captain Tom," said one person.

"What is it to you how it was done, Mick Henly? If Father Giles is satisfied, isn't that enough for the likes of you? Get out of that, and let the gentleman pass." Then Captain Tom pushed

Mick away roughly, and the others let us enter the house. "Only they wouldn't do it unless somebody gave them the wink, they'd pull you in pieces this moment for a dandy of punch, — they would indeed." Perhaps Captain Tom exaggerated the prevailing feeling, thinking thereby to raise the value of his own service in protecting me; but I was quite alive to the fact that I had done a most dangerous deed, and had a most narrow escape.

I found Father Giles sitting up in his bed, while Mrs. Kirwan was rubbing his shoulder diligently with an embrocation of arnica. The girl was standing by with a basin half full of the same, and I could see that the priest's neck and shoulders were as red as a raw beefsteak. He winced grievously under the rubbing, but he bore it like a man.

"And here comes the hero," said Father Giles. "Now stop a minute or two, Mrs. Kirwan, while we have a mouthful of break-fast, for I'll go bail that Mr. Green is hungry after his night's rest. I hope you got a better bed, Mr. Green, than the one I found you in when I was unfortunate enough to waken you last night. There it is, all ready for you still," said he, "and if you accept of it to-night, take my advice and don't let a trifle stand in the way of your dhraims."

"I hope, thin, the gintleman will conthrive to suit hisself else-where," said Mrs. Kirwan.

"He'll be very welcome to take up his quarters here if he likes," said the priest. "And why not? But, bedad, sir, you'd better be a little more careful the next time you see a sthranger using your clothes-brush. They are not so strict here in their ideas of meum and tuum as they are perhaps in England; and if you'd broken my neck for so small an offence, I don't know but what they'd have stretched your own."

We then had breakfast together, Father Giles, Captain Tom, and I, and a very good breakfast we had. By degrees even Mrs. Kirwan was induced to look favourably at me, and before the day was over I found myself to be regarded as a friend in the establish-ment. And as a friend I certainly was regarded by Father Giles — then, and for many a long day afterwards. And many times when he has, in years since that, but years nevertheless which are now long back, come over and visited me in my English home, he has told the story of the manner in which we first became acquainted. "When you find a gentleman asleep," he would say, "always ask his leave before you take a liberty with his clothes-brush."

"Father Giles of Ballymoy" appeared first in the May issue of *The Argosy* for 1866.

The Last Austrian Who Left Venice

IN THE SPRING AND EARLY SUMMER of the year now past, — the year 1866, — the hatred felt by Venetians towards the Austrian soldiers who held their city in thraldom, had reached its culminating point. For years this hatred had been very strong; — how strong can hardly be understood by those who never recognised the fact that there had been, so to say, no mingling of the conquered and the conquerors, no process of assimilation between the Italian vassals and their German masters. Venice as a city was as purely Italian as though its barracks were filled with no Hungarian long-legged soldiers, and its cafés crowded with no white-coated Austrian officers. And the regiments which held the town, lived as completely after their own fashion as though they were quartered in Pesth or Prague or Vienna, — with this exception, that in Venice they were enabled, — and indeed from circumstances were compelled, — to exercise a palpable ascendancy which belonged to them nowhere else. They were masters, daily visible as such to the eye of everyone who merely walked the narrow ways of the city or strolled through the open squares; and as masters they were as separate as the gaoler is separate from the prisoner. The Austrian officers sat together in the chief theatre, — having the best part of it to themselves. Few among them spoke Italian. None of the common soldiers did so. The Venetians seldom spoke German; and could hold no intercourse what-

ever with the Croats, Hungarians, and Bohemians, of whom the
garrison was chiefly composed. It could not be otherwise than
that there should be intense hatred in a city so ruled. But the
hatred which had been intense for years had reached its boiling
point in the May preceding the outbreak of the war.

Whatever other nations might desire to do, Italy at any rate
was at this time resolved to fight. It was not that the King and the
Government were so resolved. What was the purpose just then of
the powers of the state, if any purpose had then been definitely
formed by them, no one now knows. History perhaps may some
day tell us. But the nation was determined to fight. Hitherto all
had been done for the Italians, and now the time had come in
which Italians would do something for themselves! The people
hated the French aid by which they had been allowed to live, and
burned with a desire to prove that they could do something great
without aid. There was an enormous army, and that army should
be utilised to the enfranchisement of Venetia and to the great
glory of Italy. The king and the ministers appreciated the fact
that the fervour of the people was too strong to be repressed, and
were probably guided to such resolutions as they did make by that
appreciation. The feeling was as strong in Venice as it was in
Florence or in Milan; but in Venice only, — or rather in Venetia
only — all outward signs of such feeling were repressible, and
were repressed. All through Lombardy and Tuscany any young
man who pleased might volunteer with Garibaldi; but to volunteer with Garibaldi was not, at first, so easy for young men in
Verona or in Venice. The more complete was this repression, the
greater was this difficulty, the stronger of course arose the hatred
of the Venetians for the Austrian soldiery. I have never heard
that the Austrians were cruel in what they did; but they were
determined; and, as long as they had any intention of holding the
province, it was necessary that they should be so.

During the past winter there had been living in Venice a certain Captain von Vincke, — Hubert von Vincke, — an Austrian
officer of artillery who had spent the last four or five years among
the fortifications of Verona, and who had come to Venice, originally, on account of ill health. Some military employment had
kept him in Venice, and he remained there till the outbreak of
the war; going backwards and forwards, occasionally, to Verona,

but still having Venice as his headquarters. Now Captain von Vincke had shown so much consideration for the country which he assisted in holding under subjection as to learn its language, and to study its manners; and had by these means found his way more or less into Italian society. He was a thorough soldier, good looking, perhaps eight-and-twenty or thirty years of age, well educated, ambitious, very free from the common vice of thinking that the class of mankind to which he belonged was the only class in which it would be worth a man's while to live, but nevertheless imbued with a strong feeling that Austria ought to hold her own, that an Austrian army was indomitable, and that the quadrilateral fortresses, bound together as they were now bound by Austrian strategy, were impregnable. So much Captain von Vincke thought and believed on the part of his country; but in thinking and believing this, he was still desirous that much should be done to relieve Austrian Italy from the grief of foreign rule. That Italy should succeed in repelling Austria from Venice was to him an absurdity.

He had become intimate at the house of a widow lady, who lived in the Campo San Luca, one Signora Pepé, whose son had first become acquainted with Captain von Vincke at Verona. Carlo Pepé was a young advocate, living and earning his bread at Venice, but business had taken him for a time to Verona; and when leaving that city he had asked his Austrian friend to come and see him in his mother's house. Both Madame Pepé and her daughter Nina, Carlo's only sister, had somewhat found fault with the young advocate's rashness in thus seeking the close intimacy of home life with one whom, whatever might be his own peculiar virtues, they could not but recognise as an enemy of their country.

"That would be all very fine if it were put into a book," said the Signora to her son, who had been striving to show that an Austrian, if good in himself, might be as worthy as friend as an Italian; "but it is always well to live on the safe side of the wall. It is not convenient that the sheep and the wolves should drink at the same stream."

This she said with all that caution which everywhere forms so marked a trait in the Italian character. "Who goes softly goes soundly." Half of the Italian nature is told in that proverb, —

though it is not the half which was becoming most apparent in the doings of the nation in these days. And the Signorina was quite of one mind with her mother.

"Carlo," she said, "how is it that one never sees one of these Austrians in the house of any friend? Why is it that I have never yet found myself in a room with one of them?"

"Because men and women are generally so pigheaded and unreasonable," Carlo had replied. "How am I, for instance, ever to learn what a German is at the core, — or a Frenchman, or an Englishman, — if I refuse to speak to one."

It ended by Captain von Vincke being brought to the house in the Campo San Luca, and there becoming as intimate with the Signora and the Signorina as he was with the advocate. Our story must be necessarily too short to permit us to see how the affair grew in all its soft and delicate growth; but by the beginning of April Nina Pepé had confessed her love to Hubert von Vincke, and both the captain and Nina had had a few words with the Signora on the subject of their projected marriage.

"Carlo will never allow it," the old lady had said, trembling as she thought of the danger that was coming upon the family.

"He should not have brought Captain von Vincke to the house, unless he was prepared to regard such a thing as possible," said Nina, proudly.

"I think he is too good a fellow to object to anything that you will ask him," said the captain, holding by the hand the lady whom he hoped to call his mother-in-law.

Throughout January and February Captain von Vincke had been an invalid. In March he had been hardly more than convalescent, and had then had time and all that opportunity which convalescence gives for the sweet business of love-making. During this time, — through March and in the first weeks of April, — Carlo Pepé had been backwards and forwards to Verona, and had in truth had more business on hand than that which simply belonged to him as a lawyer. Those were the days in which the Italians were beginning to prepare for the great attack which was to be made, and in which correspondence was busily carried on between Italy and Venetia as to the enrolment of Venetian Volunteers. It will be understood that no Venetian was allowed to go into Italy without an Austrian passport, and that at this time the

Austrians were becoming doubly strict in seeing that the order was not evaded. Of course it was evaded daily, and twice in that April did young Pepé travel between Verona and Bologna in spite of all that Austria could say to the contrary.

When at Venice he and von Vincke discussed very freely the position of the country, — nothing of course being said as to those journeys to Bologna. Indeed, of them no one in the Camp San Luca knew aught. They were such journeys that a man says nothing of them to his mother or his sister, — or even to his wife, unless he has as much confidence in her courage as he has in her love. But of politics he would talk freely, as would also the German; and though each of them would speak of the cause as though they two were simply philosophical lookers on, and were not and could not become actors, — and though each had in his mind a settled resolve to bear with the political opinion of the other, yet it came to pass that they now and again were on the verge of quarrelling. The fault, I think, was wholly with Carlo Pepé, whose enthusiasm of course was growing as those journeys to Bologna were made successfully, and who was beginning to feel assured that Italy at last would certainly do something for herself. But there had not come any open quarrel, — not as yet, — when Nina, in her lover's presence, was arguing as to the impropriety of bringing Captain von Vincke to the house, if Captain von Vincke was to be regarded as altogether unfit for matrimonial purposes. At that moment Carlo was absent at Verona, but was to return on the following morning. It was decided at this conference between the two ladies and the lover, that Carlo should be told on his return of Captain von Vincke's intentions. Captain von Vincke himself would tell him.

There is a certain hotel or coffee-house, or place of general public entertainment in Venice, kept by a German, and called the Hotel Bauer, — probably from the name of the German who keeps it. It stands near the church of St. Moses, behind the grand piazza, between that and the great canal, in a narrow intricate throng of little streets, and is approached by a close dark waterway which robs it of any attempt at hotel grandeur. Nevertheless it is a large and commodious house, at which good dinners may be eaten at prices somewhat lower than are compatible with the grandeur of the grand canal. It used to be much affected by Germans, and had, perhaps, acquired among Venetians a character of being attached to Austrian interests. There was not much in this, or Carlo Pepé would not have frequented the house, even in company with his friend von Vincke. He did so frequent it, and now, on this occasion of his return home, von Vincke left word for him that he would breakfast at the hotel at eleven o'clock. Pepé by that time would have gone home after his journey, and would have visited his office. von Vincke also would have done the greatest part of his day's work. Each understood the habits of the other, and they met at Bauer's for breakfast.

It was the end of April, and Carlo Pepé had returned to Venice full of schemes for that revolution which he now regarded as immiment. The alliance between Italy and Prussia was already discussed. Those Italians who were most eager said that it was a thing done, and no Italian was more eager than Carlo Pepé. And it was believed at this time, — and more thoroughly believed in Italy than elsewhere, — that Austria and Prussia would certainly go to war. Now, if ever, Italy must do something for herself. Carlo Pepé was in this mood, full of these things, when he sat down to breakfast at Bauer's with his friend Captain von Vincke.

"Von Vincke," he said, "in three months' time you will be out of Venice."

"Shall I?" said the other; "and where shall I be?"

"In Vienna, as I hope; or at Berlin if you can get there. But you will not be here, or in the Quadrilatere, unless you are left behind as a prisoner."

The captain went on for a while cutting his meat and drinking his wine, before he made any reply to this. And Pepé said more of the same kind, expressing strongly his opinion that the empire of the Austrians in Venice was at an end. Then the captain wiped his moustaches carefully with his napkin, and did speak.

"Carlo, my friend," he said, "you are rash to say all this."

"Why rash?" said Carlo; "you and I understand each other."

"Just so, my friend; but we do not know how far that long-eared waiter may understand either of us."

"The waiter has heard nothing, and I do not care if he did."

"And beyond that," continued the captain, "you make a difficulty for me. What am I to say when you tell me these things? That you should have one political opinion and I another is nat-

114

ural. The question between us, in an abstract point of view, I can discuss with you willingly. The possibility of Venice contending with Austria I could discuss, if no such rebellion were imminent. But when you tell me that it is imminent, that it is already here, I cannot discuss it."

"It is imminent," said Carlo.

"So be it," said von Vincke. And then they finished their breakfast in silence. All this was very unfortunate for our friend the captain, who had come to Bauer's with the intention of speaking on quite another subject. His friend Pepé had evidently taken what he had said in a bad spirit, and was angry with him. Nevertheless, as he had told Nina and her mother that he would declare his purpose to Carlo on this morning, he must do it. He was not a man to be frightened out of his purpose by his friend's ill-humour. "Will you come into the Piazza, and smoke a cigar?" said von Vincke, feeling that he could begin upon the other subject better as soon as the scene should be changed.

"Why not let me have my cigar and coffee here?" said Carlo.

"Because I have something to say, which I can say better walking than sitting. Come along." Then they paid the bill and left the house, and walked in silence through the narrow ways to the piazza. von Vincke said no word till he found himself in the broad passage leading into the great square. Then he put his hand through the other's arm and told his tale at once. "Carlo," said he, "I love your sister, and would have her for my wife. Will you consent?"

"By the body of Bacchus, what is this you say?" said the other, drawing his arm away, and looking up into the German's face.

"Simply that she has consented and your mother. Are you willing that I should be your brother?"

"This is madness," said Carlo Pepé.

"On their part, you mean?"

"Yes, and on yours. Were there nothing else to prevent it, how could there be marriage between us when this war is coming?"

"I do not believe in the war; — that is, I do not believe in war between us and Italy. No war can affect you here in Venice. If there is to be a way in which I shall be concerned, I am quite willing to wait till it be over."

"You understand nothing about it," said Carlo, after a pause; "nothing! You are in the dark altogether. How should it not be so, when those who are over you never tell you anything? No, I will not consent. It is a thing out of the question."

"Do you think that I am personally unfit to be your sister's husband?"

"Not personally, — but politically and nationally. You are not one of us; and now, at this moment, any attempt at close union between an Austrian and a Venetian must be ruinous. Von Vincke, I am heartily sorry for this. I blame the women and not you."

Then Carlo Pepé went home, and there was a rough scene between him and his mother, and a scene still rougher between him and his sister. And in these interviews he told something, though not the whole of the truth as to the engagements into which he had entered. That he was to be the officer second in command in a regiment of Venetian volunteers, of those volunteers whom it was hoped that Garibaldi would lead to victory in the coming war, he did not tell them; but he did make them understand that when the struggle came he would be away from Venice, and would take a part in it. "And how am I to do this," he said, "if you here are joined, hand and heart, to an Austrian? A house divided against itself must fall."

Let the reader understand that Nina Pepé, in spite of her love and of her lover, was as good an Italian as her brother, and that their mother was equally firm in her political desires and national antipathies. Where would you have found the Venetian, man or woman, who did not detest Austrian rule, and look forward to the good day coming when Venice should be a city of Italia? The Signora and Nina had indeed, some six months before this, been much stronger in their hatred of all things German, than had the son and brother. It had been his liberal feeling, his declaration that even a German might be good, which had induced them to allow this Austrian to come among them. Then the man and the soldier had been two; and von Vincke had himself shown tendencies so strongly at variance with those of his comrades that he had disarmed their fears. He had read Italian, and condescended to speak it; he knew the old history of their once great city, and would listen to them when they talked of their old doges. He loved their churches, and their palaces, and their pictures. Gradually he had come to love Nina Pepé with all his heart, and Nina loved him too with all her heart. But when her brother spoke to her and to her mother with more than his customary vehemence of what was due from them to their country, of the debt which certainly should be paid by him, of obligations to him from which they could not free themselves; and told them also, that by that time six months not an Austrian would be found in Venice, they trembled and believed him, and Nina felt that her love would not run smooth.

"You must be with us or against us," said Carlo.

"Why then did you bring him here?" Nina replied.

"Am I to suppose that you cannot see a man without falling in love with him?"

"Carlo, that is unkind, — almost unbrotherly. Was he not your friend, and were not you the first to tell us how good he is? And he is good; no man can be better."

"He is a honest young man," said the Signora.

"He is Austrian to the back-bone," said Carlo.

"Of course he is," said Nina. "What should he be?"

"And will you be Austrian?" her brother asked.

"Not if I must be an enemy of Italy," Nina said. "If an Austrian may be a friend to Italy, then I will be an Austrian. I wish to be Hubert's wife. Of course I shall be an Austrian if he is my husband."

"Then I trust that you may never be his wife," said Carlo.

By the middle of May Carlo Pepé and Captain von Vincke had absolutely quarrelled. They did not speak, and von Vincke had been ordered by the brother not to show himself at the house in the Campo San Luca. Every German in Venice had now become more Austrian than before, and every Venetian more Italian. Even our friend the captain had come to believe in the war. Not only Venice but Italy was in earnest, and Captain von Vincke foresaw, or thought that he foresaw, that a time of wretched misery was coming upon that devoted town. He would never give up Nina, but perhaps it might be well that he should cease to press his suit till he might be enabled to do so with something of the éclat of Austrian success. And now at last it became necessary that the two women should be told of Carlo's plans, for Carlo was

going to leave Venice till the war should be over and he could re-
enter Venice as an Italian should enter a city of his own.

"Oh! my son, my son," said the mother; "why should it be
you?"

"Many must go, mother. Why not I as well as another?"

"In other houses there are fathers; and in other families more
sons than one."

"The time has come, mother, in which no woman should
grudge either husband or son to the cause. But the things is settled. I am already second colonel in a regiment which will serve
with Garibaldi. You would not ask me to desert my colours?"
There was nothing further to be said. The Signora threw herself
on her son's neck and wept, and both mother and sister felt that
their Carlo was already a second Garibaldi. When a man is a hero
to women, they will always obey him. What could Nina do at
such a time, but promise that she would not see Hubert von
Vincke during his absence. Then there was a compact made
between the brother and sister.

During three weeks past, — that is, since the breakfast at
Bauer's, — Nina had seen Hubert von Vincke but once, and had
then seen him in the presence of her mother and brother. He had
come in one evening in the old way, before the quarrel, to take
his coffee, and had been received, as heretofore, as a friend, —
Nina sitting very silent during the evening, but with a gracious
silence; and after that the mother had signified to the lover that
he had better come no more for the present. He therefore came
no more. I think it is the fact that love, though no doubt it may
run as strong with an Italian or with an Austrian as it does with
us English, is not allowed to run with so uncontrollable a stream.
Young lovers, and especially young women, are more subject to
control, and are less inclined to imagine that all things should go
as they would have them. Nina, when she was made to understand that the war was come, — that her brother was leaving her
and her mother and Venice, that he might fight for them, — that
an Austrian soldier must for the time be regarded as an enemy in
that house, — resolved, with a slow melancholy firmness, that
she would accept the circumstances of her destiny.

"If I fall," said Carlo, "you must then manage for yourself. I
would not wish to bind you after my death."

"Do not talk like that, Carlo."

"Nay, my child, but I must talk like that; and it is at least well that we should understand each other. I know that you will keep your promise to me."

"Yes," said Nina; "I will keep my promise."

"Till I come back, or till I be dead, you will not again see Captain von Vincke; or till the cause be gained."

"I will not see him, Carlo, till you come back, — or till the cause be gained."

"Or till I be dead. Say it after me."

"Or till you be dead, if I must say it."

But there was a clause in the contract that she was to see her lover once before her brother left them. She had acknowledged the propriety of her brother's behests, backed as they came to be at last by their mother; but she declared through it all that she had done no wrong, and that she would not be treated as though she were an offender. She would see her lover and tell him what she pleased. She would obey her brother, but she would see her lover first. Indeed, she would make no promise of obedience at all, — would promise disobedience instead, — unless she were allowed to see him. She would herself write to him and bid him come. This privilege was at last acceded to her, and Captain von Vincke was summoned to the Campo San Luca.

The morning sitting-room of the Signora Pepé was up two pairs of stairs, and the stairs were not paved as are the stairs of the palaces in Venice. But the room was large and lofty, and seemed to be larger than its size from the very small amount of furniture which it contained. The floor was of hard, polished cement, which looked like variegated marble, and the amount of carpet upon it was about four yards long, and was extended simply beneath the two chairs in which sat habitually the Signora and her daughter. There were two large mirrors and a large gold clock, and a large table and a small table, a small sofa and six chairs, and that was all. In England the room would have received ten times as much furniture, or it would not have been furnished at all. And there were in it no more than two small books — belonging both to Nina, for the Signora read but little. In England, in such a sitting-room, tables, — various tables, would have been strewed with books; but then, perhaps, Nina

Pepé's eye required the comfort of no other volumes than those she was actually using.

Nina was alone in the room when her lover came to her. There had been a question whether her mother should or should not be present; but Nina had been imperative, and she received him alone. "It is to bid you good-bye, Hubert," she said, as she got up and touched his hand, — just touched his hand.

"Not for long, my Nina."

"Who can say for how long, now that the war is upon us? As far as I can see, it will be for very long. It is better that you shold know it all. For myself, I think, — I fear that it will be for ever."

"For ever! Why for ever?"

"Because I cannot marry an enemy of Italy. I do not think that we can ever succeed."

"You can never succeed."

"Then I can never be your wife. It is so, Hubert; I see that it must be so. The loss is to me, not to you."

"No, no — no. The loss is to me, — to me."

"You have your profession. You are a soldier. I am nothing."

"You are all in all to me."

"I can be nothing, — I shall be nothing, — unless I am your wife. Think how I must long for that which you say is so impossible. I do long for it; I shall long for it. Oh, Hubert! go and lose your cause; let our men have their Venice. Then come to me, and your country shall be my country, and your people my people." As she said this she gently laid her hand upon his arm, and the touch of her fingers thrilled through his whole frame. He put out his arms as though to grasp her in his embrance. "No, Hubert — no; that must not be till Venice is our own."

"I wish it were," he said; "but it will never be so. You may make me a traitor in heart, but that will not drive out fifty thousand troops from the fortresses."

"I do not understand these things, Hubert, and I have felt your country's power to be so strong, that I cannot now doubt it."

"It is absurd to doubt it."

"But yet they say that we shall succeed."

"It is impossible. Even though Prussia should be able to stand against us, we should not leave Venetia. We shall never leave the fortresses."

"Then, my love, we may say farewell for ever. I will not forget you. I will never be false to you. But we must part."

He stood there arguing with her, and she argued with him, but they always came round to the same point. There was to be the war, and she would not become the wife of her brother's enemy. She had sworn, she said, and she would keep her word. When his arguments became stronger than hers, she threw herself back upon her plighted word. "I have said it, and I must not depart from it. I have told him that my love for you should be eternal, — and I tell you the same. I told him that I would see you no more, — and I can only tell you so also." He could ask her no questions as to the cause of her resolution, because he could not make inquiries as to her brother's purpose. He knew that Carlo was at work for the Venetian cause; or, at least, he thought that he knew it. But it was essential for his comfort that he should really know as little of this as might be possible. That Carlo Pepé was coming and going in the service of the cause, he could not but surmise; but should authenticated information reach him as to whither Carlo went, and how he came, it might become his duty to put a stop to Carlo's comings and Carlo's goings. On this matter, therefore, he said nothing, but merely shook his head, and smiled with a melancholy smile when she spoke of the future struggle.

"And now, Hubert, you must go. I was determined that I would see you, that I might tell you that I would be true to you."

"What good will be such truth?"

"Nay, it is for you to say that. I ask you for no pledge."

"I shall love no other woman. I would if I could. I would if I could — to-morrow."

"Let us have our own, and then come and love me. Or you need not come. I will go to you, though it be the furthest end of Galicia. Do not look like that at me. You should be proud when I tell you that I love you. No, you shall not kiss me. No man shall ever kiss me till Venice is our own. There, — I have sworn it. Should that time come, and should a certain Austrian gentleman care for Italian kisses then, he will know where to seek for them. God bless you now, and go." She made her way to the door, and opened it, and there was nothing for him but that he must go. He touched her hand once more as he went, but there was no other word spoken between them.

"Mother," she said, when she found herself again with the Signora, "my little dream of life is over. It has been very short."

"Nay, my child, life is long for you yet. There will be many dreams, and much of reality."

"I do not complain of Carlo," Nina continued. "He is sacrificing much, perhaps everything, for Venice. And why should his sacrifice be greater than mine? But I feel it to be severe, — very severe. Why did he bring him here if he felt thus?"

June came, that month of June that was to be so fatal to Italian glory, so fraught with success for the Italian cause, and Carlo Pepé was again away. Those who knew nothing of his doings, knew only that he had gone to Verona — on matters of law. Those who were really acquainted with the circumstances of his present life were aware that he had made his way out of Verona, and that he was already with his volunteers near the lakes, waiting for Garibaldi, who was then expected from Caprera. For some weeks to come, for some months probably, during the war perhaps, the two women in the Campo San Luca would know nothing of the whereabouts or of the fate of him whom they loved. He had gone to risk all for the cause, and they too must be content to risk all in remaining desolate at home without the comfort of his presence; — and she also, without the sweeter comfort of that other presence. It is thus that women fight their battles. In these days men by hundreds were making their way out of Venice, and by thousands out of the province of Venetia, and the Austrians were endeavouring in vain to stop the emigration. Some few were caught, and kept in prison; and many Austrian threats were uttered against those who should prove themselves to be insubordinate. But it is difficult for a garrison to watch a whole people, and very difficult indeed when there is a war on hand. It at last became a fact, that any man from the province could go and become a volunteer under Garibaldi if he pleased, and very many did go. History will say that they were successful, — but their success certainly was not glorious.

It was in the month of June that all the battles of that short war were fought. Nothing will ever be said or sung in story to the honour of the volunteers who served in that campaign with Garibaldi, amidst the mountains of the Southern Tyrol; but nowhere, probably, during the war was there so much continued fighting, or an equal amount endured of the hardships of military life. The task they had before them, of driving the Austrians from the fortresses amidst their own mountains, was an impossible one, impossible even had Garibaldi been supplied with ordinary military equipments, — but ridiculously impossible for him in all the nakedness in which he was sent. Nothing was done to enable him to succeed. That he should be successful was neither intended nor desired. He was, in fact, — then, as he has been always, since the days in which he gave Naples to Italy, — simply a stumbling block in the way of the king, of the king's ministers, and of the king's generals. "There is that Garibaldi again, — with volunteers flocking to him by thousands: — what shall we do to rid ourselves of Garibaldi and his volunteers? How shall we dispose of them?" That has been the feeling of those in power in Italy, — and not unnaturally their feeling, — with regard to Garibaldi. A man so honest, so brave, so patriotic, so popular, and so impracticable, cannot but have been a trouble to them. And here he was with 25,000 volunteers, all armed after a fashion, all supplied, at least, with a red shirt. What should be done with Garibaldi and his army? So they sent him away up into the mountains, where his game of play might at any rate detain him for some weeks; and in the meantime everything might get itself arranged by the benevolent and impotent interference of the emperor. Things did get themselves arranged while Garibaldi was up among the mountains, kicking with unarmed toes against Austrian pricks, — with sad detriment to his feet. Things did get themselves arranged very much to the advantage of Venetia, but not exactly by the interference of the emperor.

The facts of the war became known more slowly in Venice than they did in Florence, in Paris, or in London. That the battle of Custozza had been fought and lost by the Italian troops was known. And then it was known that the battle of Lissa also had been fought and lost by Italian ships. But it was not known, till the autumn was near at hand, that Venetia had, in fact, been surrendered. There were rumours, but men in Venice doubted these rumours; and women, who knew that their husbands had been beaten, could not believe that success was to be the result of such calamities.

There were weeks in which came no news from Carlo Pepé to the women in the Campo San Luca, and then came simply tidings that he had been wounded. "I shall see my son never again," said the widow in her ecstasy of misery. And Nina was able to talk to her mother only of Carlo. Of Hubert von Vincke she spoke not then a word. But she repeated to herself over and over again the last promise she had given him. She had sent him away from her, and now she knew nothing of his whereabouts. That he would be fighting she presumed. She had heard that most of the soldiers from Venice had gone to the fortresses. He too might be wounded, — might be dead. If alive at the end of the war, he would hardly return to her after what had passed between them. But if he did not come back no lover should ever take a kiss from her lips.

Then there was the long truce, and a letter from Carlo reached Venice. His wound had been slight, but he had been very hungry. He wrote in great anger, abusing, not the Austrians, but the Italians. There had been treachery, and the Italian general-in-chief had been the head of the traitors. The king was a traitor! The emperor was a traitor! All concerned were traitors, but yet Venetia was to be surrendered to Italy. I think that the two ladies in the Campo San Luca never really believed that this would be so until they received that angry letter from Carlo. "When I may get home, I cannot tell," he said. "I hardly care to return, and I shall remain with the general as long as he may wish to have any one remaining with him. But you may be sure that I shall never go soldiering again. Venetia may, perhaps, prosper, and become a part of Italy; but there will be no glory for us. Italy has been allowed to do nothing for herself."

The mother and sister endeavoured to feel some sympathy for the young soldier who spoke so sadly of his own career, but they could hardly be unhappy because his fighting was over and the cause was won. The cause was won. Gradually there came to be no doubt about that. It was now September, and as yet it had not come to pass that shop windows were filled with wonderful portraits of Victor-Emmanuel and Garibaldi, cheek by jowl, — they being the two men who at that moment were, perhaps, in all Italy, the most antagonistic to each other; nor were there as yet fifty different new journals cried day and night under the arcades of the Grand Piazza, all advocating the cause of Italy, one and indivisible, as there came to be a month afterwards; but still it was known that Austria was to cede Venetia, and that Venice would hencefore be a city of Italy. This was known; and it was also known in the Campo San Luca that Carlo Pepé, though very hungry up among the mountains, was still safe.

Then Nina thought that the time had come in which it would become her to speak of her lover.

"Mother, she said, "I must know something of Hubert."

"But how, Nina; how will you learn? Will you not wait till Carlo comes back?"

"No," she said. "I cannot wait longer. I have kept my promise. Venice is no longer Austrian, and I will seek for him. I have kept my word to Carlo, and now I will keep my word to Hubert."

But how to seek for him? The widow, urged by her daughter, went out and asked at barrack doors, but new regiments had come and gone, and everything was in confusion. It was supposed that any officer of artillery who had been in Venice and had left it during the war must be in one of the four fortresses. "Mother," she said, "I shall go to Verona." And to Verona she went, all alone, in search of her lover. At that time the Austrians still maintained a sort of rule in the province; and there were still current orders against private traveling, orders that passports should be investigated, orders that the communication with the four fortresses should be specially guarded; but there was an intense desire on the part of the Austrians themselves that the orders should be regarded as little as possible. They had to go, and the more quietly they went the better. Why should they care now who passed hither and thither? It must be confessed on their behalf that in their surrender of Venetia they gave as little trouble as it was possible in them to cause. The chief obstruction to Nina's journey she experienced in the Campo San Luca itself. But in spite of her mother, in spite of the not yet defunct Austrian mandates, she did make her way to Verona. "As I was true in giving him up," she said to herself, "so will I be true in clinging to him." Even in Verona her task was not easy, but she did at last find all that she sought. Captain von Vincke had been in command of a battery at Custozza, and was now lying wounded in an Austrian hospital. She contrived to see an old grey-haired surgeon before she saw Hubert himself. Captain von Vincke had been terribly mauled; so the surgeon told her; his left arm had been amputated, and — and — and —. It seemed as though wounds had been showered on him. The surgeon did not think that his patient would die; but he did think that he must be left in Verona when the Austrians were marched out of the fortress. "Can he not be taken to Venice?" said Nina Pepé.

At last she found herself by her lover's bedside; but with her there were two hospital attendants, both of them worn-out Austrian soldiers, —and there was also there the grey-haired surgeon. How was she to tell her love all that she had in her heart before such witnesses? The surgeon was the first to speak.

"Here is your friend, Captain," he said; but as he spoke in German Nina did not understand him.

"Is it really you, Nina?" said her lover. "I could hardly believe that you should be in Verona."

"Of course it is I. Who could have so much business to be in Verona as I have? Of course I am here."

"But — but — what has brought you here, Nina?"

"If you do not know, I cannot tell you."

"And Carlo?"

"Carlo is still with the General; but he is well."

"And the Signora?"

"She also is well; well, but not easy in mind while I am here."

"And when do you return?"

"Nay, I cannot tell you that. It may be to-day. It may be to-morrow. It depends not on myself at all."

He spoke not a word of love to her then; nor she to him, unless there was love in such greeting as has been here repeated. Indeed, it was not till after that first interview that he fully understood that she had made her journey to Verona, solely in quest of him. The words between them for the first day or two were very tame, as though neither had full confidence in the other; and she had taken her place as nurse by his side, as a sister might have done by a brother, — and was established in her work, — nay, had nearly completed her work, before there came to be any full understanding between them. More than once she had told herself that she would go back to Venice and let there be an end of it.

"The great work of the war," said she to herself, "has so filled his mind, that the idleness of his days in Venice and all that he did then, are forgotten. If so, my presence here is surely a sore burden to him, and I will go." But she could not now leave him without a word of farewell.

"Hubert," she said, for she had called him Hubert when she first came to his bed-side, as though she had been his sister, "I think I must return now to Venice. My mother will be lonely without me."

At that moment it appeared almost miraculous to her that she should be sitting there by his bed-side, that she should have loved him, that she should have had the courage to leave her home and seek him after the war, that she should have found him; — and that she should now be about to leave him, almost without a word between them.

"She must be very lonely," said the wounded man.

"And you, I think, are stronger than you were."

"For me, I am strong enough. I have lost my arm, and I shall carry this gaping scar athwart my face to the grave, as my cross of honour won in the Italian war; but otherwise I shall soon be well."

"It is a fair cross of honour."

"Yes; they cannot rob us of our wounds when our service is over. And so you will go, Signorina?"

"Yes; I will go. Why should I remain here? I will go, and Carlo will return, and I will tend upon him. Carlo also was wounded."

"But you have told me that he is well again."

"Nevertheless, he will value the comfort of a woman's care after his sufferings. May I say farewell to you now, my friend?" And she put her hand down upon the bed so that he might reach it. She had been with him for days, and there had been no word of love. It had seemed as though he had understood nothing of what she had done in coming to him; that he had failed altogether in feeling that she had come as a wife goes to her husband. She had made a mistake in this journey, and must now rectify her error with as much of dignity as might be left to her.

He took her hand in his, and held it for a moment before he answered her. "Nina," he said, "why did you come hither?"

"Why did I come?"

"Why are you here in Verona, while your mother is alone in Venice?"

"I had business here, — a matter of some moment. It is finished now, and I shall return."

"Was it other business than to sit at my bed-side?"

She paused a moment before she answered him. "Yes," she said; "it was other business than that."

"And you have succeeded?"

"No; I have failed."

He still held her hand; and she, though she was thus fencing with him, answering him with equivokes, felt that at last there was coming from him some word which would at least leave her no longer in doubt. "And I too, — have I failed?" he said. "When I left Venice I told myself heartily that I had failed."

"You told yourself, then," said she, "that Venetia would never be ceded. You know that I would not triumph over you, now that your cause has been lost. We Italians have not much cause for triumphing."

"You will admit always that the fortresses have not been taken from us," said the sore-hearted soldier.

"Certainly we shall admit that."

"And my own fortress; — the stronghold that I thought I had made altogether mine, — is that, too, lost for ever to the poor German?"

"You speak in riddles, Captain von Vincke," she said. She had now taken back her hand; but she was sitting quietly by his bed-side, and made no sign of leaving him.

"Nina," he said, "Nina, — my own Nina. In losing a single share of Venice, one soldier's share of the province, shall I have gained all the world for myself? Nina, tell me truly, what brought you to Verona?"

She knelt slowly down by his bed-side, and again taking his one hand in hers, pressed it first to her lips and then to her bosom. "It was an unmaidenly purpose," she said. "I came to find the man I loved."

"But you said you had failed?"

"And I now say that I have succeeded. Do you not know that success in great matters always trembles in the balance before it turns the beam, — thinking, fearing, all but knowing that failure has weighed down the scale."

"But now —?"

"Now I am sure that — Venice has been won!"

It was three months after this, and half of December had passed away, and all Venetia had in truth been ceded, and Victor-Emmanuel had made his entry into Venice and exit out of it, with as little of real triumph as ever attended a king's progress through a new province, and the Austrian army had moved itself off very quietly, and the city had become as thoroughly Italian as Florence itself, and was in a way to be equally discontented, when a party of four, two ladies and two gentlemen, sat down to breakfast in the Hotel Bauer. The ladies were the Signora Pepé and her daughter, and the men were Carlo Pepé and his brother-in-law, Hubert von Vincke. It was but a poor fête, this family breakfast at an obscure inn, but it was intended as a gala feast to mark the last day of Nina's Italian life. To-morrow, very early in the morning, she was to leave Venice for Trieste, — so early that it would be necessary that she should be on board this very night.

"My child," said the Signora, "do not say so; you will never cease to be Italian. Surely, Hubert, she may still call herself Venetian?"

"Mother," she said, "I love a losing cause. I will be Austrian now. I told him that he could not have both. If he kept his Venice, he could not have me; but as he has lost his province, he shall have his wife entirely."

"I told him that it was fated that he should lose Venetia," said Carlo, "but he would never believe me."

"Because I knew how true were our soldiers," said Hubert, "and could not understand how false were our statesmen."

"See how he regrets it," said Nina. "What he has lost, and what he has won, will, together, break his heart for him."

"Nina," he said, "I learned this morning in the city, that I shall be the last Austrian soldier to leave Venice, and I hold that of all who have entered it, and all who have left it, I am the most successful and most triumphant."

"The Last Austrian Who Left Venice" appeared first in the January issue of *Good Words* for 1867.

The House of Heine Brothers
in Munich

THE HOUSE OF HEINE BROTHERS in Munich was of good repute at the time of which I am about to tell — a time not long ago — and is so still, I trust. It was of good repute in its own way, seeing that no man doubted the word or solvency of Heine Brothers; but they did not possess, as bankers, what would in England be considered a large or profitable business. The operations of English bankers are bewildering in their magnitude. Legions of clerks are employed. The senior bookkeepers, though only salaried servants, are themselves great men; while the real partners are inscrutable, mysterious, opulent beyond measure, and altogether unknown to their customers. Take any firm at random — Brown, Jones and Cox, let us say; the probability is that Brown has been dead these fifty years, that Jones is a cabinet minister, and that Cox is master of a pack of hounds in Leicestershire. But it was by no means so with the house of Heine Brothers of Munich. Three there were; the two elderly men daily to be seen at their dingy office in the Schrannen Platz: and if any business was to be transacted requiring the interchange of more than a word or two, it was the younger brother with whom the customer was, as a matter of course, brought into contact. There were three clerks in the establishment, an old man, namely, who sat within with the elder brother, and had no personal dealings with the public; a young Englishman, of whom we shall anon hear more; and a boy who ran messages, put the wood on to the stoves, and swept out the bank. Truly the house of Heine Brothers was of no great importance; but, nevertheless, it was of good repute.

The office, I have said, was in the Schrannen Platz, or old market-place. Munich, as every one knows, is chiefly to be noted as a new town, so new that many of the streets and most of the palaces look as though they had been sent home last night from the builders, and had only just been taken out of their band-boxes. It is angular, methodical, unfinished, and palatial. But there is an old town; and though the old town be not of surpassing interest, it is as dingy, crooked, intricate, and dark as other old towns in Germany. Here, in the old market-place, up one long, broad staircase, were situated the two rooms in which was held the bank of Heine Brothers.

Of the elder member of the firm we shall have something to say before this story be completed. He was an old bachelor, and was possessed of a bachelor's dwelling somewhere out in the suburb of the city. The junior brother was a married man, with a wife some twenty years younger than himself, with two daughters, the elder of whom was now one-and-twenty, and one son. His name was Ernest Heine, whereas the senior brother was known as Uncle Hatto. Ernest Heine and his wife inhabited a portion of one of those new palatial residences at the further end of the Ludwig's Strasse; but not because they there lived must it be conceived that they were palatial people. By no means let it be so thought, as such an idea would altogether militate against whatever truth of character-painting there may be in this tale. They were not palatial people, but the very reverse, living in homely guise, pursuing homely duties, and satisfied with homely pleasures; up two pair of stairs, however, in that street of palaces they lived, having there a commodious suite of large rooms, furnished after the manner of the Germans, somewhat gaudily as regarded their best *salon*, and with somewhat meagre comfort as regarded their other rooms. But, whether in respect of that which was meagre, or whether in respect of that which was gaudy, they were as well off as their neighbours; and this, as I take it, is the point of excellence which is desirable.

Ernest Heine was at this time over sixty; his wife was past forty; and his eldest daughter, as I have said, was twenty-one years of age. His second child, also a girl, was six years younger; and the boy had not been born till another similar interval had elapsed. He was named Hatto after his uncle, and the two girls had been christened Isa and Agnes. Such in number and mode of life was the family of the Heines.

We English folk are apt to imagine that we are nearer akin to Germans than to our other continental neighbours. This may be so in blood, but, nevertheless, the difference in manners is so striking, that it could hardly be enhanced. An Englishman moving himself off to a city in the middle of Central America will find the customs to which he must adapt himself less strange to him there, than he would in many a German town. But in no degree of life is this difference more remarkable then among unmarried but marriageable young women. It is not my purpose at the present moment to attribute a superiority in this matter to either nationality. Each has its own charm, its own excellence, its own heaven-given grace, whereby men are led up to pure thoughts and sweet desires; and each may possibly have its own defects. I will not here describe the excellence or defects of either; but will, if it be in my power, say a word as to their difference. The German girl of one-and-twenty—our Isa's age—is more sedate, more womanly, more meditative than her English sister. The world's work is more in her thoughts, and the world's amusement less so. She probably knows less of those things which women learn than the English girl, but that which she does not know is nearer to her hand for use. She is not so much accustomed to society, but, nevertheless, she is more mistress of her own manner. She is not taught to think so much of those things which flurry and disturb the mind, and therefore she is seldom flurried or disturbed. To both of them love—the idea of love—must be the thought of all the most absorbing; for is it not fated for them that the joys and sorrows of their life must depend upon it? But the idea of the German girl is the more realistic, and the less romantic. Poetry and fiction she may have read, though of the latter sparingly; but they will not have imbued her with that hope for some transcendent Paradise of affection which so often fills and exalts the hearts of our daughters here at home. She is moderate in her aspirations, requiring less excitement than the English girl; and never forgetting the solid necessities of life — as they are so often forgotten

133

here in England. In associating with young men an English girl always remembers that in each one she so meets she may find an admirer whom she may possibly love, or an admirer whom she may probably be called on to repel. She is ever conscious of the fact of this position, and a romance is thus engendered which, if it may possibly at times be dangerous, is at any rate always charming. But the German girl in her simplicity has no such consciousness. As you and I, my reader, might possibly become dear friends were we to meet and know each other, so may the German girl learn to love the fair-haired youth with whom chance has for a time associated her; but to her mind there occurs no suggestive reason why it should be so, no probability that the youth may regard her in such light, because that chance has come to pass. She can therefore give him her hand without trepidation, and talk with him for half-an-hour when called on to do so, as calmly as she might do with his sister.

Such an one was Isa Heine at the time of which I am writing. We English, in our passion for daily excitement, might call her phlegmatic, but we should call her so unjustly. Life to her was a serious matter, of which the daily duties and daily wants were sufficient to occupy her thoughts. She was her mother's companion, the instructress of both her brother and her sister, and the charm of her father's vacant hours. With such calls upon her time, and so many realities around, her imagination did not teach her to look for joys beyond those of her present life and home. When love and marriage should come to her, as come they probably might, she would endeavour to attune herself to a new happiness and a new sphere of duties; in the meantime she was contented to keep her mother's accounts, and look after her brother and sister, up two pairs of stairs in the Ludwig's Strasse. But that changes would certainly come we may prophesy, for Isa Heine was a beautiful girl, tall and graceful, comely to the eye, and fit in every way to be loved and cherished as the partner of a man's home.

I have said that an English clerk made a part of that small establishment in the dingy banking-office of the Schrannen Platz, and I must say a word or two of Herbert Onslow. In his early career he had not been fortunate. His father, with means sufficiently moderate, and with a family more than sufficiently large, had sent him to a public school, at which he had been very idle, and then to one of the universities, at which he had run into debt, and had therefore left without a degree. When this occurred, a family council had been held among the Onslows, and it was decided that Herbert should be sent off to the banking-house of the Heines, at Munich, there being a cousinship between the families, and some existing connexions of business. It was therefore so settled; and Herbert, willing enough to see the world — as he considered he should do by going to Munich — started for his German home, with injunctions very tender from his mother, and very solemn from his aggrieved father. But there was nothing bad at the heart about young Onslow, and if the solemn father had well considered it, he might perhaps have felt that those debts at Cambridge reflected more fault on him than on his son. When Herbert arrived at Munich, his cousins, the Heines, far-away cousins though they were, behaved kindly to him. They established him at first in lodgings, where he was boarded with many others, having heard somewhat of his early youth; but when Madame Heine, at the end of twelve months, perceived that he was punctual at the bank, and that his allowance, which, though moderate in England was handsome in Munich, carried him on without debt, she opened her motherly heart and arms, and suggested to his mother and himself that he should live with them. In this way he also was domiciled up two pairs of stairs in the palatial residence of the Ludwig's Strasse.

But all this had happened long ago. Isa Heine had been only seventeen when her cousin had first come to Munich, and had made acquaintance with him rather as a child than as a woman; and when, as she was ripening into womanhood, this young man came more closely among them, it did not strike her that the change would affect her more powerfully than it would the others. Her uncle and father she knew had approved of Herbert at the bank, and Herbert had showed that he could be steady; therefore, he was to be taken into their family, paying his annual subsidy, instead of being left with strangers at the boarding-house. All this was very simple to her. She assisted in mending his linen as she did her father's; she visited his room daily, as she visited all the others; she took notice of his likings and dislikings, as touching their table arrangements, but by no means such notice as she did of her father's; and, without any flutter inwardly in her imagination, or outwardly as regarded the world, she made him one of the family. So things went on for a year — nay, so things went on for two years with her, after Herbert Onslow had come to the Ludwig's Strasse.

But the matter had been regarded in a very different light by Herbert himself. When the proposition had been made to him, his first idea had been, that so close a connection with a girl so very pretty would be delightful. He had blushed as he had given in his adhesion, but Madame Heine, when she saw the blush, had attributed it to anything but the true cause. When Isa had asked him as to his wants and wishes, he had blushed again; but she also had been as ignorant as her mother. Her father had merely stipulated, that as the young Englishman paid for his board, he should have the full value of his money; so that Isa and Agnes gave up their pretty front room, going into one that was inferior, and Hatto was put to sleep in the little closet that had been papa's own peculiar property. But nobody complained of this, for it was understood that the money was of service.

For the first year Herbert found that nothing especial happened. He always fancied that he was in love with Isa, and wrote some poetry about her. But the poetry was in English, and Isa could not have read it, even had he dared to show it to her. During the second year, he went home to England for three months, and by confessing a passion to one of his sisters, really brought himself to feel one. He returned to Munich, resolved to tell Isa that the possibility of his remaining there depended upon her acceptance of his heart; but for months he did not find himself able to put his resolution in force. She was so sedate, so womanly, so attentive as regarded cousinly friendship, and so cold as regarded everything else, that he did not know how to speak to her. With an English girl whom he had met three times at a ball, he might have been much more able to make progress. He was alone with her frequently, for neither father, mother, nor Isa herself objected to such communion, but yet things so went between them that he could not take her by the hand and tell her that he loved her. And then the third year of his life in Munich, and the second of his residence in the Ludwig's Strasse, went by him. So the years went by, and Isa was now passed twenty. To Herbert, in his reveries, it seemed as though life and the joys of life were slipping away from him. But no such feeling disturbed any of the Heines. Life, of course, was slipping away; but then, is it not the destiny of man that life should slip away? Their wants were all satisfied, and for them that, with their close family affection, was happiness enough.

At last, however, Herbert so spoke and so looked that both Isa and her mother knew that his heart was touched. He still declared to himself that he had made no sign, and that he was an oaf, an ape, a coward, in that he had not done so. But he had made some sign, and the sign had been read. There was no secret — no necessity for a secret on the subject between the mother and daughter; but yet it was not spoken of all at once. There was some little increase of caution between them as Herbert's name was mentioned, so that gradually each knew what the other thought; but for weeks that was all. Then at last the mother spoke out.

"Isa," she said, "I think that Herbert Onslow is becoming attached to you."

"He has never said so, mamma."

"No, I am sure he has not. Had he done so you would have told me; nevertheless, is it not true?"

"Well, mamma, I cannot say. It may be so. Such an idea has occurred to me, but I have abandoned it as needless. If he has anything to say, he will say it."

"And if he were to speak, how should you answer him?"

"I should take time to think. I do not at all know what means he has for a separate establishment."

Then the subject was dropped between them for that time, and Isa, in her communications with her cousin, was somewhat more reserved than she had been.

"Isa, are you in love with Herbert?" Agnes asked her, as they were together in their room one night.

"In love with him — no; why should I be in love with him?"

"I think he is in love with you," said Agnes.

"That is quite another thing," said Isa, laughing. "But if so, he has not taken me into his confidence, — perhaps he has you."

"Oh, no, he would not do that, I think. Not but what we are great friends, and I love him dearly. Would it not be nice for you and him to be betrothed?"

137

"That depends on many things, my dear."

"Oh, yes, I know. Perhaps he has not got money enough. But you could live here, you know; and he has got some money, because he so often rides on horseback."

And then the matter was dropped between the two sisters.

Herbert had given English lessons to the two girls, but the lessons had been found tedious, and had dwindled away. Isa, nevertheless, had kept up her exercises, duly translating German into English and English into German; and occasionally she had shewn them to her cousin. Now, however, she altogether gave over such shewing of them; but, nevertheless, worked at the task with more energy than before.

"Isa," he said to her one day, having with some difficulty found her alone in the parlour; "Isa, why should not we go on with our English?"

"Because it is troublesome; — to you, I mean."

"Troublesome — well, yes; it is troublesome. Nothing good is to be had without trouble. But I should like it, if you would not mind."

"You know how sick you were of it before; — besides, I shall never be able to speak it."

"I shall not get sick of it now, Isa —"

"Oh, yes, you would, in two days."

"And I want you to speak it. I desire it especially."

"Why especially?" asked Isa. And even she, with all her tranquillity of demeanour, could hardly preserve her even tone and quiet look as she asked the necessary question.

"I will tell you why," said Herbert; — and as he spoke he got up from his seat, and took a step or two over towards her, where she was sitting near the window. Isa, as she saw him, still continued her work, and strove hard to give to the stitches all that attention which they required. "I will tell you why I would wish you to talk my language — because I love you, Isa; and would have you for my wife, if that be possible."

She still continued her work, and the stitches, if not quite as perfect as usual, sufficed for their purpose.

"That is why I wish it. Now will you consent to learn from me again?"

"If I did, Herbert, that consent would include another."

"Yes, certainly it would. That is what I intend; — and now will you learn from me again?"

"That is, — you mean to ask, will I marry you?"

"Will you have me? Can you learn to love me? Oh, Isa, I have thought of thee so long, but you have seemed so cold that I have not dared to speak. Isa, can you love me?" And he sat himself close behind her. Now that the ice was broken he was quite prepared to become an ardent lover — if she would allow of such ardour. But as he sat down, she rose.

"I cannot answer such a question on the sudden," she said. "Give me till to-morrow, Herbert, and then I will make you a reply."

Thereupon she left him, and he stood alone in room, having done the deed on which he been meditating for the last two years. About half-an-hour afterwards he met her on the stairs as he was going to his chamber.

"May I speak to your father about this?" he said, hardly stopping on the stairs as he asked the question.

"Oh, yes, surely," she answered, and then again they parted. To him this last accorded permission sounded as though it carried with it more weight than it in truth possessed. In his own country a reference to the lady's father is taken as indicating a full consent on the lady's part, should the stern paterfamilias raise no objection. But Isa had no such meaning. She had told him that she could not give her answer till the morrow. If, however, he chose to consult her father on the subject, she had no objection. It would probably be necessary that she should discuss the whole matter in family conclave before she could bring herself to give any reply.

On that night, before he went to bed, he did speak to her father; and Isa also, before she went to rest, spoke to her mother. It was singular to him that there should appear to be so little privacy on the subject; — that there should be held to be so little necessity for a secret. Had he made a suggestion that an extra room should be allotted to him at so much per annum, the proposition could not have been discussed with simpler ease. At last, after a three days' debate, the matter ended thus, with by no means a sufficiency of romance for his taste: — Isa had agreed to become his betrothed if certain pecuniary conditions should or could be fulfilled. It appeared now that Herbert's father had promised that some small modicum of capital should be forthcoming after a term of years, and that Heine Brothers had agreed that the Englishman should have a proportionate share in the bank when that promise should have been brought to bear. Let it not be supposed that Herbert would thus become a millionaire. If all went well, the best would be that some three hundred a-year would accrue to him from the bank, instead of the quarter of that income which he at present received. But three hundred a-year goes a long way at Munich, and Isa's parents were willing that she should be Herbert's wife if such an income should be forthcoming.

But even of this there was much doubt. Application to Herbert's father could not be judiciously made for some months. The earliest period at which, in accordance with old Hatto Heine's accorded consent, young Onslow might be admitted to the bank, was still distant by four years; and the present moment was thought to be inopportune for applying to him for any act of grace. "Let them wait patiently," said papa and mamma Heine, — "at any rate, till new-year's day," then ten months distant. Isa quietly said that she would wait till new-year's day. Herbert fretted, fumed, and declared that he was ill-treated. But, in the end, he also agreed to wait. What else could he do?

"But we shall see each other daily, and be close to each other," he said to Isa, looking tenderly into her eyes.

"Yes," she replied, "we shall see each other daily, of course; but, Herbert —"

Herbert looked up at her and paused for her to go on.

"I have promised mamma that there shall be no change between us —in our manner to each other I mean. We are not betrothed as yet, you know, and perhaps we may never be so."

"Isa!"

"It may not be possible, you know. And therefore we will go on as before. Of course we shall see each other, and of course we shall be friends."

Herbert Onslow again fretted and again fumed, but he did not have his way. He had looked forward to the extasies of a lover's life, but very few of those extasies were awarded to him. He rarely found himself alone with Isa, and when he did do so her coldness overawed him. He could dare to scold her, and sometimes did do so; but he could not dare to take the slightest liberty. Once, on that night when the qualified consent of papa and mamma Heine had first been given, he had been allowed to touch her lips with his own; but since that day there had been for him no such delights as that. She would not even allow her hand to remain in his. When they all passed their evenings together in the beer garden, she would studiously manage that his chair should not be close to her own. Occasionally she would waltz with him, but not more frequently now than of yore — but few indeed of a lover's privileges did he enjoy — and in this way the long year wore itself out, and Isa Heine was one-and-twenty.

All those family details which had made it inexpedient to apply either to old Hatto or to Herbert's father before the end of the year need not be specially explained. Old Hatto, who had by far the greater share in the business, was a tyrant, somewhat feared both by his brother and sister-in-law; and the elder Onslow, as was known to them all, was a man straitened in circumstances. But soon after new-year's day the proposition was made in the Schrannen Platz, and the letter was written. On this occasion Madame Heine went down to the bank, and together with her husband was closeted for an hour with old Hatto. Uncle Hatto's verdict was not favourable. As to the young people's marriage, that was his brother's affair, not his. But as to the partnership — that was a serious matter. Who had ever heard of a partnership being given away merely because a young man wanted to marry. He would keep to his promise, and if the stipulated moneys were forthcoming, Herbert Onslow should become a partner — in four years. Nor was the reply from England more favourable. The alliance was regarded by all the Onslows very favourably. Nothing could be nicer than such a marriage! They already knew dear Isa so well, by description! But as for the money — that could not in any way be made to be forthcoming till the end of the stipulated period.

"And what shall we do?" said Herbert to papa Heine.

"You must wait," said he.

"For four years!" asked Herbert.

"You must wait, as I did," said papa Heine. "I was forty before I could marry."

141

Papa Heine, however, should not have forgotten to say that his bride was only twenty, and that if he had waited, she had not.

"Isa," Herbert said to her, when all this had been fully explained to her, "what do you say now?"

"Of course, it is all one," said she, very calmly.

"Oh, Isa! is that your love?"

"No, Herbert, that is not my love; that is my discretion"—and she even laughed with her mild, low laughter, as she answered him. "You know you are too impatient to wait four years, and what else, therefore, can I say?"

"I wonder whether you love me?" said Herbert, with a grand look of injured sentiment.

"Well, in your sense of the word, I do not think I do. I do not love you so that I need make everyone around us unhappy because circumstances forbid me to marry you. That sort of love would be baneful."

"Ah, no; you do not know what love means!"

"Not your boisterous, heart-breaking, English love, Herbert. And, Herbert, sometimes I think you had better go home and look for a bride there. Though you fancy that you love me, in your heart you hardly approve of me."

"Fancy that I love you! Do you think, Isa, that a man can carry his heart round to one customer after another, as the huckster carries his wares?"

"Yes, I think he can — I know that men do. What did your hero Waverley do with his heart, in that grand English novel which you gave me to read? I am not Flora MacIvor, but you may find a Rose Bradwardine."

"And you really wish me to do so?"

"Look here, Herbert. It is bad to boast, but I will make this boast: I am so little selfish, that I desire above all that you should do that which may make you most happy and contented. I will be quite frank with you. I love you well enough to wait these four yers with the hopes of becoming your wife when they are over; but you will think but little of my love when I tell you that this waiting would not make me unhappy. I should go on as I do now, and be contented."

"Oh heavens!" sighed Herbert.

"But, as I know that this would not suit you; as I feel sure that such delay would gall you every day; as I doubt whether it would not make you sick of me long before the four years be over — my advice is, that we should let the matter drop."

He now walked up to her, and took her hand; and, as he did so, there was something in his gait and look and tone of voice that stirred her heart more sharply than it had yet been stirred.

"And even that would not make you unhappy," he said.

She paused before she replied, leaving her hand in his, for he was contented to hold it without peculiar pressure.

"I will not say so," she replied; "but, Herbert, I think that you press me too hard. Is it not enough that I leave you to be the arbiter of my destiny?"

"I would learn the very truth of your heart," he replied.

"I cannot tell you that truth more plainly; methinks I have told it too plainly already. If you wish it, I will hold myself as engaged to you — to be married to you when these four years are past. But, remember, I do not advise it. If you wish it, you shall have back your troth — and that, I think, will be the wiser course."

But neither alternative contented Herbert Onslow, and at the time he did not resolve on either. He had some little present income from home — some fifty pounds a-year or so; and he would be satisifed to marry on that and his salary as a clerk. But to this papa and mamma Heine would not consent; neither would Isa.

"You are not a saving, close man," she said to him when he boasted of his economies; "no Englishmen are. You could not live comfortably in two small rooms and with bad dinners."

"I do not care a straw about my dinner."

"Not now that you are a lover, but you would do when you were a husband; and you change your linen almost every day."

"Bah!"

"Yes, bah, if you please. But I know what these things cost. You had better go to England and fetch a rich wife, then you will become a partner at once, and uncle Hatto won't snub you; and you will be a grand man, and have a horse to ride on."

Whereupon Herbert went away in disgust. Nothing in all this made him so unhappy as the feeling that Isa, under all their joint

143

privations, would not be unhappy herself. As far as he could see, all this made no difference in Isa.

But in truth he had not yet read Isa's character very thoroughly. She had spoken truly in saying that she knew nothing of that boisterous love which was now tormenting him and making him gloomy; but nevertheless she loved him. She, in her short life, had learned many lessons of self-denial: and now with reference to this half-promised husband she should again have practised such a lesson. Had he agreed at once to go from her, she would have balanced her own account within her own breast, and have kept to herself all her sufferings. There would have been no outward show of baffled love — none even in the colour of her cheek; for such was the nature of her temperament. But she did suffer for him. Day by day she began to think that his love, though boisterous as she had at first called it, was more deep-seated than she had believed. He made no slightest sign that he would accept any of those proffers which she had made him of release. Though he said so loudly that this waiting for four years was an impossibility, he spoke of no course that would be more possible, — except that evidently impossible course of an early marriage. And thus, while he, with redoubled vehemence, charged her with coldness and want of love, her love waxed warmer and warmer, and his happiness became the chief object of her thoughts. What could she do that he might no longer suffer?

And then he took a step which was very strange to them all. He banished himself altogether from the house, going away again into other lodgings.

"No," he said, on the morning of his departure, "I do not release you — I will never release you. You are mine, and I have a right so to call you. If you choose to release yourself, I cannot help it; but in doing so you will be forsworn."

"Nay, but, Herbert, I have sworn to nothing," said she, meaning that she had not been formally betrothed to him.

"You can do as you please; it is a matter of conscience. But I tell you what are my feelings. Here I cannot stay, for I should go mad; but I shall see you occasionally — perhaps on Sundays."

"Oh, Herbert!"

"Well, what would you have? If you really cared to see me it would not be thus. All I ask of you now is this: that if you decide, absolutely decide, on throwing me over, you will tell me at once; then I shall leave Munich."

"Herbert, I will never throw you over!"

So they parted, and young Onslow went forth to his new lodgings.

Her promise that she would never throw him over was the warmest word of love that she had ever spoken; but even that was said in her own quiet, unimpassioned way. There was in it but a little show of love, though there might be an assurance of constancy. But her constancy he did not, in truth, much doubt. Four years, fourteen, or twenty-four, would be the same to her, he said, as he seated himself in the dull, cold room which he had chosen. While living in the Ludwig's Strasse he did not know how much had been daily done for his comfort by that hand which he had been so seldom allowed to press; but he knew that he was now cold and comfortless, and he wished himself back in the Ludwig's Strasse.

"Mamma," said Isa, when they were alone, "is not uncle Hatto rather hard on us? Papa said that he would ask this as a favor from his brother."

"So he did, my dear, and offered to give up more of his own time. But your uncle Hatto is hard."

"He is rich, is he not?"

"Well, your father says not. Your father says that he spends all his income. Though he is hard and obstinate, he is not selfish; he is very good to the poor. But I believe he thinks that early marriages are foolish."

"Mamma," said Isa again, when they had sat for some minutes in silence over their work.

"Well, my love."

"Have you spoken to uncle Hatto about this?"

"No, dear; not since that day when your papa and I first went to him. To tell the truth, I am almost afraid to speak to him. But, if you wish, I will do so."

"I do wish it, mamma. But you must not think that I am discontented or impatient. I do not know that I have any right to ask my uncle for his money, for it comes to that."

"I suppose it does, my dear."

"And as for myself, I am happy here with you and with papa. I do not think so much of these four years."

"You would still be young, Isa — quite young enough."

"And what if I were not young! what does it matter? But, mamma, there has been that between Herbert and me which makes me feel myself bound to think of him. As you and Papa have sanctioned it, you are bound to think of him also. I know that he is unhappy living there all alone."

"But why did he go, dear?"

"I think he was right to go; I could understand his doing that. He is not like us, and would have been fretful here, wanting that which I could not give him. He became worse from day to day, and was silent and morose. I am glad he went. But, mama, for his sake, I wish that this should be shortened."

Madame Heine again told her daughter that she would, if Isa so wished it, herself go down to the Schrannen Platz, and see what could be done by talking to uncle Hatto. "But," she added, "I fear that no good will come of it."

"Can harm come, mamma?"

"No; I do not think harm can come."

"I'll tell you what, mamma; I will go to uncle Hatto myself, if you will let me. He is cross, I know; but I shall not be afraid of him. I feel that I ought to do something."

And so the matter was settled, Madame Heine being by no means averse to escape a further personal visit to the head of the banking establishment.

Madame Heine well understood what her daughter meant when she said that she ought to do something, though Isa feared that she had but imperfectly expressed her meaning. When he (Herbert) was willing to do so much to prove his love — when he was ready to sacrifice all the little comforts of comparative wealth to which he had been accustomed, in order that she might be his companion and wife — did it not behove her to give some proof of her love also. She could not be demonstrative as he was. Such exhibition of feeling would be contrary to her ideas of female delicacy, and to her very nature. But if called on to make any great sacrifice, that she could have done for him; and if called on to work for him, that she could do, as long as strength remained to her. But there was no sacrifice which would be of service, nor any work which would avail. Therefore, she was driven to think what deed she might do on his behalf; and at last she resolved to make her personal appeal to uncle Hatto.

"Shall I tell papa?" Isa asked of her mother.

"I will do so," said Madame Heine.

And then the younger member of the firm was informed as to the step which was to be taken; and he, though he said nothing to forbid the attempt, held out no hope that it would be successful.

Uncle Hatto was a little snuffy man, now full seventy years of age, who passed seven hours of every week-day of his life in the dark, back chamber behind the banking room of the firm, and he had so passed every week-day of his life for more years than any of the family could now remember. He had made the house what it was, and had taken his brother into partnership, when that brother married. All the family were somewhat afraid of him, including even his partner. He rarely came to the apartments in the Ludwig's Strasse, as he himself lived in one of the older and shabbier suburbs on the other side of the town. Thither he always walked, starting punctually from the bank at four o'clock, and from thence he always walked in the morning, reaching the bank as punctually at nine. His two nieces knew him well, — for on certain stated days they were wont to attend on him at his lodgings, where they would be regaled with cakes, and afterwards go with him to some old-fashioned beer-garden in his neighbourhood. But these festivities were of a sombre kind; and if on any occasion circumstances prevented the fulfilment of the ceremony, neither of the girls would be loud in their lamentation.

In London a visit, paid by a niece to her uncle, would, in all probability, be made at the uncle's private residence; but at Munish private and public matters were not so effectually divided. Isa, therefore, having put on her hat and shawl, walked off by herself to the Schrannen Platz. "Is uncle Hatto inside?" she asked. And the answer was given to her by her own lover. Yes, he was within; but the old clerk was with him. Isa, however, signified her wish to see her uncle alone, and in a few minutes the ancient, gray-haired servant of the house came out into the larger room. "You can go in now, Miss Isa," he said. And Isa found herself in the presence of her uncle before she had been two minutes under the roof. In the meantime Ernest Heine, her father, had said not a word, and Herbert knew that something very special must be about to occur.

"Well, my bonny bird," said uncle Hatto, "and what do you want at the bank?" Cheery words such as these were by no means uncommon with uncle Hatto, but Isa knew very well that no presage could be drawn from them of any special good-nature or temporary weakness on his part.

"Uncle Hatto," she began, making at once into the middle of her affairs, "you know, I believe, that I am engaged to marry Herbert Onslow?"

"I know no such thing," said he. "I thought I understood your father specially to say that there had been no betrothal."

"No, uncle Hatto, there has been no betrothal; that certainly is true. But, nevertheless, we are engaged to each other."

"Well," said uncle Hatto, very sourly; and now there was no longer any cheery tone, or any calling of pretty names.

"Perhaps you may think all this very foolish," said Isa, who, in spite of her resolves to do so, was hardly able to look up gallantly into her uncle's face as she thus talked of her own love affairs.

"Yes, I do," said uncle Hatto. "I do think it foolish for young people to hold themselves as betrothed before they have got anything to live on, and so I have told your father. He answered me by saying that you were not betrothed."

"Nor are we. Papa is quite right in that."

"Then, my dear, I would advise you to tell the young man that, as neither of you have means of your own, the thing must be at an end. It is the only step for you to take. If you agreed to wait—one of you might die, or his money might never be forthcoming, or you might see somebody else that you liked better."

"I don't think I shall do that."

"You can't tell. And if you don't, the chances are ten to one that he will."

This little blow, which was intended to be severe, did not hit Isa at all hard. That plan of a Rose Bradwardine she herself had proposed in good faith, thinking that she could endure such a termination to the affair without flinching. She was probably wrong in the estimate of her power; but, nevertheless, her present object was his release from unhappiness and doubt, not her own.

"It might be so," she said.

"Take my word for it, — it would. Look all around. There was Adelaide Schropner's —. But that was before your time, and you won't remember."

Considering that Adelaide Schropner had been for many years a grandmother, it was probable that Isa would not remember.

"But, uncle Hatto, you have not heard me. I want to say something to you, if it will not take too much of your time."

In answer to which, uncle Hatto muttered something which was intended to signify that Isa might speak.

"I also think that a long engagement is a foolish thing, and so does Herbert."

"But he wants to marry at once."

"Yes, he wants to marry — perhaps not at once, but soon."

"And I suppose you have come to say that you want the same thing."

Isa blushed ever so faintly as she commenced her answer. "Yes, uncle, I do wish the same thing. What he wishes, I wish."

"Very likely, very likely."

"Don't be scornful to me, uncle. When two people love each other, it is natural that each should wish that which the other earnestly desires."

"Oh, very natural, my dear, that you should wish to get married."

"Uncle Hatto, I did not think that you would be unkind to me, though I knew that you would be stern."

"Well, go on; what have you to say? I am not stern; but, I have no doubt you will think me unkind. People are always unkind who do not do what they are asked."

"Papa says that Herbert Onslow is some day to become a partner in the bank."

"That depends on certain circumstances. Neither I nor your papa can say whether he will or no."

But Isa went on as though she had not heard the last reply. "I have come to ask you to admit him to a partnership at once."

"Ah, I supposed so. Just as you might ask me to give you a new ribbon."

"But, uncle, I never asked you to give me a new ribbon. I never asked you to give me anything for myself; — nor do I ask this for myself."

"Do you think that if I could do it, — which, of course, I can't, — I would not sooner do it for you, who are my own flesh and blood, than for him who is a stranger?"

"Nay, he is no stranger. He has sat at your desk and obeyed your orders for nearly four years. Papa says that he has done well in the bank."

"Humph. If every clerk that does well — pretty well that is — wanted a partnership, where should we be, my dear? No, my dear, go home and tell him, when you see him this evening, that all this must be at an end. Men's places in the world are not given away so easily as that. They must either be earned or purchased. Herbert Onslow has as yet done neither, and therefore he is not entitled to take a wife. I should have been glad to have had a wife at his age; — at least, I suppose I should; but at any rate I could not afford it."

But Isa had by no means as yet done. So far the interview had progressed exactly as she had anticipated. She had never supposed it possible that her uncle would grant her so important a request, as soon as she opened her mouth to ask it. She had not for a moment expected that things would go so easily with her. Indeed, she had never expected that any success would attend her efforts; but if any success were possible, the work which must achieve that success must now commence. It was necessary that she should first state her request plainly, before she began to ask it with such eloquence as she had at her command.

"I can understand what you say, uncle Hatto."

"I am glad of that, at any rate."

"And I know that I have no right to ask you for anything."

"I do not say that. Anything in reason, that a girl like you should ask of her old uncle, I would give you."

"I have no such reasonable request to make, uncle. I have never wanted new ribbons from you, or gay toys. Even from my own mother I have not wanted them; — not wanted them faster than they seemed to come without any asking."

"No, no; you have been a good girl."

"I have been a happy girl; quite happy with those I loved, and with what Providence had given us. I had nothing to ask for. But now I am no longer happy, nor can I be unless you do for me this which I ask of you. I have wanted nothing till now, and now, in my need, I come to you."

"And now you want a husband with a fortune!"

"No!" And that single word she spoke, not loudly, for her voice was low and soft, but with an accent which carried it sharply into his ear and on to his brain. And then she rose from her seat as she went on. "Your scorn, uncle, is unjust, — unjust and untrue. I have ever acted maidenly, as has become my mother's daughter."

"Yes, yes, yes; I believe that."

"And I can say more than that for myself. My thoughts have been the same; — nor have my wishes, even, ever gone beyond them. And when this young man came to me, telling me of his feelings, I gave him no answer till I had consulted my mother."

"She should have bade you not think of him."

"Ah! you are not a mother, and cannot know. Why should I not think of him, when he is so good and kind, honest and hard-working? And then he had thought of me first—why should I not think of him? Did not mama listen to my father when he came to her?"

"But your father was forty years old, and had a business."

"You gave it him, uncle Hatto—I have heard him say so."

"And, therefore, I am to do as much for you. And then next year Agnes will come to me; and so before I die I shall see you all in want—with large families. No, Isa; I will not scorn you, but this thing cannot be."

"But I have not told you all yet. You say that I want a husband."

"Well, well: I did not mean to say it harshly."

"I do want—to be married." And here her courage failed her a little, and for a moment her eye fell to the ground. "It is true, uncle, he has asked me whether I could love him, and I have told him that I could. He has asked me whether I would be his wife, and I have given him a promise. After that must not his happiness be my happiness, and his misery my misery? Am I not his wife already before God?"

"No, no!" said uncle Hatto, loudly.

"Ah, but I am. None feel the strength of the bands but those who are themselves bound. I know my duty to my father and mother, and with God's help I will do it, but I am not the less bound to him. Without their approval, I will not stand with him at the altar; but not the less is my lot joined to his for this world: nothing could release me from that but his wish."

"And he will wish it in a month or two."

"Excuse me, uncle Hatto, but in that I can only judge for myself as best I may. He has loved me now for two years."

"Psha!"

"And whether it be wise or foolish, I have sanctioned it. I cannot now go back with honour — even if my own heart would let me. His welfare must be my welfare, and his sorrow my sorrow. Therefore I am bound to do for him anything that a girl may do for the man she loves; and as I knew of no other resource, I came to you to help me."

"And he, sitting out there, knows what you are saying."

"Most certainly not. He knows no more than that he has seen me enter this room."

"I am glad of that, because I would not wish that he should be disappointed. In this matter, my dear, I cannot do anything for you."

"And is that your last answer, uncle?"

"Yes, indeed. When you come to think over this some twenty years hence, you will know then that I was right, and that your request was unreasonable."

"It may be so," she replied. "But I do not think it."

"It will be so. Such favours as you now ask are not granted for light reasons."

"Light reasons! Well, uncle, I have said my say, and will not take up your time longer."

"Good-bye, my dear; I am sorry that I cannot oblige you; — that it is quite out of my power to oblige you."

Then she went, giving him her hand as she parted from him; and he, as she left the room, looking anxiously at her, watching her countenance and her gait, and listening to the very sound of her footfall. "Ah!" he said to himself, when he was alone. "The young people have the best of it. The sun shines for them. But why should they have all? Poor as he is, he is a happy dog — a happy dog. But she is twice too good for him. Why did she not take to one of her own country?"

Isa as she passed through the bank smiled sweetly at her father, and then smiled sweetly at her lover, nodding to him with a pleasant, kindly nod. If he could have heard all that had passed at that interview, how much more would he have known of her than now he knew; and how proud might he have been of her love! No word was spoken as she went out, and then she walked home with even step as she had walked thither. It can hardly be said that she was disappointed, as she had expected nothing. But people hope who do not expect; and though her step was even, and her face calm, yet her heart was sad.

"Mama," she said, "there is no hope from uncle Hatto."

"So I feared, my dear."

"But I thought it right to try — for Herbert's sake."

"I hope it will not do him an injury in the bank."

"Oh, mama, do not put that into my heart. If that were added to it all, I should indeed be wretched."

"No, he is too just for that. Poor young man! Sometimes I almost think it would be better that he should go back to England."

"Mama, if he did, I should — break my heart."

"Isa!"

"Well, mama! But do not suppose that I mean to complain, whatever happens."

"But I had been so sure that you had restrained your feelings."

"So had I — till I knew myself. Mama, I could wait for years, if he were contented to wait by my side. If I could see him happy, I could watch him and love him and be happy also. I do not want to have him kneeling to me, and making sweet speeches; but it has gone too far now; — and I could not bear to lose him." And thus to her mother she confessed the truth.

There was nothing more said between Isa and her mother on the subject, and for two days the matter remained as it then stood. Madame Heine had been deeply grieved at hearing those last words which her daughter had spoken. To her also that state of quiescence which Isa had so long affected seemed to be the proper state in which a maiden's heart should stand till after her marraige vow had been pronounced. She watched her Isa, and had approved of everything; — of everything till her last avowal had been made. But, now, though she could not approve, she expressed no disapproval in words. She pressed her daughter's hand and sighed, and then the two said no more upon the matter. In this way for two days there was silence in the apartments in the Ludwig's Strasse, for even when the father returned from his work, the whole circle felt that their old family mirth was for the present necessarily laid aside.

On the morning of the third day, about noon, Madame Heine returned home from the market with Isa, and as they reached their landing Agnes met them with a packet. "Fritz brought it from the bank," said Agnes. Now Fritz was the boy who ran of messages and swept out the office, and Madame Heine put out her hand for the parcel, thinking, not unnaturally, that it was for her. But Agnes would not give it to her mother. "It is for you, Isa," she said. Then Isa, looking at the address, recognised the handwriting of her uncle.

"Mama," she said, "I will come to you directly;" and then passed quickly away into her own room.

The parcel was soon opened, and contained a note from her uncle, and a stiff, large document, looking as though it had come from the hands of a lawyer. Isa glanced at the document, and read some few of the words on the outer fold, but they did not carry home to her mind any clear perception of their meaning. She was flurried at the moment, and the words perhaps were not very plain. Then she took up the note, and that was plain enough. It was very short, and ran as follows: — "MY DEAR NIECE,

"You told me on Monday that I was stern, and harsh, and unjust. Perhaps I was. If so, I hope the enclosed will make amends, and that you will not think me such an old fool as I think myself.

"Your affectionate uncle,

"HATTO HEINE.

"I have told nobody yet, and the enclosed will require my brother's signature; but I suppose he will not object."

"But he does not know it, mama," said Isa. "Who is to tell him. Oh, mama, you must tell him."

"Nay, my dear; but it must be your own present to him."

"I could not give it to him. It is uncle Hatto's present. Mama, when I left him I thought that his eye was kind to me."

"His heart at any rate has been very kind." And then again they looked over the document, and talked of the wedding which must now be near at hand. But still they had not as yet decided how Herbert should be informed.

At last Isa decided that she herself would write to him. She did write, and this was her letter.

"DEAR HERBERT,

"Mama and I wish to see you, and beg that you will come up to us this evening. We have tidings for you which we hope you will receive with joy. I may as well tell you at once, as I do not wish to flurry you. Uncle Hatto has sent to us a document which admits you as a partner into the bank. If, therefore, you wish to go on with our engagement, I suppose there is nothing now to cause any very great delay."

"ISA."

The letter was very simple, and Isa, when she had written it, subsided into all her customary quiescence. Indeed, when Herbert came to the Ludwig's Strasse, not in the evening, as he was bidden to do, but immediately, leaving his own dinner uneaten, and coming upon the Heines in the midst of their dinner, she was more than usually tranquil. But his love was, as she had told him, boisterous. He could not contain himself, but embraced them all, and then scolded Isa because she slipped from him, and was so calm.

"Why should I not be calm," said she, "now that I know you are happy."

The house in the Schrannen Platz still goes by the name of Heine Brothers, but the mercantile world in Bavaria, and in some cities out of Bavaria, is well aware that the real pith and marrow of the business is derived from the energy of the young English partner.

"The House of Heine Brothers in Munich" appeared first in the November 16 and 23 issues of *Public Opinion: Literary Supplement* for 1861.

La Mère Bauche

THE PYRENEEAN VALLEY in which the baths of Vernet are situated is not much known to English, or indeed to any travellers. Tourists in search of good hotels and picturesque beauty combined do not generally extend their journeys to the Eastern Pyrenees. They rarely get beyond Luchon, and in this they are right, as they thus end their peregrinations at the most lovely spot among these mountains; and are as a rule so deceived, imposed on, and bewildered by guides, innkeepers, and horse-owners at this otherwise delightful place as to become undesirous of further travel. Nor do invalids from distant parts frequent Vernet. People of fashion go to the Eaux Bonnes and to Luchon, and people who are really ill to Barèges and Cauterets. It is at these places that one meets crowds of Parisians, and the daughters and wives of rich merchants from Bordeaux, with an admixture, now by no means inconsiderable, of Englishmen and Englishwomen. But the Eastern Pyrenees are still unfrequented. And probably they will remain so; for though there are among them lovely valleys — and of all such the valley of Vernet is perhaps the most lovely — they cannot compete with the mountain scenery of other tourists-loved regions in Europe. At the Port de Venasquez and the Brèche de Roland in the Western Pyrenees, or rather, to speak more truly, at spots in the close vicinity of these famous mountain entrances from France into Spain, one can make comparisons with Switzerland, Northern Italy, the Tyrol, and Ireland, which will not be injurious to the scenes then under view.

But among the eastern mountains this can rarely be done. The hills do not stand thickly together so as to group themselves; the passes from one valley to another, though not wanting in altitude, are not close pressed together with overhanging rocks, and are deficient in grandeur as well as loveliness. And then, as a natural consequence of all this, the hotels — are not quite as good as they should be.

But there is one mountain among them which can claim to rank with the Píc du Midi or the Maledetta. No one can pooh-pooh the stern old Canigou, standing high and solitary, solemn and grand, between the two roads which run from Perpignan into Spain, the one by Prades and the other by Le Boulon. Under the Canigou, towards the west, lie the hot baths of Vernet, in a close secluded valley, which, as I have said before, is, as far as I know, the sweetest spot in these Eastern Pyrenees.

The frequenters of these baths were a few years back gathered almost entirely from towns not very far distant, from Perpignan, Narbonne, Carcassonne, and Bézières, and were not therefore famous, expensive, or luxurious; but those who believed in them believed with great faith; and it was certainly the fact that men and women who went thither worn with toil, sick with excesses, and nervous through over-care, came back fresh and strong, fit once more to attack the world with all its woes. Their character in latter days does not seem to have changed, though their circle of admirers may perhaps be somewhat extended.

In those days, by far the most noted and illustrious person in the village of Vernet was La Mère Bauche. That there had once been a Père Bauche was known to the world, for there was a Fils Bauche who lived with his mother; but no one seemed to remember more of him than that he had once existed. At Vernet he had never been known. La Mère Bauche was a native of the village, but her married life had been passed away from it, and she had returned in her early widowhood to become proprietress and manager, or, as one may say, the heart and soul of the Hôtel Bauche at Vernet.

This hotel was a large and somewhat rough establishment, intended for the accommodation of invalids who came to Vernet for their health. It was built immediately over one of the thermal springs, so that the water flowed from the bowels of the earth directly into the baths. There was accommodation for seventy people, and during the summer and autumn months the place was always full. Not a few also were to be found there during the winter and spring, for the charges of Madame Bauche were low, and the accommodation reasonably good.

And in this respect, as indeed in all others, Madame Bauche had the reputation of being an honest woman. She had a certain price, from which no earthly consideration would induce her to depart; and certain returns for this price in the shape of déjeuners and dinners, baths and beds, which she never failed to give in accordance with the dictates of a strict conscience. These were traits in the character of an hotelkeeper which cannot be praised too highly, and which had met their due reward in the custom of the public. But nevertheless there were those who thought that there was occasionally ground for complaint in the conduct even of Madame Bauche.

In the first place she was deficient in that pleasant smiling soft-ness which should belong to any keeper of a house of public entertainment. In her general mode of life she was stern and silent with her guests, autocratic, authoritative, and sometimes contradictory in her house, and altogether irrational and uncon-ciliatory when any change even for a day was proposed to her, or when any shadow of a complaint reached her ears.

Indeed of complaint, as made against the establishment, she was altogether intolerant. To such she had but one answer. He or she who complained might leave the place at a moment's notice if it so pleased them. There were always others ready to take their places. The power of making this answer came to her from the lowness of her prices; and it was a power which was very dear to her.

The baths were taken at different hours according to medical advice, but the usual time was from five to seven in the morning. The déjeuner or early meal was at nine o'clock, the dinner was at four. After that, no eating or drinking was allowed in the Hôtel Bauche. There was a café in the village, at which ladies and gentlemen could get a cup of coffee or a glass of eau sucré; but no such accommodation was to be had in the establishment. Not by any possible bribery or persuasion could any meal be procured at any other than the authorized hours. A visitor who should enter the salle à manger more than ten minutes after the last bell would be looked at very sourly by Madame Bauche, who on all occasions sat at the top of her own table. Should any one appear as much as half an hour late, he would receive only his share of what had not been handed round. But after the last dish had been so handed, it was utterly useless for any one to enter the room at all.

Her appearance at the period of our tale was perhaps not altogether in her favour. She was about sixty years of age and was very stout and short in the neck. She wore her own gray hair, which at dinner was always tidy enough; but during the whole day previous to that hour she might be seen with it escaping from under her cap in extreme disorder. Her eyebrows were large and bushy, but those alone would not have given to her face that look of indomitable sternness which it possessed. Her eyebrows were serious in their effect, but not so serious as the pair of green spectacles which she always wore under them. It was thought by those who had analyzed the subject that the great secret of Madame Bauche's power lay in her green spectacles.

Her custom was to move about and through the whole establishment every day from breakfast till the period came for her to dress for dinner. She would visit every chamber and every bath, walk once or twice round the salle à manger, and very repeatedly round the kitchen; she would go into every hole and corner, and peer into everything through her green spectacles: and in these walks it was not always thought pleasant to meet her. Her custom was to move very slowly, with her hands generally clasped behind her back: she rarely spoke to the guests unless she was spoken to, and on such occasions she would not often diverge into general conversation. If any one had aught to say connected with the business of the establishment, she would listen, and then she would make her answers, — often not pleasant in the hearing.

And thus she walked her path through the world, a stern, hard, solemn old woman, not without gusts of passionate explosion; but honest withal, and not without some inward benevolence and true tenderness of heart. Children she had had many, some seven or eight. One or two had died, others had been married; she had sons settled far away from home, and at the time of which we are now speaking but one was left in any way subject to parental authority.

Adolphe Bauche was the only one of her children of whom much was remembered by the present denizens and hangers-on of the hotel. He was the youngest of the number, and having been born only very shortly before the return of Madame Bauche to Vernet, had been altogether reared there. It was thought by the world of those parts, and rightly thought, that he was his mother's darling — more so than had been any of his brothers and sisters, — the very apple of her eye, and gem of her life. At this time he was about twenty-five years of age, and for the last two years had been absent from Vernet — for reasons which will shortly be made to appear. He had been sent to Paris to see something of the world, and learn to talk French instead of the patois of his valley; and having left Paris had come down south into Languedoc, and remained there picking up some agricultural lore which it was thought might prove useful in the valley farms of Vernet. He was now expected home again very speedily, much to his mother's delight.

That she was kind and gracious to her favourite child does not perhaps give much proof of her benevolence; but she had also been kind and gracious to the orphan child of a neighbour; nay, to the orphan child of a rival innkeeper. At Vernet there had been more than one water establishment, but the proprietor of the second had died some few years after Madame Bauche had settled herself at the place. His house had not thrived, and his only child, a little girl, was left altogether without provision.

This little girl, Marie Clavert, La Mère Bauche had taken into her own house immediately after the father's death, although she had most cordially hated that father. Marie was then an infant, and Madame Bauche had accepted the charge without much thought, perhaps, as to what might be the child's ultimate destiny. But since then she had thoroughly done the duty of a mother by the little girl, who had become the pet of the whole establishment, the favourite plaything of Adolphe Bauche, — and at last of course his early sweetheart.

And then and therefore there had come troubles at Vernet. Of course all the world of the valley had seen what was taking place and what was likely to take place, long before Madame Bauche knew anything about it. But at last it broke upon her senses that her son, Adolphe Bauche, the heir to all her virtues and all her riches, the first young man in that or any neighbouring valley, was absolutely contemplating the idea of marrying that poor little orphan, Marie Clavert!

That any one should ever fall in love with Marie Clavert had never occurred to Madame Bauche. She had always regarded the child as a child, as the object of her charity, and as a little thing to be looked on as poor Marie by all the world. She, looking through her green spectacles, had never seen that Marie Clavert was a beautiful creature, full of ripening charms, such as young men love to look on. Marie was of infinite daily use to Madame Bauche in a hundred little things about the house, and the old lady thoroughly recognized and appreciated her ability. But for this very reason she had never taught herself to regard Marie otherwise than as a useful drudge. She was very fond of her protégée — so much so that she would listen to her in affairs about the house when she would listen to no one else; — but Marie's prettiness and grace and sweetness as a girl had all been thrown away upon Maman Bauche, as Marie used to call her.

But unluckily it had not been thrown away upon Adolphe. He had appreciated, as it was natural that he should do, all that had been so utterly indifferent to his mother; and consequently had fallen in love. Consequently also he had told his love; and consequently also, Marie had returned his love. Adolphe had been hitherto contradicted but in few things, and thought that all difficulty would be prevented by his informing his mother that he wished to marry Marie Clavert. But Marie, with a woman's instinct, had known better. She had trembled and almost crouched with fear when she confessed her love; and had absolutely hid herself from sight when Adolphe went forth, prepared to ask his mother's consent to his marriage.

The indignation and passionate wrath of Madame Bauche were past and gone two years before the date of this story, and I need not therefore much enlarge upon that subject. She was at first abusive and bitter, which was bad for Marie; and afterwards bitter and silent, which was worse. It was of course determined that poor Marie should be sent away to some asylum for orphans or penniless paupers — in short anywhere out of the way. What mattered her outlook into the world, her happiness, or indeed her very existence? The outlook and happiness of Adolphe Bauche, — was not that to be considered as everything at Vernet?

But this terrible sharp aspect of affairs did not last very long. In the first place La Mère Bauche had under those green spectacles a heart that in truth was tender and affectionate, and after the first two days of anger she admitted that something must be done for Marie Clavert; and after the fourth day she acknowledged that the world of the hotel, her world, would not go as well without Marie Clavert as it would with her. And in the next place Madame Bauche had a friend whose advice in grave matters she would sometimes take. This friend had told her that it would be much better to send away Adolphe, since it was so necessary that there should be a sending away of some one; that he would be much benefited by passing some months of his life away from his native valley; and that an absence of a year or two would teach him to forget Marie, even if it did not teach Marie to forget him.

And we must say a word or two about this friend. At Vernet he was usually called M. le Capitaine, though in fact he had never reached that rank. He had been in the army, and having been wounded in the leg while still a sous-lieutenant, had been pensioned, and had thus been interdicted from treading any further the thorny path that leads to glory. For the last fifteen years he had resided under the roof of Madame Bauche, at first as a casual visitor, going and coming, but now for many years as constant there as she was herself.

He was so constantly called Le Capitaine that his real name was seldom heard. It may however as well be known to us that this was Theodore Campan. He was a tall, well-looking man; always dressed in black garments, of a coarse description certainly, but scrupulously clean and well brushed; of perhaps fifty years of age, and conspicuous for the rigid uprightness of his back — and for a black wooden leg.

This wooden leg was perhaps the most remarkable trait in his character. It was always jet black, being painted, or polished, or japanned, as occasion might require, by the hands of the capitaine himself. It was longer than ordinary wooden legs, as indeed the capitaine was longer than ordinary men; but nevertheless it never seemed in any way to impede the rigid punctilious propriety of his movements. It was never in his way as wooden legs usually are in the way of their wearers. And then to render it more illustrious it had round its middle, round the calf of the leg we may so say, a band of bright brass which shone like burnished gold.

It had been the capitaine's custom, now for some years past, to retire every evening at about seven o'clock into the sanctum sanctorum of Madame Bauche's habitation, the dark little private sitting-room in which she made out her bills and calculated her profits, and there regale himself in her presence — and indeed at her expense, — for the items never appeared in the bill, with coffee, and cognac. I have said that there was neither eating nor drinking at the establishment after the regular dinner-hours; but in so saying I spoke of the world at large. Nothing further was allowed in the way of trade; but in the way of friendship so much was now-a-days always allowed to the capitaine.

It was at these moments that Madame Bauche discussed her private affairs, and asked for and received advice. For even Madame Bauche was mortal; nor could her green spectacles without other aid carry her through all the troubles of life. It was now five years since the world of Vernet discovered that La Mère Bauche was going to marry the capitaine; and for eighteen months the world of Vernet had been full of this matter: but any amount of patience is at last exhausted, and as no further steps in that direction were ever taken beyond the daily cup of coffee, that subject died away — very much unheeded by La Mère Bauche.

But she, though she thought of no matrimony for herself, thought much of matrimony for other people; and over most of those cups of evening coffee and cognac a matrimonial project was discussed in these latter days. It has been seen that the capitaine pleaded in Marie's favour when the fury of Madame Bauche's indignation broke forth; and that ultimately Marie was kept at home, and Adolphe sent away by his advice.

"But Adolphe cannot always stay away," Madame Bauche had pleaded in her difficulty. The truth of this the capitaine had admitted; but Marie, he said, might be married to some one else before two years were over. And so the matter had commenced.

But to whom should she be married? To this question the capitaine had answered in perfect innocence of heart, that La Mère

Bauche would be much better able to make such a choice than himself. He did not know how Marie might stand with regard to money. If madame would give some little 'dot,' the affair, the capitaine thought, would be more easily arranged.

All these things took months to say, during which period Marie went on with her work in melancholy listlessness. One comfort she had. Adolphe, before he went, had promised to her, holding in his hand as he did so a little cross which she had given him, that no earthly consideration should sever them; — that sooner or later he would certainly be her husband. Marie felt that her limbs could not work nor her tongue speak were it not for this one drop of water in her cup.

And then, deeply meditating, La Mère Bauche hit upon a plan, and herself communicated it to the capitaine over a second cup of coffee into which she poured a full teaspoonful more than the usual allowance of cognac. Why should not he, the capitaine himself, be the man to marry Marie Clavert?

It was a very startling proposal, the idea of matrimony for himself never having as yet entered into the capitaine's head at any period of his life; but La Mère Bauche did contrive to make it not altogether unacceptable. As to that matter of dowry she was prepared to be more than generous. She did love Marie well, and could find it in her heart to give her anything — anything except her son, her own Adolphe. What she proposed was this. Adolphe, himself, would never keep the baths. If the capitaine would take Marie for his wife, Marie, Madame Bauche declared, should be the mistress after her death; subject of course to certain settlements as to Adolphe's pecuniary interests.

The plan was discussed a thousand times, and at last so far brought to bear that Marie was made acquainted with it—having been called to sit in presence with La Mère Bauche and her future proposed husband. The poor girl manifested no disgust to the stiff ungainly lover whom they assigned to her, — who through his whole frame was in appearance almost as wooden as his own leg. On the whole, indeed, Marie liked the capitaine, and felt that he was her friend; and in her country such marriages were not uncommon. The capitaine was perhaps a little beyond the age at which a man might usually be thought justified in demanding the services of a young girl as his nurse and wife, but then Marie had so little to give — except her youth, and beauty, and goodness.

But yet she could not absolutely consent; for was she not absolutely pledged to her own Adolphe? And therefore, when the great pecuniary advantages were, one by one, displayed before her, and when La Mère Bauche, as a last argument, informed her that as wife of the capitaine she would be regarded as a second mistress in the establishment and not as a servant, — she could only burst out into tears, and say that she did not know.

"I will be very kind to you," said the capitaine; "as kind as a man can be."

Marie took his hard withered hand and kissed it; and then looked up into his face with beseeching eyes which were not without avail upon his heart.

"We will not press her now," said the capitaine. "There is time enough."

But let his heart be touched ever so much, one thing was certain. It could not be permitted that she should marry Adolphe. To that view of the matter he had given in his unrestricted adhesion; nor could he by any means withdraw it without losing altogether his position in the establishment of Madame Bauche. Nor indeed did his conscience tell him that such a marriage should be permitted. That would be too much. If every pretty girl were allowed to marry the first young man that might fall in love with her, what would the world come to?

And it soon appeared that there was not time enough — that the time was growing very scant. In three months Adolphe would be back. And if everything was not arranged by that time, matters might still go astray.

And then Madame Bauche asked her final question: "You do not think, do you, that you can ever marry Adolphe?" And as she asked it the accustomed terror of her green spectacles magnified itself tenfold. Marie could only answer by another burst of tears.

The affair was at last settled among them. Marie said that she would consent to marry the capitaine when she should hear from Adolphe's own mouth that he, Adolphe, loved her no longer. She declared with many tears that her vows and pledges prevented her from promising more than this. It was not her fault, at any rate not now, that she loved her lover. It was not her fault, —

not now at least — that she was bound by these pledges. When she heard from his own mouth that he had discarded her, then she would marry the capitaine — or indeed sacrifice herself in any other way that La Mère Bauche might desire. What would anything signify then?

Madame Bauche's spectacles remained unmoved; but not her heart. Marie, she told the capitaine, should be equal to herself in the establishment, when once she was entitled to be called Madame Campan, and she should be to her quite as a daughter. She should have her cup of coffee every evening, and dine at the big table, and wear a silk gown at church, and the servants should all call her Madame; a great career should be open to her, if she would only give up her foolish girlish childish love for Adolphe. And all these great promises were repeated to Marie by the capitaine.

But nevertheless there was but one thing in the whole world which in Marie's eyes was of any value; and that one thing was the heart of Adolphe Bauche. Without that she would be nothing; with that, — with that assured, she could wait patiently till doomsday.

Letters were written to Adolphe during all these eventful doings; and a letter came from him saying that he greatly valued Marie's love, but that as it had been clearly proved to him that their marriage would be neither for her advantage, nor for his, he was willing to give it up. He consented to her marriage with the capitaine, and expressed his gratitude to his mother for the immediate pecuniary advantages which she had held out to him. Oh, Adolphe, Adolphe! But, alas, alas! is not such the way of most men's hearts — and of the hearts of some women?

This letter was read to Marie, but it had no more effect upon her than would have had some dry legal document. In those days and in those places men and women did not depend much upon letters; nor when they were written, was there expressed in them much of heart or feeling. Marie would understand, as she was well aware, the glance of Adolphe's eye and the tone of Adolphe's voice; she would perceive at once from them what her lover really meant, what he wished, what in the innermost corner of his heart he really desired that she should do. But from that stiff constrained written document she could understand nothing.

It was agreed therefore that Adolphe should return, and that she would accept her fate from his mouth. The capitaine, who knew more of human nature than did poor Marie, felt tolerably sure of his bride. Adolphe, who had seen something of the world, would not care very much for the girl of his own valley. Money and pleasure, and some little position in the world would soon wean him from his love; and then Marie would accept her destiny — as other girls in the same position had done since the French world began.

And now it was the evening before Adolphe's expected arrival. La Mère Bauche was discussing the matter with the capitaine over the usual cup of coffee. Madame Bauche had of late become rather nervous on the matter, thinking that they had been some- what rash in acceding so much to Marie. It seemed to her that it was absolutely now left to the two young lovers to say whether or no they would have each other or not. Now nothing on earth could be further from Madame Bauche's intention than this. Her decree and resolve was to heap down blessings on all persons con- cerned — provided always that she could have her own way; but, provided she did not have her own way, to heap down, — any- thing but blessings. She had her code of morality in this matter. She would do good if possible to everybody around her. But she would not on any score be induced to consent that Adolphe should marry Marie Clavert. Should that be in the wind she would rid the house of Marie, of the capitaine, and even of Adolphe himself.

She had become therefore somewhat querulous, and self- opinionated in her discussions with her friend.

"I don't know," she said on the evening in question; "I don't know. It may be all right; but if Adolphe turns against me, what are we to do then?"

"Mère Bauche," said the capitaine, sipping his coffee and puff- ing out the smoke of his cigar, "Adolphe will not turn against us." It had been somewhat remarked by many that the capitaine was more at home in the house, and somewhat freer in his manner of talking with Madame Bauche, since this matrimonial alliance had been on the tapis than he had ever been before. La Mère herself observed it, and did not quite like it; but how could she prevent it now? When the capitaine was once married she would make him know his place, in spite of all her promises to Marie.

"But if he says he likes the girl?" continued Madame Bauche.

"My friend, you may be sure that he will say nothing of the kind. He has not been away two years without seeing girls as pretty as Marie. And then you have his letter."

"That is nothing, capitaine; he would eat his letter as quick as you would eat an omelet aux fines herbes." Now the capitaine was especially quick over an omelet aux fines herbes.

"And, Mère Bauche, you also have the purse; he will know that he cannot eat that, except with your good will."

"Ah!" exclaimed Madame Bauche, "poor lad! He has not a sous in the world unless I give it to him." But it did not seem that this reflection was in itself displeasing to her.

"Adolphe will now be a man of the world," continued the capitaine. "He will know that it does not do to throw away everything for a pair of red lips. That is the folly of a boy, and Adolphe will be no longer a boy. Believe me, Mère Bauche, things will be right enough."

"And then we shall have Marie sick and ill and half dying on our hands," said Madame Bauche.

This was not flattering to the capitaine, and so he felt it. "Perhaps so, perhaps not," he said. "But at any rate she will get over it. It is a malady which rarely kills young women — especially when another alliance awaits them."

"Bah!" said Madame Bauche; and in saying that word she avenged herself for the too great liberty which the capitaine had lately taken. He shrugged his shoulders, took a pinch of snuff, and uninvited helped himself to a teaspoonful of cognac. Then the conference ended, and on the next morning before breakfast Adolphe Bauche arrived.

On that morning poor Marie hardly knew how to bear herself. A month or two back, and even up to the last day or two, she had felt a sort of confidence that Adolphe would be true to her; but the nearer came that fatal day the less strong was the confidence of the poor girl. She knew that those two long-headed, aged counsellors were plotting against her happiness, and she felt that she could hardly dare hope for success with such terrible foes opposed to her. On the evening before the day Madame Bauche had met her in the passages, and kissed her as she wished her good night. Marie knew little about sacrifices, but she felt that it was a sacrificial kiss.

In those days a sort of diligence with the mails for Olette passed through Prades early in the morning, and a conveyance was sent from Vernet to bring Adolphe to the baths. Never was prince or princess expected with more anxiety. Madame Bauche was up and dressed long before the hour, and was heard to say five several times that she was sure he would not come. The capitaine was out and on the high road, moving about with his wooden leg, as perpendicular as a lamp-post and almost as black. Marie also was up, but nobody had seen her. She was up and had been out about the place before any of them were stirring; but now that the world was on the move she lay hidden like a hare in its form.

And then the old char-à-banc clattered up to the door, and Adolphe jumped out of it into his mother's arms. He was fatter and fairer than she had last seen him and certainly looked more like a man. Marie also saw him out of her little window, and she thought that he looked like a god. Was it probable, she said to herself, that one so godlike would still care for her?

The mother was delighted with her son, who rattled away quite at his ease. He shook hands very cordially with the capitaine — of whose intended alliance with his own sweetheart he had been informed, and then as he entered the house with his hand under his mother's arm, he asked one question about her. "And where is Marie?" said he. "Marie! oh upstairs; you shall see her after breakfast," said La Mère Bauche. And so they entered the house, and went in to breakfast among the guests. Everybody had heard something of the story, and they were all on the alert to see the young man whose love or want of love was considered to be of so much importance.

"You will see that it will be all right," said the capitaine, carrying his head very high.

"I think so, I think so," said La Mère Bauche, who, now that the capitaine was right, no longer desired to contradict him.

"I know that it will be all right," said the capitaine. "I told you that Adolphe would return a man; and he is a man. Look at him; he does not care this for Marie Clavert;" and the capitaine, with much eloquence in his motion, pitched over a neighbouring wall a small stone which he held in his hand.

And then they all went to breakfast with many signs of out- ward joy. And not without some inward joy; for Madame Bauche thought she saw that her son was cured of his love. In the mean time Marie sat up stairs still afraid to show herself.

"He has come," said a young girl, a servant in the house, run- ning up to the door of Marie's room.

"Yes," said Marie; "I could see that he has come."

"And, oh, how beautiful he is!" said the girl, putting her hands together and looking up to the ceiling. Marie in her heart of hearts wished that he was not half so beautiful, as then her chance of having him might be greater.

"And the company are all talking to him as though he were the préfet," said the girl.

"Never mind who is talking to him," said Marie; "go away, and leave me — you are wanted for your work." Why before this was he not talking to her? Why not, if he were really true to her? Alas, it began to fall upon her mind that he would be false! And what then? What should she do then? She sat still gloomily, thinking of that other spouse that had been promised to her.

As speedily after breakfast as was possible Adolphe was invited to a conference in his mother's private room. She had much debated in her own mind whether the capitaine should be invited to this conference or no. For many reasons she would have wished to exclude him. She did not like to teach her son that she was unable to manage her own affairs, and she would have been well pleased to make the capitaine understand that his assistance was not absolutely necessary to her. But then she had an inward fear that her green spectacles would not now be as efficacious on Adolphe, as they had once been, in old days, before he had seen the world and become a man. It might be necessary that her son, being a man, should be opposed by a man. So the capitaine was invited to the conference.

What took place there need not be described at length. The three were closeted for two hours, at the end of which time they came forth together. The countenance of Madame Bauche was serene and comfortable; her hopes of ultimate success ran higher than ever. The face of the capitaine was masked, as are always the

171

faces of great diplomatists; he walked placid and upright, raising his wooden leg with an ease and skill that was absolutely marvellous. But poor Adolphe's brow was clouded. Yes, poor Adolphe! for he was poor in spirit. He had pledged himself to give up Marie, and to accept the liberal allowance which his mother tendered him; but it remained for him now to communicate these tidings to Marie herself.

"Could not you tell her?" he had said to his mother, with very little of that manliness in his face on which his mother now so prided herself. But La Mère Bauche explained to him that it was a part of the general agreement that Marie was to hear his decision from his own mouth.

"But you need not regard it," said the capitaine, with the most indifferent air in the world. "The girl expects it. Only she has some childish idea that she is bound till you yourself release her. I don't think she will be troublesome." Adolphe at that moment did feel that he should have liked to kick the capitaine out of his mother's house.

And where should the meeting take place? In the hall of the bath-house, suggested Madame Bauche; because, as she observed, they could walk round and round, and nobody ever went there at that time of day. But to this Adolphe objected; it would be so cold and dismal and melancholy.

The capitaine thought that Mère Bauche's little parlour was the place; but La Mère herself did not like this. They might be overheard, as she well knew; and she guessed that the meeting would not conclude without some sobs that would certainly be bitter and might perhaps be loud.

"Send her up to the grotto, and I will follow her," said Adolphe. On this therefore they agreed. Now the grotto was a natural excavation in a high rock, which stood precipitously upright over the establishment of the baths. A steep zigzag path with almost never-ending steps had been made along the face of the rock from a little flower garden attached to the house which lay immediately under the mountain. Close along the front of the hotel ran a little brawling river, leaving barely room for a road between it and the door; over this there was a wooden bridge leading to the garden, and some two or three hundred yards from the bridge began the steps by which the ascent was made to the grotto.

When the season was full and the weather perfectly warm the place was much frequented. There was a green table in it, and four or five deal chairs; a green garden seat also was there, which however had been removed into the innermost back corner of the excavation, as its hinder legs were somewhat at fault. A wall about two feet high ran along the face of it, guarding its occupants from the precipice. In fact it was no grotto, but a little chasm in the rock, such as we often see up above our heads in rocky valleys, and which by means of these steep steps had been turned into a source of exercise and amusement for the visitors at the hotel.

Standing at the wall one could look down into the garden, and down also upon the shining slate roof of Madame Bauche's house; and to the left might be seen the sombre silent snow-capped top of the stern old Canigou, king of mountains among those Eastern Pyrenees.

And so Madame Bauche undertook to send Marie up to the grotto, and Adolphe undertook to follow her thither. It was now spring; and though the winds had fallen and the snow was no longer lying on the lower peaks, still the air was fresh and cold, and there was no danger that any of the few guests at the establishment would visit the place.

"Make her put on her cloak, Mère Bauche," said the capitaine, who did not wish that his bride should have a cold in her head on their wedding-day. La Mère Bauche pished and pshawed, as though she were not minded to pay any attention to recommendations on such subjects from the capitaine. But nevertheless when Marie was seen slowly to creep across the little bridge about fifteen minutes after this time, she had a handkerchief on her head, and was closely wrapped in a dark brown cloak.

Poor Marie herself little heeded the cold fresh air, but she was glad to avail herself of any means by which she might hide her face. When Madame Bauche sought her out in her own little room, and with a smiling face and kind kiss bade her go to the grotto, she knew, or fancied that she knew that it was all over.

"He will tell you all the truth, — how it all is," said La Mère. "We will do all we can, you know, to make you happy, Marie. But you must remember what Monsieur le Curé told us the other day. In this vale of tears we cannot have everything; as we shall have some day, when our poor wicked souls have been purged of all their wickedness. Now go, dear, and take your cloak."

"Yes, maman."

"And Adolphe will come to you. And try and behave well, like a sensible girl."

"Yes, maman," — and so she went, bearing on her brow another sacrificial kiss — and bearing in her heart such an unutterable load of woe!

Adolphe had gone out of the house before her; but standing in the stable yard, well within the gate so that she should not see him, he watched her slowly crossing the bridge and mounting the first flight of the steps. He had often seen her tripping up those stairs, and had, almost as often, followed her with his quicker feet. And she, when she would hear him, would run; and then he would catch her breathless at the top, and steal kisses from her when all the power of refusing them had been robbed from her by her efforts at escape. There was no such running now, no such following, no thought of such kisses.

As for him, he would fain have skulked off and shirked the interview had he dared. But he did not dare; so he waited there, out of heart, for some ten minutes, speaking a word now and then to the bath-man, who was standing by, just to show that he was at his ease. But the bath-man knew that he was not at his ease. Such would-be lies as those rarely achieve deception; — are rarely believed. And then, at the end of the ten minutes, with steps as slow as Marie's had been, he also ascended to the grotto.

Marie had watched him from the top, but so that she herself should not be seen. He however had not once lifted up his head to look for her; but, with eyes turned to the ground had plodded his way up to the cave. When he entered she was standing in the middle, with her eyes downcast, and her hands clasped before her. She had retired some way from the wall, so that no eyes might possibly see her but those of her false lover. There she stood when he entered, striving to stand motionless, but trembling like a leaf in every limb.

It was only when he reached the top step that he made up his mind how he would behave. Perhaps after all, the capitaine was right; perhaps she would not mind it.

"Marie," said he, with a voice that attempted to be cheerful; "this is an odd place to meet in after such a long absence," and he held out his hand to her. But only his hand! He offered her no salute. He did not even kiss her cheek as a brother would have done! Of the rules of the outside world it must be remembered that poor Marie knew but little. He had been a brother to her, before he had become her lover.

But Marie took his hand saying, "Yes, it has been very long."

"And now that I have come back," he went on to say, "it seems that we are all in a confusion together. I never knew such a piece of work. However, it is all for the best, I suppose."

"Perhaps so," said Marie still trembling violently, and still looking down upon the ground. And then there was silence between them for a minute or so.

"I tell you what it is, Marie," said Adolphe at last, dropping her hand and making a great effort to get through the work before him. "I am afraid we two have been very foolish. Don't you think we have now? It seems quite clear that we can never get ourselves married. Don't you see it in that light?"

Marie's head turned round and round with her, but she was not of the fainting order. She took three steps backwards and leant against the wall of the cave. She also was trying to think how she might best fight her battle. Was there no chance for her? Could no eloquence, no love prevail? On her own beauty she counted but little; but might not prayers do something, and a reference to those old vows which had been so frequent, so eager, so solemnly pledged between them?

"Never get outselves married!" she said, repeating his words. "Never, Adolphe? Can we never be married?"

"Upon my word, my dear girl, I fear not. You see my mother is so dead against it."

"But we could wait; could we not?"

"Ah, but that's just it, Marie. We cannot wait. We must decide now, — to-day. You see I can do nothing without money from her — and as for you, you see she won't even let you stay in the house unless you marry old Campan at once. He's a very good

175

sort of fellow though, old as he is. And if you do marry him, why you see you'll stay here, and have it all your own way in every-thing. As for me, I shall come and see you all from time to time, and shall be able to push my way as I ought to do."

"Then, Adolphe, you wish me to marry the capitaine?"

"Upon my honour I think it is the best thing you can do; I do indeed."

"Oh, Adolphe!"

"What can I do for you, you know? Suppose I was to go down to my mother and tell her that I had decided to keep you myself, what would come of it? Look at it in that light, Marie."

"She could not turn you out — you her own son!"

"But she would turn you out; and deuced quick, too, I can assure you of that; I can, upon my honour."

"I should not care that," and she made a motion with her hand to show how indifferent she would be to such treatment as regarded herself. "Not that —; if I still had the promise of your love."

"But what would you do?"

"I would work. There are other houses besides that one," and she pointed to the slate roof of the Bauche establishment.

"And for me — I should not have a penny in the world," said the young man.

She came up to him and took his right hand between both of hers and pressed it warmly, oh, so warmly. "You would have my love," said she; "my deepest, warmest, best heart's love. I should want nothing more, nothing on earth, if I could still have yours." And she leaned against his shoulder and looked with all her eyes into his face.

"But, Marie; that's nonsense, you know."

"No, Adolphe; it is not nonsense. Do not let them teach you so. What does love mean, if it does not mean that? Oh, Adolphe, you do love me, you do love me; you do love me?"

"Yes; — I love you," he said slowly; — as though he would not have said it, if he could have helped it. And then his arm crept slowly round her waist, as though in that also he could not help himself.

"And do not I love you?" said the passionate girl. "Oh I do, so dearly; with all my heart, with all my soul. Adolphe, I so love you, that I cannot give you up. Have I not sworn to be yours; sworn, sworn a thousand times? How can I marry that man! Oh Adolphe, how can you wish that I should marry him?" And she clung to him, and looked at him, and besought him with her eyes.

"I shouldn't wish it; — only —" and then he paused. It was hard to tell her that he was willing to sacrifice her to the old man because he wanted money from his mother.

"Only what! But, Adolphe, do not wish it at all! Have you not sworn that I should be your wife? Look here, look at this;" and she brought out from her bosom a little charm that he had given her in return for that cross. "Did you not kiss that when you swore before the figure of the virgin that I should be your wife? And do you not remember that I feared to swear too, because your mother was so angry; and then you made me? After that, Adolphe! Oh, Adolphe! Tell me that I may have some hope. I will wait; oh, I will wait so patiently."

He turned himself away from her and walked backwards and forwards uneasily through the grotto. He did love her; — love her as such men do love sweet, pretty girls. The warmth of her hand, the affection of her touch, the pure bright passion of her tear-laden eye had reawakened what power of love there was within him. But what was he to do? Even if he were willing to give up the immediate golden hopes which his mother held out to him, how was he to begin, and then how carry out this work of self-devotion? Marie would be turned away, and he would be left a victim in the hands of his mother, and of that stiff, wooden-legged militaire; — a penniless victim, left to mope about the place without a grain of influence or a morsel of pleasure.

"But what can we do?" he exclaimed again, as he once more met Marie's searching eye.

"We can be true and honest, and we can wait," she said, coming close up to him and taking hold of his arm. "I do not fear it; and she is not my mother, Adolphe. You need not fear your own mother."

"Fear; no, of course I don't fear. But I don't see how the very devil we can manage it."

"Will you let me tell her that I will not marry the capitaine; that I will not give up your promises; and then I am ready to leave the house?"

"It would do no good."

"It would do every good, Adolphe, if I had your promised word once more; if I could hear from your own voice one more tone of love. Do you not remember this place? It was here that you forced me to say that I loved you. It is here also that you will tell me that I have been deceived."

"It is not I that would deceive you," he said. "I wonder that you should be so hard upon me. God knows that I have trouble enough."

"Well; if I am a trouble to you, be it so. Be it as you wish," and she leaned back against the wall of the rock, and crossing her arms upon her breast looked away from him and fixed her eyes upon the sharp granite peaks of Canigou.

He again betook himself to walk backwards and forwards through the cave. He had quite enough of love for her to make him wish to marry her; quite enough, now, at this moment, to make the idea of her marriage with the capitaine very distasteful to him; enough probably to make him become a decently good husband to her, should fate enable him to marry her; but not enough to enable him to support all the punishment which would be the sure effects of his mother's displeasure. Besides, he had promised his mother that he would give up Marie; — had entirely given in his adhesion to that plan of the marriage with the capitaine. He had owned that the path of life as marked out for him by his mother was the one which it behoved him, as a man, to follow. It was this view of his duties as a man which had been specially urged on him with all the capitaine's eloquence. And old Campan had entirely succeeded. It is so easy to get the assent of such young men, so weak in mind and so weak in pocket, when the arguments are backed by a promise of two thousand francs a year.

"I'll tell you what I'll do," at last he said. "I'll get my mother by herself, and will ask her to let the matter remain as it is for the present."

"Not if it be a trouble, M. Adolphe;" and the proud girl still held her hands upon her bosom, and still looked towards the mountain.

"You know what I mean, Marie. You can understand how she and the capitaine are worrying me."

"But tell me, Adolphe, do you love me?"

"You know I love you, only —"

"And you will not give me up?"

"I will ask my mother. I will try and make her yield."

Marie could not feel that she received much confidence from her lover's promise; but still, even that, weak and unsteady as it was, even that was better than absolute fixed rejection. So she thanked him, promised him with tears in her eyes that she would always, always be faithful to him, and then bade him go down to the house. She would follow, she said, as soon as his passing had ceased to be observed.

Then she looked at him as though she expected some sign of renewed love. But no such sign was vouchsafed to her. Now that she thirsted for the touch of his lip upon her cheek, it was denied to her. He did as she bade him; he went down, slowly loitering, by himself; and in about half an hour she followed him and unobserved crept to her chamber.

Again we will pass over what took place between the mother and son; but late in that evening, after the guests had gone to bed, Marie received a message, desiring her to wait on Madame Bauche in a small salon which looked out from one end of the house. It was intended as a private sitting-room should any special stranger arrive who required such accommodation, and therefore was but seldom used. Here she found La Mère Bauche sitting in an arm-chair behind a small table on which stood two candles; and on a sofa against the wall sat Adolphe. The capitaine was not in the room.

"Shut the door, Marie, and come in and sit down," said Madame Bauche. It was easy to understand from the tone of her voice that she was angry and stern, in an unbending mood, and resolved to carry out to the very letter all the threats conveyed by those terrible spectacles.

Marie did as she was bid. She closed the door and sat down on the chair that was nearest to her.

"Marie," said La Mère Bauche — and the voice sounded fierce in the poor girl's ears, and an angry fire glimmered through the green glasses — "what is all this about that I hear? Do you dare to say that you hold my son bound to marry you?" And then the august mother paused for an answer.

But Marie had no answer to give. She looked suppliantly towards her lover, as though beseeching him to carry on the fight for her. But if she could not do battle for herself, certainly he could not do it for her. What little amount of fighting he had had in him had been thoroughly vanquished before her arrival.

"I will have an answer, and that immediately," said Madame Bauche. "I am not going to be betrayed into ignominy and disgrace by the object of my own charity. Who picked you out of the gutter, miss, and brought you up and fed you, when you would otherwise have gone to the foundling? And is this your gratitude for it all? You are not satisfied with being fed and clothed and cherished by me, but you must rob me of my son! Know this then, Adolphe shall never marry a child of charity such as you are."

Marie sat still, stunned by the harshness of these words. La Mère Bauche had often scolded her; indeed, she was given to much scolding; but she had scolded her as a mother may scold a child. And when this story of Marie's love first reached her ears, she had been very angry; but her anger had never brought her to such a pass as this. Indeed, Marie had not hitherto been taught to look at the matter in this light. No one had heretofore twitted her with eating the bread of charity. It had not occurred to her that on this account she was unfit to be Adolphe's wife. There, in that valley, they were all so nearly equal, that no idea of her own inferiority had ever pressed itself upon her mind. But now —!

When the voice ceased she again looked at him; but it was no longer with a beseeching look. Did he also altogether scorn her? That was now the inquiry which her eyes were called upon to make. No; she could not say that he did. It seemed to her that his energies were chiefly occupied in pulling to pieces the tassel of the sofa cushion.

"And now, miss, let me know at once whether this nonsense is to be over or not," continued La Mère Bauche; "and I will tell you at once, I am not going to maintain you here, in my house, to plot against our welfare and happiness. As Marie Clavert you shall not stay here. Capitaine Campan is willing to marry you; and as his wife I will keep my word to you, though you little deserve it. If you refuse to marry him, you must go. As to my son, he is there; and he will tell you now, in my presence, that he alto-gether declines the honour you propose for him."

And then she ceased, waiting for an answer, drumming the table with a wafer stamp which happened to be ready to her hand; but Marie said nothing. Adolphe had been appealed to; but Adophe had not yet spoken.

"Well, miss?" said La Mère Bauche.

Then Marie rose from her seat, and walking round she touched Adolphe lightly on the shoulder. "Adolphe," she said, "it is for you to speak now. I will do as you bid me."

He gave a long sigh, looked first at Marie and then at his mother, shook himself slightly, and then spoke: "Upon my word, Marie, I think mother is right. It would never do for us to marry; it would not indeed."

"Then it is decided," said Marie, returning to her chair.

"And you will marry the capitaine?" said La Mère Bauche.

Marie merely bowed her head in token of acquiescence.

"Then we are friends again. Come here, Marie, and kiss me. You must know that it is my duty to take care of my own son. But I don't want to be angry with you if I can help it; I don't indeed. When once you are Madame Campan, you shall be my own child; and you shall have any room in the house you like to choose — there!" And she once more imprinted a kiss on Marie's cold forehead.

How they all got out of the room, and off to their own cham-bers, I can hardly tell. But in five minutes from the time of this last kiss they were divided. La Mère Bauche had patted Marie, and smiled on her, and called her her dear good little Madame Campan, her young little mistress of the Hôtel Bauche; and had then got herself into her own room, satisfied with her own victory.

Nor must my readers be too severe on Madame Bauche. She had already done much for Marie Clavert; and when she found herself once more by her own bedside, she prayed to be forgiven for the cruelty which she felt that she had shown to the orphan.

But in making this prayer, with her favourite crucifix in her hand and the little image of the Virgin before her, she pleaded her duty to her son. Was it not right, she asked the Virgin, that she should save her son from a bad marriage? And then she promised ever so much of recompense, both to the Virgin and to Marie; a new trousseau for each, with candles to the Virgin, with a gold watch and chain for Marie, as soon as she should be Marie Campan. She had been cruel; she acknowledged it. But at such a crisis was it not defensible? And then the recompense should be so full!

But there was one other meeting that night, very short indeed, but not the less significant. Not long after they had all separated, just so long as to allow of the house being quiet, Adolphe, still sitting in his room, meditating on what the day had done for him, heard a low tap at his door. "Come in," he said, as men always do say; and Marie opening the door, stood just within the verge of his chamber. She had on her countenance neither the soft look of entreating love which she had worn up there in the grotto, nor did she appear crushed and subdued as she had done before his mother. She carried her head somewhat more erect than usual, and looked boldly out at him from under her soft eyelashes. There might still be love there but it was love proudly resolving to quell itself. Adolphe as he looked at her, felt that he was afraid of her.

"It is all over then between us, M. Adolphe?" she said.

"Well, yes. Don't you think it had better be so, eh, Marie?"

"And this is the meaning of oaths and vows, sworn to each other so sacredly?"

"But, Marie, you heard what my mother said."

"Oh, sir! I have not come to ask you again to love me. Oh, no! I am not thinking of that. But this, this would be a lie if I kept it now; it would choke me if I wore it as that man's wife. Take it back;" and she tendered to him the little charm which she had always worn round her neck since he had given it to her. He took it abstractedly, without thinking what he did, and placed it on his dressing-table.

"And you," she continued, "can you still keep that cross? Oh, no! you must give me back that. It would remind you too often of vows that were untrue.'

"Marie," he said, "do not be so harsh to me."

"Harsh!" said she, "no; there has been enough of harshness. I would not be harsh to you, Adolphe. But give me the cross; it would prove a curse to you if you kept it."

He then opened a little box which stood upon the table, and taking out the cross gave it to her.

"And now good-bye," she said. "We shall have but little more to say to each other. I know this now, that I was wrong ever to have loved you. I should have been to you as one of the other poor girls in the house. But, oh! how was I to help it?" To this he made no answer, and she, closing the door softly, went back to her chamber. And thus ended the first day of Adolphe Bauche's return to his own house.

On the next morning the capitaine and Marie were formally betrothed. This was done with some little ceremony, in the presence of all the guests who were staying at the establishment, and with all manner of gracious acknowledgments of Marie's virtues. It seemed as though La Mère Bauche could not be courteous enough to her. There was no more talk of her being a child of charity; no more allusion now to the gutter. La Mère Bauche with her own hand brought her cake with a glass of wine after her betrothal was over, and patted her on the cheek, and called her her dear little Marie Campan. And then the capitaine was made up of infinite politeness, and the guests all wished her joy, and the servants of the house began to perceive that she was a person entitled to respect. How different was all this from that harsh attack that was made on her the preceding evening! Only Adolphe, — he alone kept aloof. Though he was present there he said nothing. He, and he only, offered no congratulations.

In the midst of all these gala doings Marie herself said little or nothing. La Mère Bauche perceived this, but she forgave it. Angrily as she had expressed herself at the idea of Marie's daring to love her son, she had still acknowledged within her own heart that such love had been natural. She could feel no pity for Marie as long as Adolphe was in danger; but now she knew how to pity her. So Marie was still petted and still encouraged, though she went through the day's work sullenly and in silence.

As to the capitaine it was all one to him. He was a man of the world. He did not expect that he should really be preferred, con amore, to a young fellow like Adolphe. But he did expect that

Marie, like other girls, would do as she was bid; and that in a few days she would regain her temper and be reconciled to her life.

And then the marriage was fixed for a very early day; for as La Mère said, "What was the use of waiting? All their minds were made up now, and therefore the sooner the two were married the better. Did not the capitaine think so?"

The capitaine said that he did think so.

And then Marie was asked. It was all one to her, she said. Whatever Maman Bauche liked, that she would do; only she would not name a day herself. Indeed she would neither do nor say anything herself which tended in any way to a furtherance of these matrimonials. But then she acquiesced, quietly enough if not readily, in what other people did and said; and so the marriage was fixed for the day week after Adolphe's return.

The whole of that week passed much in the same way. The servants about the place spoke among themselves of Marie's perverseness, obstinacy, and ingratitude, because she would not look pleased, or answer Madame Bauche's courtesies with gratitude; but La Mère herself showed no signs of anger. Marie had yielded to her, and she required no more. And she remembered also the harsh words she had used to gain her purpose; and she reflected on all that Marie had lost. On these accounts she was forbearing and exacted nothing — nothing but that one sacrifice which was to be made in accordance with her wishes.

And it was made. They were married in the great salon, the dining-room, immediately after breakfast. Madame Bauche was dressed in a new puce silk dress and looked very magnificent on the occasion. She simpered and smiled, and looked gay even in spite of her spectacles; and as the ceremony was being performed, she held fast clutched in her hand the gold watch and chain which were intended for Marie as soon as ever the marriage should be completed.

The capitaine was dressed exactly as usual, only that all his clothes were new. Madame Bauche had endeavoured to persuade him to wear a blue coat; but he answered that such a change would not, he was sure, be to Marie's taste. To tell the truth, Marie would hardly have known the difference had he presented himself in scarlet vestments.

Adolphe, however, was dressed very finely, but he did not make himself prominent on the occasion. Marie watched him closely, though none saw that she did so; and of his garments she could have given an account with much accuracy — of his garments, ay! and of every look. "Is he a man," she said at last to herself, "that he can stand by and see all this?"

She too was dressed in silk. They had put on her what they pleased, and she bore the burden of her wedding finery without complaint and without pride. There was no blush on her face as she walked up to the table at which the priest stood, nor hesitation in her low voice as she made the necessary answers. She put her hand into that of the capitaine when required to do so; and when the ring was put on her finger she shuddered, but ever so slightly. No one observed it but La Mère Bauche. "In one week she will be used to it, and then we shall all be happy," said La Mère to herself. "And I, — I will be so kind to her!"

And so the marriage was completed, and the watch was at once given to Marie. "Thank you, maman," said she, as the trinket was fastened to her girdle. Had it been a pincushion that had cost three sous, it would have affected her as much.

And then there was cake, and wine, and sweetmeats; and after a few minutes Marie disappeared. For an hour or so the capitaine was taken up with the congratulations of his friends, and with the efforts necessary to the wearing of his new honours with an air of ease; but after that time he began to be uneasy because his wife did not come to him. At two or three in the afternoon he went to La Mère Bauche to complain. "This lackadaisical nonsense is no good," he said. "At any rate it is too late now. Marie had better come down among us and show herself satisfied with her husband."

But Madame Bauche took Marie's part. "You must not be too hard on Marie," she said. "She has gone through a good deal this week past, and is very young; whereas, capitaine, you are not very young."

The capitaine merely shrugged his shoulders. In the mean time Mère Bauche went up to visit her protégée in her own room, and came down with a report that she was suffering from a headache. She could not appear at dinner, Madame said; but would make

185

one at the little party which was to be given in the evening. With this the capitaine was forced to be content.

The dinner therefore went on quietly without her, much as it did on other ordinary days. And then there was a little time of vacancy, during which the gentlemen drank their coffee and smoked their cigars at the café, talking over the event that had taken place that morning, and the ladies brushed their hair and added some ribbon or some brooch to their usual apparel. Twice during this time did Madame Bauche go up to Marie's room with offers to assist her. "Not yet, maman; not quite yet," said Marie piteously through her tears, and then twice did the green spectacles leave the room, covering eyes which also were not dry. Ah! what had she done? What had she dared to take upon herself to do? She could not undo it now.

And then it became quite dark in the passages and out of doors, and the guests assembled in the salon. La Mère came in and out three or four times, uneasy in her gait and unpleasant in her aspect, and everybody began to see that things were wrong. "She is ill, I am afraid," said one. "The excitement has been too much," said a second; "and he is so old," whispered a third. And the capitaine stalked about erect on his wooden leg, taking snuff, and striving to look indifferent; but he also was uneasy in his mind.

Presently La Mère came in again with a quicker step than before, and whispered something, first to Adolphe and then to the capitaine, whereupon they both followed her out of the room.

"Not in her chamber?" said Adolphe.

"Then she must be in yours," said the capitaine.

"She is in neither," said La Mère Bauche, with her sternest voice; "nor is she in the house."

And now there was no longer an affectation of indifference on the part of any of them. They were anything but indifferent. The capitaine was eager in his demands that the matter should still be kept secret from the guests. She had always been romantic, he said, and had now gone out to walk by the river-side. They three and the old bath-man would go out and look for her.

"But it is pitch dark," said La Mère Bauche.

"We will take lanterns," said the capitaine. And so they sallied forth with creeping steps over the gravel, so that they might not be heard by those within, and proceeded to search for the young wife.

"Marie! Marie!" said La Mère Bauche, in piteous accents; "do come to me; pray do!"

"Hush!" said the capitaine. "They'll hear you if you call." He could not endure that the world should learn that a marriage with him had been so distasteful to Marie Clavert.

"Marie, dear Marie!" called Madame Bauche, louder than before, quite regardless of the capitaine's feelings; but no Marie answered. In her innermost heart now did La Mère Bauche wish that this cruel marriage had been left undone.

Adolphe was foremost with his lamp, but he hardly dared to look in the spot where he felt that it was most likely that she should have taken refuge. How could he meet her again, alone, in that grotto? Yet he alone of the four was young. It was clearly for him to ascend. "Marie!" he shouted, "are you there?" as he slowly began the long ascent of the steps.

But he had hardly begun to mount when a whirring sound struck his ear, and he felt that the air near him was moved; and then there was a crash upon the lower platform of rock, and a moan, repeated twice but so faintly, and a rustle of silk, and a slight struggle somewhere as he knew within twenty paces of him; and then all was again quiet and still in the night air.

"What was that?" asked the capitaine in a harsh voice. He made his way half across the little garden, and he also was within forty or fifty yards of the flat rock. But Adolphe was unable to answer him. He had fainted and the lamp had fallen from his hands, and rolled to the bottom of the steps.

But the capitaine, though even his heart was all but quenched within him, had still strength enough to make his way up to the rock; and there, holding the lantern above his eyes, he saw all that was left to see of his bride.

As for La Mère Bauche, she never again sat at the head of that table — never again dictated to guests — never again laid down laws for the management of any one. A poor bedridden old woman, she lay there in her house at Vernet for some seven tedious years, and then was gathered to her fathers.

As for the capitaine—but what matters? He was made of sterner stuff. What matters either the fate of such a one as Adolphe Bauche?

"La Mère Bauche" appeared first in *Tales of All Countries, First Series* (London: Chapman & Hall, 1861). (Trollope had intended the story for *Harper's New Monthly Magazine*. According to a letter written to Fletcher Harper on September 1, 1859, Trollope was sending him the story within the week. Why the story was not published in the magazine is not known.)

The Gentle Euphemia;
or,
"Love Shall Still Be Lord of All"

"Lo, I must tell a tale of chivalry,
For large white plumes are dancing in mine eye."
                                        KEATS[1]

Chapter I

"—Knowledge, so my daughter, held,
Was all in all." —TENNYSON[2]

THE GENTLE EUPHEMIA lived in a castle, and her father was the Count Grandnostrel. The wise Alasco, who had dwelt for fifty years in the mullioned chamber of the North Tower, was her tutor, and he taught her poetry, arithmetic and philosophy, to love virtue, and the use of the globes.

And there came the lord of Mountfidget to her father's halls to drink the blood-red wine, and make exchange of the beeves and swine of Mountfidget against the olives and dried fruits which grow upon the slopes of Grandnostrel. For the pastures of Mountfidget are very rich, and its beeves and swine are fat.

"And peradventure I shall see the fair Euphemia," said the young lord to Lieutenant Hossbach, of the Marines, who sojourned oft at Grange of Mountfidget, and delighted more in the racket-court, the billiard-table, and the game of cards, than in guiding the manœuvres of his trusty men-at-arms. "Peradventure," said the young lord, "I shall see the fair Euphemia, — for the poets of Grandnostrel sing of her peerless beauty, and declare her to be the pearl of pearls."

"Nay, my lord," said the lieutenant, "but an you behold the girl once in that spirit, thou art but a lost man, a kestrel with a broken wing, a spavined steed, a noseless hound, a fish out of water; for credit me, the fair Euphemia wants but a husband; — and therefore do the poets sing so loudly." For lieutenant Hossbach knew that were there a lady at the Grange the spigot would not turn so freely.

"By my halidome," said the young lord, "I will know whether the poets sing sooth or not."

So the lord of Mountfidget departed for the Castle of Grandnostrel, and his beeves and his swine were driven before him.

Alasco the Wise sat in the mullioned chamber, with the globes before him and Aristotle's volume under his arm, and the gentle Euphemia sat lowly on a stool at his feet. And she asked him as to the lore of the ancient schools. "Teach me," she said, "as Plato taught, and the learned Esculapius and Aristides the Just; for I would fain walk in the paths of knowledge, and be guided by the rules of virtue." But he answered her not at all, nor did he open the books of wisdom. "Nay, my father," she said; "but the winged hours pass by, and my soul is athirst!"

Then he answered her and said; "My daughter, there cometh hither this day the young lord of Mountfidget, whose beeves and swine are as the stars of heaven in number, and whose ready money in many banks brings in rich harvest of interest. He cometh hither to drink the blood-red wine with your father, and to exchange his beeves and swine for the olives and the dried fruits which grow upon the slopes of Grandnostrel; and peradventure he will ask to see thy father's daughter. Then wilt thou no longer desire to hear what Plato teaches, or how the just man did according to justice."

But Euphemia replied; "Nay, my father. Am I no better than other girls that I should care for the glance of the young man's eye? Have I not sat at your feet since I was but as high as your knee? Teach me still as Plato taught."

But Alasco said; "Love will still be lord of all."

"He shall never be lord of me," said Euphemia.

Chapter II

"And from the platform spare ye not
To fire a noble salvo shot —
Lord Marmion waits below." — SCOTT[3]

And in those days there was the rinderpest in the land among the cattle, and the swine were plagued with a sore disease, and there had gone forth an edict and a command from the Queen's Councillors that no beeves or swine should be driven on the Queen's highways. So there came upon the lord of Mountfidget men armed with authority from the Queen, and they slew his beeves and his swine, and buried their carcases twenty fathom deep beneath the ground.

And the young lord was angered much, for he loved his beeves and his swine, and he said to himself, "What will my lord, the Count Grandnostrel, say unto me, if I visit him with empty hands? Will the blood-red wine be poured, or shall I see the gentle Euphemia?" For the Count Grandnostrel was a hard man, and loved a bargain well. "But I have much money in many banks," said the lord of Mountfidget, in council with himself. "And though my beeves and my swine are slain and buried, yet will he receive me; for the rich are ever welcome, though their hands be empty." So he went up the slopes which led to the Castle of Grandnostrel.

And at the portal, within the safeguard of the drawbridge, there were huge heaps of dried fruits, and mountains of olives. And there came out to him the Count Grandnostrel, and demanded of him where were his beeves and his swine. And the lord told the count how men in authority from the Queen had come upon him on the road, and had slain the beasts, and buried them twenty fathom beneath the earth, — because of the disease among the swine. Then said the Count Grandnostrel: "And art thou come empty-handed to drink the blood-red wine; and hast thou never a horn or a tusk? If my butler draw but a sorry pint for thee, I'll butler him with a bastinado! No; — not a cork! Get thee gone to thy Grange." So he drew up the drawbridge, and the sweet scents of the olives and of the dried fruits were borne aloft

191

by the zephyrs, and struck upon the envious senses of the young lord.

"And shall I not see thy daughter, the gentle Euphemia?" said he.

Then the Count Grandnostrel called to his archers and bade them twang their bows; and the archers twanged their bows, and seven arrows struck the Lord Mountfidget full upon his breast. But their points availed nought against his steel cuirass; so he smiled and turned away.

"Nay, my lord, Count Grandnostrel," said he, "thou shalt rue the day when thou treated thus one who has ready money in many banks; I will set the lawyers at thee, and ruin thee with many costs."

Then, as he walked away, the archers twanged again, and struck him on the back. The good steel turned the points, and the arrows of Grandnostrel fell blunted to the ground. But I fear there was one arrow which entered just above the joint of the knight's harness, and galled the neck of the young lord.

But as he went down the slopes there waved a kerchief from the oriel window over the eastern parapet.

Chapter III

"Oh coz, coz, coz, coz, my pretty little coz,
Dost know how many fathom deep I am in love?" — SHAKESPEARE[4]

"Twas midnight, and there came a soft knock at the door of Alasco the Wise. But Alasco heard it not, for he was drinking in the wisdom of the ancients with all his senses, and his ears were deaf to all earthly sounds.

"Sleepest thou, my father?" said the gentle Euphemia, as she opened the door, "or is thy soul buried amidst thy books?"

"Daughter," said Alasco the Wise, "my soul is buried among my books. The hour is short, and the night cometh, and he who maketh not his hay while the sun of life shineth, shall hardly garner his crop beneath the cold, damp hand of death. But for thee, my child, and thy needs, all other things shall give way." Then he wiped his pen, and put a mark in his book, and closed his lexicon.

"My father," said the girl, "didst thou hear my father's archers, how their bows twanged this morn?"

"I heard a rattling as of dried peas against a window-pane," said the sage.

"It was the noise, father, of the arrows as they fell upon the breast of the Lord Mountfidget. And they fell upon his back, also, and alack! one has struck him on the nape of his neck! And then he rode away. Oh, father!"

"And is it thus with thee, my child?" said Alasco.

"Thus, father," said Euphemia. And she hid her face upon the serge of his mantle.

"Did I not say that love should still be lord of all?" said the sage.

"Spare me, father," said the damsel. "Spare the child that has stood at thy footstool since she was as high as thy knee. Spare me, and aid me to save my lord!"

Then they sallied forth from the small wicket which opens into the forest from beneath the west barbican.

Chapter IV

"Come back! come back! he cried in grief,
My daughter, oh, my daughter!" — CAMPBELL[5]

"When he found she'd levanted, the Count of Alasco
At first turned remarkably red in the face." — BARHAM[6]

And in the morning the Count of Grandnostrel called for his daughter. And his eyes were red with drinking, and his breath was thick, and he sat with his head between his hands. For he had drunk the blood-red wine sitting all alone through the night, laughing, as he quaffed down goblet after goblet, at the discomfiture of the lord of Mountfidget. "Rinderpest, indeed!" he had said. "He that cometh hither empty-handed is likely to return a-dry. Ho! there, butler! another stoup of Malvoisie, and let it be that with the yellow seal." But in the morning he had called for a cool tankard and now he demanded his daughter's presence, that she might pour for him the cup which cheers but not inebriates. "Where is the Lady Euphemia? Why tarries the Lady Euphemia?" But the attendants answered him never a word. Then he called again. "Why cometh not my child to pour for her father the beverage which he loves? Now, by cock and pie, an that old greybeard detain her, he shall hence from the mullioned chamber, — and that with a flea in each ear." But still they answered him not a word. Then he up with the tankard from which he had taken his morning's brewst, and flung it at the menial's head. "Thou churl, thou sot, thou knave, thou clod! why answerest thou not thy liege and lord?" But the menial put his hands to his bruised head, and still answered he never a word.

Then there entered Dame Ulrica, a poor and aged cousin of the house, who went abroad to dances and to tea-parties with the gentle Euphemia. "An please you, my lord count," said Dame Ulrica, "Euphemia has fled this morning by the small wicket which leads from beneath the west barbican into the forest, and Alasco the Wise has gone with her."

Then the Count Grandnostrel stood up in his wrath, and sat down in his wrath, and stood up in his wrath once again. "That tankard full of gold pieces," said he, "to him who shall bring me the greybeard's head!"

Then the archers twanged their bows, and the men-at-arms sharpened their sabres, and the volunteers looked to their rifles and the drummers drummed, and the fifers fifed, and they let down the drawbridge, and they went forth in pursuit of the wise Alasco and the gentle Euphemia.

"By cock and pie," said the Count Grandnostrel, "an it be as I expect, and that sorry knave from Mountfidget is at the bottom of this —"

"In that case it will be meetest, my lord, that she should be his wife," said the Dame Ulrica, who was riding on a palfrey at his right hand. And when she spoke the ancient virtue of the old race was to be seen in her eye, and might be heard in her voice.

"Thou sayest well, dame," answered the count.

"And the lord of Mountfidget has beeves and swine numerous as the stars, and ready money in many banks," said Dame Ulrica. For Dame Ulrica was not virtuous only, but prudent also.

"By cock and pie thou sayest sooth," said the Count Grand-nostrel. And as they had now reached the Fiery Nostril, a hostel that standeth on the hill overlooking the olive gardens of the castle, the count called loudly for the landlord's ale. "By cock and pie this is dry work," said the Count Grandnostrel. "But we will squeeze Mountfidget drier before we have done with him."

Then the menials laughed, and the pot-bellied landlord swayed his huge paunch hither and thither, as he shook his sides with merriment. "Faix, and it is my lord the count is ever ready with his joke," said the landlord.

So they paid for the beer and rode on.

Chapter V

"A breathing but devoted warrior lay.
T'was Lara bleeding fast from life away." — BYRON[7]

In the upper chamber of a small cottage, covered with ivy and vines, lay the lord of Mountfidget, hurt unto death. For one of the arrows had touched him on the nape of the neck, and the point had been dipped in the oil of strychnine. And there leaned over his couch a widow, watching him from moment to moment, touching his lips over and anon with orange juice mixed with brandy, and wiping the clammy dew from his cold brow. "Lord of Mountfidget," she said, "when my dear husband was torn from my widowed arms, thy father gave unto the poor widow this cottage. Would I could repay the debt with my heart's blood."

"Aha! alas! alack! and well-a-day," said the young lord. "Nought can repay me now, — either interest or principal. All my money at all the banks cannot prolong my life one hour. No, nor my beeves and swine, though they outnumber the stars of heaven, and are fatter than a butter-tub. It is all up with poor Mountfidget."

"Nay, say not so, my lord. If only I could reach the wise man that liveth in the mullioned chamber of the north tower, he hath a medicine that might yet be of avail."

Then Mountfidget demanded who was the wise man, and where was the mullioned chamber of the north tower; and when

he learned that aid could be had only from the Castle of Grandnostrel, he sighed amain, and sighed again, and then thus he
addressed the widow; "Ay, help from Grandnostrel; — yes; but
not such aid as that. I want no grey-bearded senior to rack my
dying brains with wise saws; but, if it might be given me to let my
eyes rest but once on the form of the gentle Euphemia, methinks
I could die contented."

Then the door of the chamber was opened, and there entered
a young page, whose slashed doublet and silken hose were foul
with the mud of many lanes, and the dirt of the forest clung to his
short cloak, and his hair was wet with the dropping of the leaves,
and his cap was crushed and his jacket was torn. "He is here! he
is here?" said the page. "I have followed him by his blood through
the forest." Then the page fell at the bed-foot, and there he
fainted.

Chapter VI

"Meanwhile war arose." —MILTON[8]

But as the page sank upon the floor, a small bottle fell from his
breast coat-pocket, and the widow saw that it was labelled "anti-
dote for the oil of strychnine." Then the widow's heart leaped for
joy, and as she poured the precious drops into the gaping wound,
she said a prayer that the page might recover also.

But what noise is this of horses and of men around the humble
vineyard of that poor widow? "Tiraloo, Tiraloo, Tiraloo-ooh,"
"Ha!" said the Mountfidget, raising himself on his elbow, "'tis the
war-cry of the Grandnostrel!" "Rowdadow, Rowdadow,
Rowdadow-dow," then greeted his ears. "Ha! ha!" he cried.
"Rowdadow, a Rowdadow, Rowdadow-dow; 'tis the war-cry of
the Mountfidget!" And he grasped the sword which lay beneath
his pillow. "Mountfidget to the rescue! Shall a man lie still and
perish beneath the bedclothes? Ho, a Hossbach! Ho, a Walker!"
For Walker was the captain of the men-at-arms at Mountfidget,
and the lord knew the voice of his trusty clansman.

Then the widow looked through the lattice-window, and told
him how the fight went. But no one thought of the page upon

whose brow the clammy hand of death was falling as he lay at the bed-foot.

Chapter VII

"Close against her heaving breast
Something in her hand is pressed." — LONGFELLOW[9]

Alasco the Wise had been left in the forest, and was unable to stir another step. "'Tis the blood of the Mountfidget," he had said, when he saw the gouts upon the path. "I know it by its purple hue, and by its violet-scented perfume. Follow it on, but take that bottle with thee. And stay, lest thy sex betray thee to ill-usage from the boors, take this page's raiment which I carry in my wallet, and put the bottle in thy breast coat-pocket. If thou find, as is too likely, a gaping wound in the nape of the neck, naught can restore him but this. Pour it in freely, and he shall live. But if he shall first have heard the war-cry of thy father to disturb him, then he shall surely die." So the gentle Euphemia had gone through the forest, and had reached the chamber of the widow in which lay the lord of Mountfidget.

And as she lay at the foot of the bed, slowly there came back upon her mind a knowledge that she was there. She put her hand to her bosom in haste, and found that the bottle was gone. Then a terrible sound greeted her ears, and she heard the war-cry of her father. Tiraloo, Tiraloo, Tiraloo-ooh! "He is dead," she cried, springing to her feet. "He is dead, and I will die also."

Then the widow knew that it was the gentle Euphemia. "No, thou gentlest one," she said; "he shall not die. He shall live to count the fat beeves and the many swine of Mountfidget, and shall be the possessor of much money in many banks; and thou, thou gentlest one, shall share his blessings. For love shall still be lord of all."

"I do confess," said the gentle Euphemia in a silvern whisper, — in a silvern whisper that was heard by him beneath the bed-clothes, — "I do confess that love is lord of me." Then she sank upon the floor.

Chapter VIII

"I charge you be his faithful and true wife,
Keep warm his hearth and clean his board; and when
He speaks, be quick in your obedience." — ELIZ. B. BROWNING[10]

And then they all returned to the Castle of Grandnostrel, and on their way they took up the wise Alasco, who had remained in the forest.

"Nay, father," said the damsel smiling, "but thou hast been right in all things, and hast taught me better than Plato ever taught."

"And was not I young once myself!" said the sage. So when the blood-red wine had warmed his old veins, and made supple the joints of his aged legs, he tripped a measure in the castle hall, and was very jocund.

So the lord of Mountfidget was married to the gentle Euphemia. But when three months were passed and gone, Lieutenant Hossbach had returned to his regimental duties.

And love shall still be lord of all.

NOTES

1"Specimen of an Induction To a Poem"
[2]*The Princess*, i, 135
[3]*Marmion*, Canto I, iv
[4]*As You Like It*, IV, i, 209-10
[5]Lord Ullin's Daughter"
[6]"The Lay of St. Odille"
[7]*Lara*, XVII, 416-17
[8]*Paradise Lost*, II, 767
[9]*Tales of a Wayside Inn*, "The Musician's Tale," VIII, 9-10.
[10]*Aurora Leigh*, 7, 344-46.

"The Gentle Euphemia; or, Love Shall Still Be Lord of All" appeared first in the May 1 issue of the *Fortnightly Review* for 1866.

The Journey to Panama

THERE IS PERHAPS NO FORM of life, in which men and women of the present day frequently find themselves for a time existing, so unlike their customary conventional life, as that experienced on board the large Ocean Steamers. On the voyages so made separate friendships are formed and separate enmities are endured. Certain lines of temporary politics are originated by the energetic, and intrigues, generally innocent in their conclusions, are carried on with the keenest spirit by those to whom excitement is necessary; whereas the idle and torpid sink into insignificance and general contempt, — it being their lot to do on board ship as in other places. But the enjoyments and activity of such life do not display themselves till the third or fourth day of the voyage. The men and women at first regard each other with distrust and ill-concealed dislike. They by no means anticipate the strong feelings which are to arise, and look forward to ten, fifteen, or twenty days of gloom and sea sickness. Sea sickness disappears, as a general condition, on the evening of the second day, and the gloom about noon on the fourth. Then the men begin to think that the women are not so ugly, vulgar, and insipid; and the women drop their monosyllables, discontinue the close adherence to their own niches which they first observed, and become affable, perhaps even beyond their wont on shore. And alliances spring up among the men themselves. On their first entrance to this new world, they generally regard each other with marked aversion, — each thinking that those nearest to him are low fellows, or perhaps worse; but by the fourth day, if not sooner, every man has his two or three intimate friends with whom he talks and smokes, and to whom he communicates the peculiar politics, and perhaps intrigues, of his own voyage. The female friendships are slower in their growth, for the suspicion of women is perhaps stronger than that of men; but when grown they also are stronger, and exhibit themselves sometimes in extremes of feminine affection.

But the most remarkable alliances are those made between gentlemen and ladies. This is a matter of course on board ship quite as much as on shore, and it is of such an alliance that the present tale purports to tell the story. Such friendships, though they may be very dear, can seldom be very lasting. Though they may be full of sweet romance, — for people become very romantic among the discomforts of a sea voyage, — such romance is generally short lived and delusive, and occasionally is dangerous.

There are several of those great ocean routes, of which, by common consent as it seems of the world, England is the centre. There is the great Eastern line — running from Southampton across the Bay of Biscay, and up the Mediterranean. It crosses the Isthmus of Suez and branches away to Australia, to India, to Ceylon, and to China. There is the great American line, transversing the Atlantic to New York and Boston with the regularity of clockwork. The voyage here is so much a matter of every day routine, that romance becomes scarce upon the route. There are one or two other North American lines, perhaps open to the same objection. Then there is the line of packets to the African coast, — very romantic, as I am given to understand; and there is the great West India route to which the present little history is attached; — great, not on account of our poor West Indian islands which cannot at the present moment make anything great, but because it spreads itself out from thence to Mexico and Cuba, to Guiana and the republics of New Grenada and Venezuela, to Central America, the Isthmus of Panamá, and from thence to California, Vancouver's Island, Peru, and Chili.

It may be imagined how various are the tribes which leave the shores of Great Britain by this route. There are Frenchmen for the French sugar islands, as a rule not very romantic; there are old Spaniards, Spaniards of Spain, seeking to renew their fortunes

amidst the ruins of their former empire; and new Spaniards, —
Spaniards, that is, of the American republics, who speak Spanish, but are unlike the Don both in manners and physiognomy, —
men and women with a touch perhaps of Indian blood, very keen
after dollars, and not much given to the graces of life. There are
Dutchmen too, and Danes, going out to their own islands. There
are citizens of the stars and stripes, who find their way everywhere
— and, alas! perhaps now also citizens of the new Southern flag
with the palmetto leaf. And there are Englishmen of every shade
and class, — and Englishwomen also.

It is constantly the case that women are doomed to make this
long voyage alone. Some are going out to join their husbands,
some to find a husband, some few peradventure to leave a husband. Girls who have been educated at home in England, return
to their distant homes across the Atlantic; and others follow their
relatives who have gone before them as pioneers into a strange
land. It must not be supposed that these females absolutely
embark in solitude, putting their feet upon the deck without the
aid of any friendly arm. They are generally consigned to some
prudent elder, and appear, as they first show themselves on the
ship, to belong to a party. But as often as not their real loneliness
shows itself after a while. The prudent elder is not, perhaps, congenial, and by the evening of the fourth day a new friendship is
created.

Not long since such a friendship was formed under the circumstances which I am now about to tell. A young man — not very
young, for he had turned his thirtieth year, but still a young man
— left Southampton by one of the large West Indian steam-boats,
purposing to pass over the Isthmus of Panamá, and thence up to
California and Vancouver's Island. It would be too long to tell
the cause which led to these distant voyages. Suffice to say it was
not the accursed greed after gold — *auri sacra fames* — which so
took him; nor had he any purpose of permanently settling himself
in those distant colonies of Great Britain. He was at the time a
widower, and perhaps his home was bitter to him without the
young wife whom he had early lost. As he stepped on board he
was accompanied by a gentleman some fifteen years his senior,
who was to be the companion of his sleeping apartment as far as
St. Thomas. The two had been introduced to each other, and

therefore appeared as friends on board the "Serrapiqui"; but their acquaintance had commenced in Southampton, and my hero, Ralph Forrest by name, was alone in the world as he stood looking over the side of the ship at the retreating shores of Hampshire.

"I say, old fellow, we'd better see about our places," said his new friend, slapping him on his back. Mr. Matthew Morris was an old traveller, and knew how to become intimate with his temporary allies at a very short notice. A long course of travelling had knocked all bashfulness out of him, and, when he had a mind to do so, he could make any man his brother in half an hour and any woman his sister in ten minutes.

"Places! what places?" said Forrest.

"A pretty fellow you are to go to California. If you don't look sharper than that, you'll get little to drink and nothing to eat till you come back again. Don't you know the ship's as full as ever she can hold?"

Forrest acknowledged that she was full.

"There are places at table for about a hundred, and we have a hundred and thirty on board. As a matter of course those who don't look sharp will have to scramble. However, I've put cards on the plates and taken the seats. We had better go down and see that none of those Spanish fellows oust us." So Forrest descended after his friend and found that the long tables were already nearly full of expectant dinner eaters. When he took his place, a future neighbour informed him, not in the most gracious voice, that he was encroaching on a lady's seat; and when he immediately attempted to leave that which he held, Mr. Matthew Morris forbade him to do so. Thus a little contest arose, which however happily was brought to a close without bloodshed. The lady was not present at the moment, and the grumpy gentleman agreed to secure for himself a vacant seat on the other side.

For the first three days the lady did not show herself. The grumpy gentleman, who, as Forrest afterwards understood, was the owner of stores in Bridgetown, Barbados, had other ladies with him. First came forth his daughter, creeping down to dinner on the second day, declaring that she would be unable to eat a morsel, and prophesying that she would be forced to retire in five minutes. On this occasion, however, she agreeably surprised herself and her friends. Then came the grumpy gentleman's wife, and the grumpy gentleman's wife's brother — on whose constitution the sea seemed to have an effect quite as violent as on that of the ladies; and lastly, at breakfast on the fourth day, appeared Miss Viner, and took her place as Mr. Forrest's neighbour at his right hand.

He had seen her before on deck, as she lay on one of the benches, vainly endeavouring to make herself comfortable, and had remarked to his companion that she was very unattractive, and almost ugly. Dear young ladies, it is thus that men always speak of you when they first see you on board ship! She was disconsolate, sick at heart, and ill at ease in body also. She did not like the sea. She did not in the least like the grumpy gentleman, in whose hands she was placed. She did not especially like the grumpy gentleman's wife, and she altogether hated the grumpy gentleman's daughter who was the partner of her berth. That young lady had been very sick and very selfish, and Miss Viner had been very sick also, and perhaps equally selfish. They might have been angels, and yet have hated each other under such circumstances. It was no wonder that Mr. Forrest thought her ugly as she twisted herself about on the hard bench, vainly striving to be comfortable.

"She'll brighten up wonderfully before we're in the tropics," said Mr. Morris; "and you won't find her so bad there. It is she that is to sit next to you."

"Heaven forbid!" said Forrest. But nevertheless he was very civil to her when she did come down on the fourth morning. On board the West Indian packets the world goes down to its meals; in crossing between Liverpool and the States, the world goes up to them.

Miss Viner was by no means a very young lady. She also was nearly thirty. In guessing her age on board the ship the ladies said that she was thirty-six, but the ladies were wrong. She possessed a good figure, and when seen on shore, in her natural state and with all her wits about her, was by no means without attraction. She was bright-eyed, with a clear dark skin and good teeth; her hair was of a dark brown and glossy, and there was a touch of feeling and also of humour about her mouth which would have saved her from Mr. Forrest's ill-natured criticism had he first met her under more favourable circumstances.

"You'll see a good deal of her," Mr. Morris said to him, as they began to prepare themselves for luncheon by a cigar immediately after breakfast. "She is going across the isthmus and down to Peru."

"How on earth do you know?"

"I pretty well know where they're all going by this time: old Grumpy told me so. He has her in tow as far as St. Thomas, but knows nothing about her. He gives her up there to the Captain. You'll have a chance of making yourself very agreeable as you run across with her to the Spanish Main."

Mr. Forrest replied that he did not suppose he should know her much better than he did now; but he made no further remarks as to her ugliness. She had spoken a word or two to him at table, and he had seen that her eyes were bright, and had found that her voice was sweet.

"I also am going to Panamá," he said to her on the morning of the fifth day. The weather at that time was very fine, and the October sun as it shone on them, while hour by hour they made more towards the South, was pleasant and genial. The big ship lay almost without motion on the bosom of the Atlantic, as she was driven through the waters at the rate of twelve miles the hour. All was as pleasant now as things can be on board a ship, and Forrest had forgotten that Miss Viner had seemed so ugly to him when he first saw her. At this moment, as he spoke to her, they were running through the Azores, and he had been assisting her with his field-glass to look for orange groves on their sloping shores. Orange groves they had not succeeded in seeing, but their failure had not disturbed their peace. "I also am going to Panamá," he said.

"Are you, indeed?" said she. "Then I shall not feel so terribly alone and disconsolate. I have been looking forward with such fear to that journey on from St. Thomas."

"You shall not be disconsolate, if I can help it," he said. "I am not much of a traveller myself, but what I can do, I will."

"Oh, thank you."

"It is a pity Mr. Morris is not going on with you. He's at home everywhere, and knows the way across the isthmus as well as he does down Regent Street."

"Your friend, you mean."

"My friend, if you call him so; and indeed I hope he is, for I like him. But I don't know more of him than I do of you. I also am as much alone as you are — perhaps more so."

"But a man never suffers in being alone."

"Oh, does he not? Don't think me uncivil, Miss Viner, if I say that you may be mistaken in that. You feel your own shoe when it pinches, but do not realize the tight boot of your neighbour."

"Perhaps not," she said. And then there was a pause, during which she pretended to look again for the orange groves. "But there are worse things, Mr. Forrest, than being alone. It is often a woman's lot to wish that she were let alone." Then she left him, and retreated to the side of the grumpy gentleman's wife, feeling perhaps, that it might be prudent to discontinue a conversation which, seeing that Mr. Forrest was quite a stranger to her, was becoming particular.

"You're getting on famously, my dear," said the lady from Barbados.

"Pretty well, thank you, ma'am," said Miss Viner.

"Mr. Forrest seems to be making himself quite agreeable. I tell Amalia," — Amalia was the young lady to whom, in their joint cabin, Miss Viner could not reconcile herself, — "I tell Amalia that she is wrong not to receive attentions from gentlemen on board ship, if it is not carried too far," — and she put great emphasis on the "too far," — "I see no harm in it."

"Nor I either," said Miss Viner.

"But then Amalia is so particular."

"The best way is to take such things as they come," said Miss Viner; perhaps meaning that such things never did come in the way of Amalia. "If a lady knows what she is about, she need not fear a gentleman's attentions."

"That's just what I tell Amalia; but then, my dear, she has not had so much experience as you and I." Such being the amenities which passed between Miss Viner and the prudent lady who had her in charge, it was not wonderful that the former should feel ill at ease with her own "party," as the family of the grumpy Barbadian was generally considered to be by those on board.

"You're getting along like a house on fire with Miss V.," said Matthew Morris to his young friend.

"Not much fire, I can assure you," said Forrest.

"She isn't so ugly as you thought her?"

"Ugly! No; she's not ugly — I don't think I ever said she was. But she is nothing particular as regards beauty."

"No; she won't be lovely for the next three days to come, I dare say. By the time you reach Panamá, she'll be all that is perfect in woman. I know how these things go."

"Those sort of things don't go at all quickly with me," said Forrest, gravely. "Miss Viner is a very interesting young woman, and as it seems that her route and mine will be together for some time, it is well that we should be civil to each other. And the more so, seeing that the people she is with are not congenial to her."

"No; they are not. There is no young man with them. I generally observe, that on board ship no one is congenial to unmarried ladies except unmarried men. It is a recognised nautical rule. Uncommon hot, isn't it? We are beginning to feel the tropical air. I shall go and cool myself with a cigar in the fiddle." The fiddle is a certain part of the ship devoted to smoking, and thither Mr. Morris betook himself. Forrest, however, did not accompany him, but going forward into the bow of the vessel, threw himself along upon the sail, and meditated on the loneliness of his life.

On board the "Serrapiqui" the upper tier of cabins opened on to a long gallery which ran round that part of the ship immediately over the *salon*, so that from thence a pleasant inspection could be made of the viands as they were being placed on the tables. The custom on board these ships is for two bells to ring preparatory to dinner, at an interval of half an hour. At the sound of the first ladies would go to their cabins to adjust their toilets, but as dressing for dinner is not carried to an extreme at sea, these operations are generally over before the second bell, and the lady passengers would assemble in the balcony for some fifteen minutes before dinner. At first they would stand there alone, but by degrees they were joined by some of the more enterprising of the men, and so at last a kind of little drawing-room was formed. The cabins of Miss Viner's party opened on to one side of this gallery, and that of Mr. Morris and Forrest on the other. Hitherto Forrest had been contented to remain on his own side, occasionally throwing a word across to the ladies on the other; but on this day he boldly went over as soon as he had washed his hands, and took his place between Amalia and Miss Viner.

"We are dreadfully crowded here, mamma," said Amalia.

"Yes, my dear, we are," said her mother. "But what can we do?"

"There's plenty of room in the ladies' cabin," said Miss Viner. Now if there be one place on board a ship more distasteful to ladies than another, it is the ladies' cabin. Mr. Forrest stood his ground, but it may be doubted whether he would have done so had he fully understood all that Amalia had intended.

Then the last bell rang. Mr. Grumpy gave his arm to Mrs. Grumpy, the brother-in-law gave his arm to Amalia, and Forrest did the same to Miss Viner. She hesitated for a moment and then took it, and by so doing transferred herself mentally and bodily from the charge of the prudent and married Mr. Grumpy to that of the perhaps imprudent and certainly unmarried Mr. Forrest. She was wrong. A kind-hearted motherly old lady from Jamaica, who had seen it all knew that she was wrong, and wished that she could tell her so. But there are things of this sort which kind-hearted old ladies cannot find it in their hearts to say. After all, it was only for the voyage. Perhaps Miss Viner was imprudent, but who in Peru would be the wiser? Perhaps indeed, it was the world that was wrong, and not Miss Viner. "*Honi soit qui mal y pense,*" she said to herself, as she took his arm, and leaning on it felt that she was no longer so lonely as she had been. On that day she allowed him to give her a glass of wine out of his decanter. "Hadn't you better take mine, Miss Viner?" asked Mr. Grumpy, in a loud voice; but before he could be answered the deed had been done.

"Don't go too fast, old fellow," Morris said to our hero that night, as they were walking the deck together before they turned in. "One gets into a hobble in such matters before one knows where one is."

"I don't think I have anything particularly to fear," said Forrest.

"I daresay not; only keep your eyes open. Such harridans as Mrs. Grumpy allow any latitude to their tongues out in these diggings. You'll find that unpleasant tidings will be put on board the ship going down to Panamá, and everybody's eye will be upon you." So warned, Mr. Forrest did put himself on his guard, and for the next day and a half his intimacy with Miss Viner progressed but little. These were, probably, the dullest hours that he had on the whole voyage.

Miss Viner saw this and drew back. On the afternoon of that second day she walked a turn or two on deck with the weak brother-in-law, and when Mr. Forrest came near her she applied herself to her book. She meant no harm, and if she were not afraid of what people might say, why should he be so? So she turned her shoulder towards him at dinner, and would not drink of his cup.

"Have some of mine, Miss Viner," said Mr. Grumpy very loudly — but on that day Miss Viner drank no wine.

The sun sets quickly as one draws near to the tropics, and the day was already gone and the dusk had come on when Mr. Forrest walked out upon the deck that evening a little after six. But the night was beautiful and mild, and there was a hum of merry voices from the benches. He was already uncomfortable and sore with a sense of being deserted. There was but one person on board the ship that he liked, and why should he avoid her, and be avoided? He soon perceived where she was standing. The Grumpy family had a bench to themselves, and she was opposite to it, on her feet, leaning against the side of the vessel. "Will you walk this evening, Miss Viner?" he asked.

"I think not," she answered.

"Then I shall persevere in asking you till you are sure. It will do you good, for I have not seen you walking all day."

"Have you not? then I will take a turn. Oh, Mr. Forrest, if you knew what it was to have to live with such people as those." And then out of that, on that evening, there grew up between them something like the confidence of real friendship. Things were told such as none but friends do tell to one another, and warm answering words were spoken such as the sympathy of friendship produces — alas! they were both foolish, for friendship and sympathy should have deeper roots.

She told him all her story. She was going out to Peru to be married to a man who was nearly twenty years her senior. It was a long engagement of ten years' standing. When first made, it was made as being contingent on certain circumstances. An option of escaping from it had then been given to her, but now there was no longer an option. He was rich, and she was penniless. He had even paid her passage money and her outfit. She had not at last given way and taken these irrevocable steps till her only means of support in England had been taken from her. She had lived the last two years with a relative who was now dead. "And he also is my cousin — a distant cousin: you understand that."

"And do you love him?"

"Love him! What; as you loved her whom you have lost. As she loved you, when she clung to you before she went. No; certanly not — I shall never know anything of that love."

"And is he good?"

"He is a hard man. Men become hard when they deal in money as he has done. He was home five years since and then I swore to myself that I would not marry him. But his letters to me are kind."

Forrest sat silent for a minute or two, — for they were up on the bow again, seated on the sail that was bound round the bowsprit; and then he answered her: "A woman should never marry a man unless she loves him."

"Ah," said she, "of course you will condemn me. That is the way in which women are always treated. They have no choice given them, and are then scolded for choosing wrongly."

"But you might have refused him."

"No; I could not — I cannot make you understand the whole; — how it first came about that the marriage was proposed and agreed to by me under certain conditions. Those conditions have come about, and I am now bound to him. I have taken his money and have no escape. It is easy to say that a woman should not marry without love; — as easy as it is to say that a man should not starve. But there are men who starve, — starve although they work hard."

"I did not mean to judge you, Miss Viner."

"But I judge myself, — and condemn myself so often! Where should I be in half an hour from this if I were to throw myself forward into the sea. I often long to do it. Don't you feel tempted sometimes to put an end to it all?"

"The waters look cool and sweet, but I own I am afraid of the bourne beyond."

"So am I; and that fear will keep me from it."

"We are bound to bear our burdens of sorrow—mine, I know, is heavy enough."

"Yours, Mr. Forrest! Have you not all the pleasure of memory to fall back on, and every hope for the future? What can I remember, or what can I hope? But, heavens! it is near eight o'clock, and they have all been at tea this hour past. What will my Cerberus say to me? I do not mind the male mouth, if only the two feminine mouths could be stopped." Then she rose and went back to the stern of the vessel; but as she slid into a seat, she saw that Mrs. Grumpy was standing over her.

From thence to St. Thomas the voyage went on in the customary manner. The sun became very powerful, and the passengers in the lower part of the ship complained loudly of having their port holes closed. The Spaniards sat grumbling in the cabin all day, and the ladies prepared for the general move which was to be made at St. Thomas. The alliance between Forrest and Miss Viner went on much the same as ever, and Mrs. Grumpy said very ill-natured things. On one occasion she ventured to lecture Miss Viner; but that lady knew how to take her own part, and Mrs. Grumpy did not get the best of it. The dangerous alliance, I have said, went on the same as ever; but it must not be supposed that either person in any way committed aught that was wrong. They sat together and talked together, each now knowing the other's circumstances; but had it not been for the prudish caution of some ladies there would have been nothing amiss. As it was there was not much amiss. Few of the passengers really cared whether or no Miss Viner had found an admirer. Those who were going to Panamá were mostly Spaniards, and as the great separation became nearer, people had somewhat else of which to think.

And then the separation came. They rode into that pretty harbour of St. Thomas early in the morning, and were ignorant, — the most of them, — that they were lying in the very worst centre of yellow fever among all those plague-spotted islands. St. Thomas is very pretty as seen from the ships; and when that has been said, all has been said that can be said in its favour. There was a busy bustling time of it then. One vessel after another was brought up alongside the big ship that had come from England, and each took its separate freight of passengers and luggage. First started the boat that ran down the Leeward Islands to Demerara, taking with her Mr. Grumpy and all his family.

"Good bye, Miss Viner," said Mrs. Grumpy. "I hope you'll get quite safely to the end of your voyage; but do take care."

"I'm sure I hope everything will be right," said Amalia, as she absolutely kissed her enemy. It is astonishing how well young women can hate each other, and yet kiss at parting.

"As to everything being right," said Miss Viner, "that is too much to hope. But I do not know that anything is going especially wrong. Good bye, sir;" and then she put out her hand to Mr. Grumpy. He was at the moment leaving the ship laden with umbrellas, sticks, and coats, and was forced to put them down in order to free his hand.

"Well, good bye," he said. "I hope you'll do till you meet your friend at the isthmus."

"I hope I shall, sir," she replied; and so they parted.

Then the Jamaica packet started. "I dare say we shall never see each other again," said Morris, as he shook his friend's hand heartily. "One never does. Don't interfere with the rights of that gentleman in Peru, or he might run a knife into you."

"I feel no inclination to injure him on that point."

"That's well; and now good bye;" and thus they also were parted. On the following morning the branch ship was despatched to Mexico; and then on the afternoon of the third day that for Colon — as we Englishmen call the town on this side of the Isthmus of Panamá. Into that vessel Miss Viner and Mr. Forrest moved themselves and their effects; and now that the three-headed Cerberus was gone she no longer hesitated in allowing him to do for her all those little things which it is well that men should do for women when they are travelling. A woman without assistance under such circumstances is very forlorn, very apt to go to the wall, very ill able to assert her rights as to accommodation; and I think few can blame Miss Viner for putting herself and her belongings under the care of the only person who was disposed to be kind to her.

Late in the evening the vessel steamed out of St. Thomas' harbour; and as she went, Ralph Forrest and Emily Viner were standing together at the stern of the boat, looking at the retreating lights of the Danish town. If there be a place on the earth's surface odious to me, it is that little Danish isle to which so many of our young seamen are sent to die, — there being no good cause whatever for such sending. But the question is one which cannot well be argued here. "I have five more days of self and liberty left me," said Miss Viner. "That is my life's allowance."

"For heaven's sake, do not say words that are so horrible!"

"But am I to lie for heaven's sake, and say words that are false; or shall I be silent for heaven's sake, and say nothing during these last hours given to me for speaking? It is so. To you I can say that it is so, and why should you begrudge me the speech."

"I would begrudge you nothing that I could do for you."

"No, you should not. Now that my incubus has gone to Barbados, let me be free for a day or two. What chance is there, I wonder, that the ship's machinery should all go wrong, and that we should be tossed about in the sea here for the next six months — I suppose it would be very wicked to wish it."

"We should all be starved; that's all."

"What with a cow on board, — and a dozen live sheep, and thousands of cocks and hens! But we are to touch at Santa Martha and Cartagena. What would happen to me if I were to run away at Santa Martha?"

"I suppose I should be bound to run with you."

"Oh, of course; and therefore as I would not wish to destroy you, I won't do it. But it wouldn't hurt you much to be shipwrecked, and wait for the next packet."

"Miss Viner," he said, after a pause — and in the meantime he had drawn nearer to her, too near to her considering all things — "in the name of all that is good, and true, and womanly, go back to England. With your feelings, if I may judge of them by words which are spoken half in jest "

"Mr. Forrest, there is no jest."

"With your feelings a poorhouse in England would be better than a palace in Peru."

"An English poorhouse would be better, but an English poorhouse is not open to me. You do not know what it is to have

212

friends — no, not friends, but people belonging to you — just so near as to make your respectability a matter of interest to them, but not so near that they should care for your happiness. Emily Viner married to Mr. Gorloch, in Peru, is put out of the way respectably. She will cause no further trouble, and her name may be mentioned in family circles without annoyance. The fact is, Mr. Forrest, that there are people who have no business to live at all.'

"I would go back to England," he added, after another pause. "When you talk to me with such bitterness of five more days of living liberty, you scare my very soul. Return, Miss Viner, and brave the worst. He is to meet you at Panamá. Remain on this side of the isthmus, and send him word that you must return. I will be the bearer of the message."

"And shall I walk back to England?" said Miss Viner.

"I had not quite forgotten all that," he replied very gently; "there are moments when a man may venture to propose that which under ordinary circumstances would be a liberty. Money, in a moderate way, is not greatly an object to me. As a return for my valiant defence of you against your West Indian Cerberus, you shall allow me to arrange that with the agent at Colon."

'I do so love plain English, Mr. Forrest. You are proposing, I think, to give me something like fifty guineas."

"Well; call it so if you will. If you will have plain English, that is what I mean."

"So that by my journey out here I should rob and deceive the man I do know, and also rob the man I don't know. I am afraid of that bourne beyond the waters of which we spoke, but I would rather face that than act as you suggest."

"Of the feelings between him and you I can, of course, be no judge."

"No, no; you cannot. But what a beast I am not to thank you. I do thank you. That which it would be mean in me to take, it is noble — very noble — in you to offer. It is a pleasure to me, I cannot tell why; but it is a pleasure to me to have had the offer. But think of me as a sister and you will feel that it could not be accepted — could not be accepted even if I could bring myself to betray that other man."

Thus they ran across the Caribbean Sea, renewing very often such conversations as that just given. They touched at Santa Martha and Cartagena on the coast of the Spanish Main, and at both places he went with her on shore. He found that she was fairly well educated, and anxious to see and to learn all that might be seen and learned in the course of her travels. On the last day, as they neared the isthmus, she became more tranquil and quiet in the expression of her feelings than before, and spoke with less gloom than she had done.

"After all, ought I not to like him?" she said. "He is coming all the way from Callao merely to meet me. What man would go from London to Moscow to pick up a wife?"

"I would — and thence round the world to Moscow again — if she were the wife I wanted."

"Yes; but a wife who has never said that she loved you! It is purely a matter of convenience. Well, I have locked my big box, and I shall give the key to him before it is ever again unlocked. He has a right to it, for he has paid for nearly all that it holds."

"You look at things from such a mundane point of view."

"A woman should, or she will always be getting into difficulty. Mind, I shall introduce you to him, and tell him all that you have done for me; how you braved Cerberus, and the rest of it."

"I shall certainly be glad to meet him."

"But I shall not tell him of your offer to send me back to England; not yet at least. If he be good and gentle with me, I shall tell him that too after a time. I am very bad at keeping secrets, as no doubt you have perceived. I think we go across the isthmus at once, do we not?"

"So the captain says."

"Look!" and she handed him back his own field-glass; 'I can see the men on the wooden platform — yes; and I can see the smoke of an engine." And then in a little more than an hour from that time the ship had swung round on her anchor.

Colon, or Aspinwall as it should be called, is a place in itself as detestable as St. Thomas. It is not so odious to an Englishman, for it is not used by Englishmen more than is necessary. We have no great depôt of traffic there which we might with advantage move elsewhere. Taken, however, on its own merits, Aspinwall is not a delectable place. Luckily, however, travellers across the isthmus to the Pacific are never doomed to remain there long. If they arrive early in the day the railway thence to Panamá takes them on at once. If it be not so, they remain on board ship till the next morning. Of course it will be understood that the transit here chiefly affects Americans, as it is the high road from New York to California.

In less than an hour from their landing, their baggage had been examined by the Custom House officers of New Granada, and they were in the railway cars crossing the isthmus. The officials in these out-of-the-way places always seem like apes imitating the doings of men. The officers at Aspinwall open and look at the trunks just as monkeys might do, having clearly no idea of any duty to be performed, nor any conception that goods of this or that class should not be allowed to pass. It is the thing in Europe to examine luggage going into a new country — and why should not they be as good as Europeans?

"I wonder whether he will be at the station," she said, when the three hours of the journey had nearly passed. Forrest could perceive that her voice trembled as she spoke and that she was becoming nervous.

"If he have already reached Panamá, he will be there. As far as I could learn, the arrival up from Peru had not been telegraphed."

"Then I have another day — perhaps two. We cannot say how many. I wish he were there. Nothing is so intolerable as suspense."

"And the box must be opened again."

When they reached the station at Panamá they found that the vessel from the South American coast was in the roads, but that the passengers were not yet on shore. Forrest therefore took Miss Viner down to the hotel, and there remained with her, sitting next to her in the common drawing-room of the house, when she had come from her own bed-room. It would be necessary that they should remain there four or five days, and Forrest had been quick in securing a room for her. He had assisted in taking up her luggage, had helped her in placing her big box, and had thus been recognised by the crowd in the hotel as her friend. Then came the tidings that the passengers were landing, and he became nervous as she was — "I will go down and meet him," said he, "and

215

tell him that you are here. I shall soon find him by his name." And so he went out.

Everybody knows the scrambling manner in which passengers arrive at an hotel out of a big ship. First came two or three energetic heated men, who, by dint of screeching and bullying, have gotten themselves first despatched. They always get the worst rooms at the inns, the innkeepers having a notion that the richest people — those with the most luggage — must be more tardy in their movements. Four or five of this nature passed by Forrest in the hall, but he was not tempted to ask questions of them. One, from his age, might have been Mr. Gorloch, but he instantly declared himself to be a Spanish count. Then came an elderly man alone, with a small bag in his hand. He was one of those who pride themselves on going from pole to pole wihtout encumbrance, and who will be behoved to no one for the carriage of their luggage. To him, as he was alone in the street, Forrest addressed himself. "Gorloch," said he — "Gorloch! Are you a friend of his?"

"A friend of mine is so," said Forrest.

"Ah, indeed; yea," said the other; and then he hesitated. "Sir," he then said. "Mr. Gorloch died at Callao just seven days before the ship sailed. You had better see Mr. Cox." And then the elderly man passed on with his little bag.

Mr. Gorloch was dead! "Dead!" said Forrest to himself, as he leaned against the wall of the hotel, still standing on the street pavement. "She has come out here; and now he is gone!" And then a thousand thoughts crowded on him. Who should tell her? And how would she bear it? Would it, in truth, be a relief to her to find that liberty for which she had sighed? Or might it be, now that this terrible test of her true feelings had come to her, that she would regret the loss of home and wealth, and such position as life in Peru would have given her? And, above all, would this sudden death of one who was to have been so near to her strike her to the heart?

But what was he to do? How was he now to show his friendship? He was returning slowly in at the hotel door, where crowds of men and women were now thronging, when he was addressed by a middle-aged, good-looking gentleman, who asked him whether his name was Forrest. "I am told," said the gentleman, when Forrest had answered him, "that you are a friend of Miss Viner's. Have you heard the sad tidings from Callao?" It then appeared that this gentleman had been a stranger to Mr. Gorloch, but had undertaken to bring a letter up to Miss Viner. This letter was handed to Mr. Forrest, and he found himself burdened with the task of breaking the news to his poor friend. Whatever he did, he must do at once, for all those who had come up by the Pacific steamer knew the story, and it was incumbent on him that Miss Viner should not hear the tidings in a sudden manner, and from a stranger's mouth.

He went up into the drawing-room, and found Miss Viner seated there, in the midst of a crowd of women. He walked up to her her and, taking her hand, asked her in a whisper whether she would come out with him for a moment.

"Where is he?" said she. "I know that something is the matter. What is it?"

"There is such a crowd here! Step out for a moment." And he led her away to her own room.

"Where is he?" she asked. "What is the matter? He has sent to say that he no longer wants me. Tell me; am I free from him?"

"Miss Viner, you are free."

Though she had asked the question herself, she was astonished by the answer; but, nevertheless, no idea of the truth had yet come upon her. "It is so," she said. "Well; what else? Has he written? He has bought me as he would a beast of burden, and has, I suppose, a right to treat me as he pleases."

"I have a letter; — but, dear Miss Viner"

"Well, tell me all — out at once. Tell me everything."

"You are free, Miss Viner, but you will be cut to the heart when you learn the manner of your freedom."

"He has lost everything in trade! He is ruined!"

"Miss Viner, he is dead."

She stood staring at him for a moment or two as though she could not realize the information which he gave her. Then gradually she retreated to the bed, and sat upon it. "Dead — Mr. Forrest," she said. He did not answer her, but handed her the letter, which she took and read as though it were mechanically. The letter was from Mr. Gorloch's partner, and told her everything which it was necessary that she should know.

217

"Shall I leave you now?" he said, when he saw that she had finished reading it.

"Leave me; yes — no. But you had better leave me, and let me think about it. Alas! me, that I should have so spoken of him."

"But you have said nothing unkind."

"Yes; much that was unkind. But spoken words cannot be recalled. Let me be alone now, but come to me soon. There is no one else here that I can speak to."

He went out, and finding that the hotel dinner was ready, he went in and dined. Then he strolled into the town among the hot, narrow, dilapidated streets; and then after two hours' absence returned to Miss Viner's room. When he knocked, she came and opened the door, and he found that the floor was strewn with clothes. "I am preparing, you see, for my return. The vessel starts back for St. Thomas the day after to-morrow."

"You are quite right to go — to go at once. Oh, Miss Viner — Emily, now, at least — you must let me help you."

He had been thinking of her much during those last two hours, and her voice had become pleasant to his ears, and her eyes very bright to his sight.

"You shall help me," she said. "Are you not helping me when at such a time you come to speak to me?"

"And you will let me think that I have a right to act as your protector?"

"My protector! I do not want such aid as that. During the days that we are here together you shall be my friend."

"You shall not return alone. My journeyings are nothing to me. Emily, I will return with you to England."

Then she rose up from her seat and spoke to him.

"Not for the world," she said. "Putting out of question the folly of your forgetting your own objects, do you think it possible that I should go with you, now that he is dead? To you I have spoken of him harshly;.and now that it is my duty to mourn for him, could I do so heartily if you were with me? While he lived, it seemed to me that in those last days I had a right to speak my thoughts plainly. You and I were to part and meet no more; and I regarded us both as people apart, who, for a while, might drop the common usages of the world. It is so no longer. Instead of going

218

with you farther, I must ask you to forget that we were ever together."

"Emily, I shall never forget you."

"Let your tongue forget me. I have given you no cause to speak good of me, and you will be too kind to speak evil."

After that she explained to him all that that letter contained. The arrangements for her journey home had been made. Money had been sent to her, and Mr. Gorloch in his will had provided for her, not liberally, seeing that he was rich, but still sufficiently.

And so they parted in Panamá. She would not allow him even to cross the isthmus with her, but pressed his hand warmly as he left her at the station. "God bless you!" he said; "And may God bless you, my friend," she answered.

Thus alone she took her departure for England, and he went on his way to California.

"The Journey to Panama" appeared first in *Victoria Regia* (London: Emily Faithfull and Company, 1861).